"The volatile and tough-minded stories in *If the Sky Falls* establish Nicholas Montemarano as a remarkable storyteller with a gift for the grittily noir. A disturbing, bracing, and brutally powerful collection."

—ADRIENNE MILLER, author of *The Coast of Akron*

"Montemarano's superb, powerful, exacting stories drive deep and hard into the teeming center of things. This book is very fine in so many ways, but most of all it is riveting. Story after story, you will be unable to stop reading. This book is also beautifully ruthless, full of grief as well as its opposite—big manic hilarious good will. The world is reproduced here in all its grainy, mysterious largeness, and the tales these people tell are unforgettable in their stubborn glory. Montemarano is a brilliant, brazen truthseeker, and his fiction is as honest and as human as it comes."

—MICHAEL BYERS, author of *Long for This World*

"Montemarano writes a visceral, dug-in, experienced prose that stays in the mind. He will win readers and reputations with these powerful stories."

—SVEN BIRKERTS, editor, *Agni*

"Montemarano's brutal vision is tempered—and complicated—by an aching humanity that pervades each story. There is much pain, much grief—and much dignity. He bleeds for his characters, and we do too. *If the Sky Falls* is a rare and exhilarating book of stories."

—PETER ORNER, author of *Esther Stories*

yellow shoe fiction

MICHAEL GRIFFITH, EDITOR

{ STORIES }

if the sky falls

NICHOLAS MONTEMARANO

Louisiana State University Press
Baton Rouge

Manufactured in the United States of America

An LSU Press Paperback Original
First Printing

Designer: Barbara Neely Bourgoyne
Typeface: Brioso Pro, display; Adobe Minion, text
Printer and binder: Edwards Brothers, Inc.

Library of Congress Cataloging-in-Publication Data
Montemarano, Nicholas, 1970–
If the sky falls : stories / Nicholas Montemarano.
p. cm. — (Yellow shoe fiction)
ISBN 0-8071-3122-9 (pbk. : alk. paper)
I. Title. II. Series.
PS3613.O5484I34 2005
813'.6—dc22
2005010257

The paper in this book meets the guidelines for permanence and durability of the Committee on Production Guidelines for Book Longevity of the Council on Library Resources. ♾

Acknowledgment and thanks are given to the following publications in which some of the stories in this book originally appeared: *Agni:* "The Usual Human Disabilities" (2003); *Alaska Quarterly Review:* "Shift" (2000); *The Antioch Review:* "The Worst Degree of Unforgivable" (2001) and "Man Throws Dog Out Window" (2005); *DoubleTake:* "The Other Man" (1999) and "Story" (2002); *Esquire:* "The November Fifteen" (2004); *The Florida Review:* "To Fall Apart" (2001); and *Zoetrope: All-Story:* "Note to Future Self" (2001).

"The Worst Degree of Unforgivable" was reprinted in *The Pushcart Prize XXVII: Best of the Small Presses.*

I would also like to thank the following: My parents, for their support; my sister, Jennifer, for letting me push my way out first; Doug Arey, for years of witnessing; Jill Grinberg, for being my friend as well as my agent; Susan Steinberg, for friendship and endless feedback; Dan Bernstein, for laughter; Beau Friedlander, for his support even when he didn't have to give it; Michael Griffith, for midwifing this book into the world; everyone at LSU Press who had a hand in this book; Peter Garfield, for the cover; and Chris Brown (I *told* you I would thank you). I'm also grateful to The MacDowell Colony and Yaddo for giving me time to work in beautiful and peaceful places, and to the National Endowment for the Arts for a surprising and much-needed grant in 2002. I received a 2005 Pennsylvania Council on the Arts Fellowship, administered by the Mid Atlantic Arts Foundation, and I would like to thank them for their support. Finally, I'd like to thank Nicole Michels for her love and support and for changing the way I see.

for my sister

contents

if the sky falls

to fall apart

The framed picture of my sister no longer hung next to the picture of me on the wall between our rooms. Her closet was empty; her dresser drawers were empty. The barrettes she wore were gone from the place on her dresser where she kept them. Missing from the table beside her bed was the music box I heard when my sister played in her room.

In the garbage, when I looked, were cracked eggshells, crumpled paper, an empty milk carton, the end of a loaf of bread inside a bread bag.

Inside my mother's closet was a locked trunk.

On top of the trunk were the three pairs of shoes my mother owned, the first for Sunday mass (black with a fake black flower near the toe, a two-inch heel), the second for everyday use (black flats with a silver buckle), the third for what she called knockaround (black slip-ons that looked more like slippers than shoes). She kept the shoes on top of the trunk in order, from Sunday to knockaround, and she placed under the shoes a red cloth, draped over the front and back and sides of the trunk. The trunk was locked with a combination lock, meaning: It could not be opened with a key; it could not be picked open with a bobby pin or safety pin or whatever else people use to pick locks, meaning: If you did not know the combination, the only way to open the trunk would be to pound the lock or break a hole in the trunk itself. The outside was black; the latch and edges were metal. The trunk was heavy enough so that it could not be lifted by a boy seven years old, but not so heavy that this boy could not tilt the trunk or slide it across the floor.

During the time of this part of the story, I was seven years old. I was the boy tilting and sliding the trunk in his mother's closet. But before I tilted and slid the trunk, I removed the shoes and laid them on the closet floor, then removed the red cloth from the top of the trunk (noticing just how far it draped over the front and back and sides) and folded it gently (so as not to make creases) and laid it on top of the shoes (so as not to get dust on the cloth)—all this before I found out that the trunk was locked and there was no possible way to open it.

I tilted the trunk to determine its weight, and also to determine if there was some way to open the trunk I had not noticed, or if there was a way to see inside, perhaps a hole in the side or on the bottom. I tilted the trunk in a way that would allow me to look at the bottom, that would allow me to get my face low enough to the ground in order to see clearly, while at the same time holding the trunk in its tilted position, but the trunk came down on my fingers, and I cried out, and my mother came running the way some mothers do when their child or any child cries out.

My mother saw that the closet door was open, and that the trunk was not in its usual position, and that her shoes were not on top of the trunk, where they were supposed to be, and that the red cloth was folded on top of the shoes, not draped over the trunk, where it was supposed to be.

She rushed at me. My head hit the wall behind me, and I fell forward.

I lay on the floor, crying, my mother standing above me.

She pulled me up by my hair. I could knock your teeth out, she said, and then she smacked my face. She waited. She held her hand high, my eyelids fluttered, and then she smacked me again. Though I knew not to back away from her, I backed away from her. I could feel my legs buckle.

To keep me on my feet she grabbed my hair; with her other hand she bent back my fingers.

She pulled me to the window and parted the drapes. Do you see that man in the black car? she said. He's the man who takes all bad children away.

This isn't make-believe, she said. He's going to take you away, and you're never coming back.

I'll be good, I said.

It's too late, she said.

She brought me a suitcase. Inside, she told me, were all my clothes and everything that belonged to me.

I don't want to go away, I said.

My mother handed me my suitcase. I'm sorry, she said. The man has a list, and your name is on the list. There's nothing I can do.

My father was sitting in the chair I will always remember when I remember my father; he did not look up from the newspaper he was reading.

My mother opened the door and led me outside. I could see the man in the black car, his arm draped out the window, a cigarette between his fingers.

We began walking across the street, but then she stopped and told me to go back in the house for a moment, she wanted to speak with the man. She was almost positive it was too late to change his mind, she explained, but she could ask if he would give me another chance. I went back inside and waited. I prayed to God and told God how sorry I was, how I would never be bad again, how I loved my mother and knew what a good mother she was, and then she came inside and told me I would be allowed to stay this time—only this time—but that if I was bad ever again—just once—the man in the black car would come back and take me where all bad children are taken, and no one would ever see me again.

Three days later I was back in the closet, working on the lock.

And the next day, and the next—my mother's shoes removed from the trunk, the red cloth folded carefully on top of the shoes.

On one particularly frustrating day, I used the bottom of one of my mother's Sunday shoes in an attempt to break the lock, but I succeeded not in opening the trunk but, rather, in scratching the metal near the lock and near where the trunk opened and closed, and also in scuffing one of my mother's shoes. I licked my fingers and wet the scuff, then rubbed the scuff with my shirttail. A racing heart may be a sign of nerves, but it may also be a sign of excitement, and so I will put forth my theory now that the seven-year-old boy of this part of the story was excited, rather than nervous, about having scratched the metal part of the trunk and about having scuffed one of his mother's shoes, excited at the possibility of getting caught, at the possibility of bringing things to a head, despite the consequences, even face-slapping, hair-grabbing, finger-bending, worse, excited that his mother might become so angry that she would open the trunk and say: There! Do you see? Take a look! Nothing inside that concerns you.

You're not going to school today, she said, and I told her I wasn't sick, I wanted to go to school, and again she said no, not today, today you will stay in your room and think about things, today you will think about what kind of son you've been to your mother, and she closed the door and left me in my room.

I could hear my mother banging pots and pans against the counter, against the stove, could hear her slamming doors, could hear her feet stomping around the apartment, and eventually into my room, where she would not look at me, where she placed my washed and ironed (*with my own hands*) clothes into my (*paid for with the money I earn making dresses*) drawer. She left me with the echo of her having been there, and in this way I knew she knew I had touched the trunk.

But there had been no satisfaction, things had not been brought to a head, she had not opened the trunk and said: There! Do you see? Nothing that concerns you.

The next day I stole matches from my father's coat hanging in the closet. I stood in front of the closet door and looked behind me. I remember the feel of the matches in my pocket. My hand on the doorknob. A glance behind. My hand turning the knob. I remember taking my mother's shoes from the trunk and folding the red cloth. I remember looking one more time for a hole in the trunk. I remember trying to pull open, then kicking, the lock. I remember lighting a match and trying to melt the lock. I remember looking at the lock to see if it had melted, and holding in my raised hand what remained of the still-lit match, and not paying attention to how close my hand was to my mother's dress, then seeing that her dress had caught fire, then, after a moment's deliberation, trying to put out the fire with my hands, then trying to put out the fire with the red cloth, then with my mother's Sunday shoes, then her everyday shoes, then my mother running into the room, my mother pulling me out of the room and running into the hallway to find help, and then one of our neighbors, a widower who lived alone and had been waiting years to feel this useful, coming in and putting out the fire with a blanket, and perhaps now, finally, everything was coming to a head (though not before three dresses and two hats were burned).

The fire was out; the smoke had escaped through an open window; the ruined dresses and hats lay blackened on the floor.

My mother kneeled beside the bed, slapped her hands against the mattress, and said *Why why why why* about her (*What, Holy Mother of God, have I done to deserve this?*) son. This was her moment to press her face into the mattress and rail. Her entire (*I want no more of it, no more, I want nothing more from it*) life had been leading to this moment, and she would never stop railing, not even when my father came home and lifted my mother onto the bed and covered her with a blanket—still, she railed at her (*Take him away from me, get him out of my sight*) son.

And then she stopped speaking—her shaking and crying replaced by depression. Days in bed, my father trying to feed her. When I could no longer take her suffering, I tried to make her speak, asked questions (*Can I do something for you, how can I make you feel better?*), made promises (*I'll never go near the trunk again, I'm sorry, never again, you don't need to have the man come and take me away*).

One year before the fire in my mother's closet, my sister and I were six. It was summer. My mother took us to the park. I don't remember what we were doing. Maybe I was throwing a rubber ball against a wall and waiting for it to bounce back to me, then feeling the rubber slap against the palm of my hand, then throwing it again. Maybe my sister, with her fingers, was digging in the dirt where the grass had ceased to grow. Maybe with a white rock we were scratching our names into the side of a water fountain or into the handball court wall. It no longer matters what we were doing. What matters is this: At some point, after we had been playing a while, an hour, maybe two, my mother said that it was time to go home, but my sister said she wanted to stay, and my mother said no, it was time to go home, we had had enough time in the park, but my sister stomped her sneakers on the ground and asked if she could please stay a little while longer, just another ten minutes, she wanted to finish whatever it was she was doing, her fingers creating a world in the dirt, but my mother said no, it was time to go home, and my mother made the face that meant she was angry, and for a moment my sister went back to whatever she was playing with, she did not move as quickly as my mother wanted her to move, and then my mother started to walk toward the car. I followed my mother.

How will she get home? I said.

That's up to her, my mother said. She has to learn to come when I tell her to come.

My mother got in the car. She opened the door for me. She started the car, then asked if I was getting in. Or did I want to be left behind with my sister?

We can't leave without her, I said.

It's your last chance to get in the car, she said.

I could see my sister in the distance, running toward us, calling for us to wait, Don't leave without me, I'm coming, I'm sorry, please wait for me. I was begging my mother not to leave without my sister, but my mother closed the door and started to pull away.

I yelled for my mother to stop, I was coming, I didn't want to be left behind.

My mother stopped the car. I got in, and then she drove away.

I can still see my sister running for the car.

* * *

It is the type of park with plenty of lights, and sometimes at night there are runners, and you can lie on the grass, even if you are alone, and watch the sky. You can close your eyes and listen to the runners breathing, their sneakers on the pavement.

On the spot of earth where the water fountain was is grass. Under the grass, dirt.

I have scraped paint from the place on the handball court wall my memory tells me is the place my sister and I carved our names.

Under the white paint was more white paint. Under that paint, more.

The story I tell myself—the story I have revised so many times that it is now more memory than imagination—is that my sister, upon seeing the car pull away, upon seeing my face on the other side of the car window, felt beneath her fear a sense of hope that she was not really being left behind, that one of us, her mother or her brother, would come back and find her, take her home, or maybe her mother would scream at her, slap her ear with such force that she, my sister, would have to sit in her room an hour, longer, waiting for the ringing in her ear to fade, or maybe her mother would pull her close by pulling her ponytail, and her brother would turn away as she knew him to turn away when her hair was pulled, as she knew herself to turn away when her brother's hair was pulled, or maybe beneath her fear was a belief, or a hope, that her mother driving around the corner to where my sister could no longer see was part of a lesson her mother wanted her to learn, which years later she and her mother would laugh about, Remember the time I left you in the park because you wouldn't come when I told you to come, when I told you enough was enough, it was time to go home so I could finish the laundry, so I could water the front garden and defrost the chicken for dinner and do all the things I did, and still do, that make me a good mother, and you went back to whatever it was you were playing with, and I told you three or four times that it was time to go, but you turned away, you ignored me the way I don't like to be ignored, the way a daughter should never ignore her mother, you were always doing that when you were young, even when you were playing on the street with your friends and I told you it was time to come in and you said just a few more minutes, that's what you always said when you were a girl, just a few more minutes, I don't want to come in yet, as if it would kill you to come in when you were told to come in, and I would say to you, Josephine, what time did we agree you would come in, and you would say whatever time we had agreed on, and I would ask you, Do you know what time it is now, and you would say, I don't know, and I would tell you, It's a half-hour past the time we agreed you would come in, do you see how I've already let you stay out longer than you should be staying out, and you would say, But can't I have just a few more minutes, and I would explain to you how, even if I gave you a few more minutes, when those few minutes had passed you would ask for a few minutes more, and this would continue until you were the last person standing on the street, and you would sulk and stomp your sneakers and make me look bad in front of all the other girls and in front of all the other mothers, who were always watching from their stoops, nosy mothers who thought they were the best mothers, and one time one of these mothers said something to me about why don't I just let you stay out a few minutes more, Would it be so terrible to allow your daughter, the poor girl, to stay out with her friends just a few minutes more, and that time, rather than give that woman a piece of my tongue, I walked out into the street and pulled you into the house by your hair, and I said to myself, No more, from now on when I say now it means now, no more dragging her by the hair, and that was why a few months later, in the park, when you didn't come when I asked you to come, I got in the car, and made your brother get in the car, and drove away.

Perhaps my sister, in the seconds after she lost sight of the car, imagined a future wherein the memory of my mother driving away would become no more important than any number of memories, a story that, from the vantage point of several years later, would become something to laugh about, though it is also possible that my sister—after she lost sight of the car, and after she hoped her mother or brother would return for her, and after she imagined one day laughing about this story with her mother—grew angry, went back to whatever she was playing with, the world she was creating in the dirt, rocks for buildings, pebbles for people, her spit for the ocean, her fingers to make waves in the ocean, to make buildings topple, to make people scatter for safety, perhaps she wanted her mother to find her like this, as if to say, Your plan to frighten me did not frighten me, you could have left me here an hour, two days, a week, still I would be here in my dirt world, which I created with my own spit and fingers, and which only I can destroy and rebuild with my own spit and fingers, and which you cannot touch. I imagine my sister's fingers deep in the dirt. Five minutes pass, five minutes that seem fifty, and now a man's voice: Was that your mother and brother that just left you? (My sister looks at the dirt below her nails: She will not look at the man standing beside her, only at his brown shoes, at his untied brown laces.) Don't be afraid, I won't hurt you. Was that your mother and brother in the red car? (My sister cannot see the dirt on her hair where her fingers have touched.) Because if that was your mother and brother in the red car, I just came running from where they got into an accident, right around the block, on the other side of the park, near the softball field, a very bad accident. But I don't want you to worry, they're going to be okay. Someone called an ambulance, and from the look of them they're probably going to the hospital, but your mother told me to find you. I was in the car behind her when it happened, and I pulled over and got out and went to see what they looked like, and there was some blood and bruises, that much I could see, and I told them not to move, that someone was going to call an ambulance, and your mother said to me, Go find my daughter, she's playing by the water fountain on the other side of the park, a girl six years old with her hair in a ponytail, brown hair, brown eyes, and I know that's you, and I think you should come with me right away to the other side of the park, just beyond those trees, where your mother and brother are waiting for you, or, if not waiting for you, then on their way to the hospital, where your mother said I should take you. (My sister is standing on her dirt world, her fingers working into her shorts, into her legs, leaving dirt marks on the skin of her legs, my sister staring at the ground the way I knew her when she was around strangers to stare at the ground.) We should hurry up and get there before they've gone. Your brother said something to me too, he said, Bring my sister, I want her with me, and I told him I would do that for him. Give me your hand and I'll lead you to where they are. We'll run together, to the other side of the park, right there where I'm pointing, just beyond those trees.

My mother took me to yard sales. I walked behind her. I pulled my wagon behind me. She bought plates and saucers and cups and glasses. A complete set for two dollars, or sometimes a quarter a plate, ten cents a glass; it did not matter if the glasses were cracked or if the patterns on the plates had faded.

She had me carry everything down to the basement. I tried to show her I was strong by carrying as much as possible. I had to walk down the stairs slowly. I had to watch out for the hole in the second-from-the-bottom step. She was always telling me to be careful. Don't carry too much at one time, she said. If you have to make trips, make trips.

Put them in the back room, she said. Against the wall with the others.

One time I dropped a stack of plates I should not have been trying to carry all at once. I made sure to pick up the broken pieces, then I placed the pieces into my wagon, then pulled my wagon to the garbage pail in the yard and dropped in the pieces, trying very hard not to make so much noise that my mother would hear. But then I heard her crying and knew she knew, and when I was finished dropping all the pieces into the pail I looked up and saw her at the kitchen window, watching me through the spaces between her fingers.

My father is not yet a character in this story because sometimes I wonder if he ever existed. During the time of this part of the story, he was a shadowy figure who, when he left for work each morning, opened the door slowly and closed it gently behind him, and who, when he came home, did the same. One moment he was there, the next he was not. One day a lung was taken from his body, and another day his body was taken from the house. But I know he existed: There are pictures. I remember the pants he wore, how they were too short, how the knees had faded. I remember the way he smoked with his legs crossed in the chair by the door. Sometimes he liked to stand near the window. I remember his hands parting drapes. I remember him picking at a sandwich. I remember him tasting a crust of bread then putting the bread back on his plate.

There may have been a time when he was someone else, when his life was life, but that father has been forgotten, replaced by the silent father who picks at a crust of bread.

We would sit in the living room, he in his chair by the door, me on the floor near his shoes, and I would watch him through the smoke between us. My memory tells me he would look at me then quickly look away.

He would stand, sometimes, when we heard my mother in the basement. He would pace to the window and back to his chair.

The sound of glass breaking came at intervals. I tried to find a pattern; there was no pattern. Sometimes ten seconds between. I counted to ten and waited, then continued counting; when I thought it was over, it wasn't. Six seconds between, then four. There was no way to prepare. I covered my ears but could feel the glass breaking. The wall my mother threw things against was almost directly below me. Only the floor beneath me and the ceiling above her were between us.

My father kept smoking; he crossed his legs.

When it was over—that is, when enough time had passed without the sound of glass breaking—my father got up from his chair and went down to the basement, and then my mother came upstairs and sat in the kitchen, where she listened to the news on the radio.

I pressed my ear against the floor.

My father sweeping. Broken glass dropped into a pail.

When he was finished, he came upstairs. Sometimes he liked to watch a ballgame. He chewed his nails.

One time, when my mother was taking a bath and my father was raking leaves in the yard, I went into the basement and picked up a plate. (I imagined another me playing on the living room floor above.) There were chips in the wall my mother threw things against. I moved my arm in the motion I imagined my mother made when she threw, but I did not let go of the plate.

When I heard my mother's footsteps, I put the plate back with the others.

When I was twelve, my mother was called to identify a body found seventy miles away, in upstate New York.

My father drove; we listened to news on the radio.

Trees were turning colors on the side of the highway. A two-lane accident slowed us. My father smoked out the window; he looked at his watch.

My mother sent my father inside; we waited in the car.

When my father came back to the car he shook his head no, then drove us home.

The present of this story is my typing these words with one hand so I can press the fingers of my other hand against the side of my nose, so I can breathe, so the tightness in my neck and chest will go away. The present of this story is a man, almost thirty years old, feeling in his body the fears he, as a child, did not feel. The nameless feeling when my mother drove around the park and came back to where we had left my sister, and saw that my sister was not where she had been playing, and when we stood where my sister had been playing, near the water fountain, and looked in all directions, and saw grass and dirt and sky and trees and people we did not know, and when we walked in every direction, together, calling my sister's name, and when my mother clutched my hand and squeezed my hand so hard I thought the bones in my hand would break, and when our voices grew tired, when the time between each call of my sister's name increased, and when we walked back to the car and sat in the car, and when my mother got out of the car and leaned her head against the top of the car so I could not see her face but could see her chest shaking, and when she walked away from the car and into the street, and when she looked at each person driving each car that passed, and when she raised her arm to signal a car to stop, and when that car did not stop, and when she came back to the car where we sat not looking at each other, and when we drove around the park, how many times, five times, fifty times, how long, two hours, longer, I don't know, and when she said loudly enough for me to hear how when she found my sister she was going to knock her teeth out, How stupid can she be to wander off like that, how many times have I told her never to wander off from the last place she was seen, I'll break that girl's teeth, I'll break every bone in her body, I'll make her swallow her teeth, and when we looked again in the park, and called my sister's name, and stood where she had been playing, and when we went back to the car and drove home, and when on the way home my mother drove too fast, and when on the way home she screamed out the window at a man who did not turn on his turn signal, and when we arrived home and discovered no one had called, and when my mother called my father at work and found out from him that no one had called, and when we got back in the car and drove to the park, and drove around the park I don't know how many times, and stood where my sister had been playing and called her name, and when we walked in every direction so many times that I knew every patch of dirt where grass had not grown, and when we walked toward the trees in the distance, and among the trees, and beyond the trees to the other side of the park, where I imagine my sister was taken—now, in my body, are all those feelings I did not, then, allow myself to feel.

I should mention:

There were times my sister and I spilled juice on the living room rug. There were times I pulled my sister's hair and she pulled mine. There were times I kicked my sister and, when she cried, kicked her again. There were times we chased each other around the house and screamed at each other and did not stop when we saw that our mother was trying to sleep. There were times my mother told us to quiet down, she had been working all day and did not feel well, could we stop screaming, could we please stop running around, could we sit down for just a few minutes?

One time my mother went away for two days.

Then my father said, I have a surprise for you.

When?

Tomorrow morning, he said.

We woke early and played on the floor near my father's shoes. He parted the drapes. We heard a car stop out front, and my father said, Here it is, here is your surprise, and we followed him down the stoop and to the car at the curb. My mother was in the backseat. My father paid the driver, then opened the back door and helped my mother out of the car. She looked at us and smiled. I looked behind her on the backseat and said, Where is the surprise? and my sister said, Where is the surprise? My father closed the door. Your mother is the surprise, he said. She was in the hospital. She had some tests. There was a lump in her chest. But everything is all right, it's nothing to worry about, and now she's home. We looked at each other and then at my father. Your mother is home, he said. That's the surprise. We could not think of what we were supposed to do. My father led us into the house.

When I was seven, and ten, and twenty-five, my mother said to me: That broke my heart that day. I thought to myself, my children don't love me.

Sometimes, now, in the present of this story, my mother asks me to come over and sleep on her couch: She is afraid of dying during the night. I can't breathe as I walk up the stoop, as I unlock the door. I go into the bathroom and take a pill. I can't breathe when I sit on the couch across from the chair I think of when I think of my father. An hour before trying to sleep, I take another pill. Sometimes, before my mother says, Good night, with the help of God I'll see you in the morning, she tells me the story of the day she came back from the hospital. She says, That broke my heart, what my children said to me.

One year after the fire in my mother's closet, I am a boy eight years old.

Let me begin with what I remember of that day in the park. I remember the look of the park (though perhaps my memory is tinted by my having been back there several times since I began writing this part of the story): a series of basketball courts, the remains of what were once red, white, and blue nets hanging from the rims; two handball courts that shared the same wall (against which older kids leaned while they smoked cigarettes and drank beer from small brown bottles); and what was called the playground area, which was separated from the handball courts by a small fence and which consisted of two slides, one seesaw, one sandbox, and monkey bars.

Here I am, in my mind, walking into the park with my mother. Here we are, sitting on a bench. She urges me to play in the playground area, where there are other children my age and some older, where there are children who are not me and who therefore (I used to think) must know everything about me, every feeling I have ever had, every secret: that sometimes my mother slipped into moods during which she stopped talking and refused to look at me; that sometimes I was afraid for and of my mother, for and of myself; that sometimes I sensed just beyond the reach of my knowing a future laden with disaster and the past from which it had come: This is me, now, projecting these thoughts onto the eight-year-old self of my memory; this is me, now, imagining a boy walking to the playground area, climbing the monkey bars while his mother watches from a park bench. He wraps his fingers around the cold bars; he pulls himself up and drapes his legs over the higher bars and pulls himself up and climbs higher; he hangs from the almost-highest bar, his body stretched by gravity; he wraps his legs around the highest bar and reaches for the ground; his hair reaches; the world is upside-down; his eyes are falling, his blood is falling, his liver and kidneys and heart are falling, in this upside-down world (though they are rising in his body, he imagines: Soon they will rise through his throat and into his mouth and he will cough them to the ground). And in this way—in his concentrating on using his hands and legs and muscles to make himself the very best at climbing these bars—he forgets about his mother.

When she sees that her son is no longer looking, she stands up from the bench and steps away from him, slowly, so as not to draw atten-

tion to herself (perhaps one of the other mothers saw her bring the boy into the park). She backs up a few steps, three or four or five, then a few steps more, and then she backs up to the entrance of the park and thinks: This is what it feels like to move away from a child, this is how to move away from a child and feel no worry.

When I came down from the monkey bars, the ground was moving, and the trees and houses around the park were spinning, and I had to wait for the world to right itself. I looked at the bench where my mother had been sitting and saw that she was no longer there. I looked at the other benches, and at the women sitting on these benches, and wondered if this was a new world in which my mother was someone else. I wanted to find a mirror or a puddle, anything I could look into, so I could know it was the same world and the same me.

I walked around the playground area, then from bench to bench (where I could see more clearly the women's faces), then onto the handball courts (a boy pressing his body against a girl backed against the graffiti-covered wall, brown glass at their feet), then onto the basketball courts (one boy boosting another so he could touch the rim), then onto the softball field (hundreds of bottle caps embedded in the concrete), then back to the playground area, where a woman touched my arm.

Where is your mother?

I don't know.

Are you here alone?

Her son, who was around my age, looked at me, then grabbed his mother's hand. She walked us around the playground area, from bench to bench, onto the handball then basketball courts, around the softball field, and back to the place where she first touched me.

Did you come to the park alone? she asked. Do you live around here?

And then suddenly my mother was there again, as if she had never been gone, pulling me away from the woman.

Are you the boy's mother? she said. I found him wandering around. I think he was looking for you. He was alone, and I wondered—

What did you wonder? my mother said.

Her eyes turned to slits, and her lips disappeared. The woman stepped back, and the boy hid behind her.

Tell me what you wondered, my mother said. Tell me what you wondered about this boy's mother. Go ahead, tell me, she said, and then the woman and her son walked away.

There are many stories my imagination has created. My favorite is the story of my sister's escape: Maybe, at the park, she runs away before getting into the man's car. Maybe she senses something is wrong the way some children have the power to sense something is wrong. Maybe she sees a woman walking a dog, or a woman crying, or a man and woman kissing, or a man and woman fighting, or a group of boys playing baseball, or a group of boys drinking beer, it doesn't matter whom she sees, she senses something is wrong and sees someone and runs toward whomever she sees; maybe her running away catches the man by surprise and he does not react quickly enough to stop her; maybe the man, afraid of being caught, runs in the opposite direction. But this story does not work for me; I can take it only so far, and then it begins to fall apart, for I do not know, nor can my imagination tell me, what happens to my sister after she runs away from the man and toward whomever she sees in the park and tells this person, or these people, that a man has been trying to take her away and her mother and brother were in a car accident and she isn't sure whom she should trust and would they, let's say the couple fighting, would they take her home or to the hospital where her mother and brother might be, would they please tell her what she should do? I don't know what happens to my sister after she asks these people for help because my brain tells me these people would have brought my sister home. But I never saw her again, except in my mind: when I can't sleep, when I open my eyes in the dark of my room and see her hanging from the ceiling, or when she is floating outside my window, or when I'm taking a shower and sense her on the other side of the shower curtain, or when I see her reflection, as I just saw her reflection, in the glass of my computer screen. So my story breaks down, my sister does not escape at the park, she does not run away from the man, she does not see a woman crying or a couple fighting or a group of boys drinking beer, or maybe she does see these people but she senses they are not safe, the man she is with is safer than these people, maybe she gets into the man's car and during the drive he allows her to play with the radio dial and asks her name and her favorite this, her favorite that, maybe she begins to forget that her mother and brother have been in a serious car accident and are on their way to the hospital, maybe she forgets how, according to this man, her brother asked for her, her brother wanted her with him when he suffered whatever a person suffers after he has been in a car accident, her brother wanted them to grow up together in the same house with the same father and mother, he did not want to grow up alone in the house he knew with the mother and father he knew, maybe my sister forgets about me and instead focuses on how this man allows her to play with the radio dial for as long as she wants to play with it and never asks her to choose one goddamn station with the tone of voice she hated when her mother used it, and how this man seems like the kind who would never slap her even if she doesn't listen when he asks her nicely to stop playing with the radio dial, maybe my sister does not feel the need to escape, maybe she senses that driving with this man is the escape she has been waiting for, maybe the man drives her to a neighborhood she does not recognize, to a house in the suburbs, say, and tells her he has to go inside and call the closest hospital and make sure he has the right one, sometimes an ambulance will transport people to the closest hospital, but sometimes, because of problems too complicated to explain, the ambulance will transport people to a hospital other than the closest, he must go inside and call to make sure, she should come inside with him, he doesn't think her mother or her brother—who, in his opinion, seemed to care about her quite a bit, asking for his sister the way he did—would want him, this man, to leave her, their daughter/sister, outside in the car while he goes inside to make a phone call, you never know these days who is going to come and snatch you away, there are all sorts of bad people in the world, and so my sister is more than happy to go into the man's house, more than happy to accept when he offers her juice, more than happy to say yes when he asks would she like to play with his new video game system, and more than willing to believe, an hour later, when he tells her her mother and brother are doing fine, and her father is there with them, but the doctors said only one visitor at a time, and her family agreed it would be best if she stayed here with him as long as necessary, they would call when it was time for her to visit, and what would she like for dinner, whatever she wants, and did she see the rest of the video games in his collection, and if she wants to take a nap, take a nap, if she wants to watch television, watch television, if she wants to play the radio, play the radio, if she wants to sing a song, sing a song, if she wants to dance, dance, but she shouldn't go outside because of what he told her before about the bad people in this world and how her family is trusting him to take care of her, and she shouldn't use the phone, in case the hospital is trying to call. But here, again, my story falls apart, for the hospital never calls, and my sister never comes home, and so the story of my sister's escape, if it is to remain a story of my sister's escape and not become the story of my sister's death, must by necessity be an escape *to* this man rather than from him, and when I think of the story this way—when I am forced to think of it this way—I begin to see my sister outside my window with more frequency, or hanging from the ceiling of my room, or reflected in my computer screen, or in my dreams.

Last night—almost the present of this story—was not the first time I have awakened from sleep because I could not breathe. I found myself running to the front door, as if something inside my house was chasing me. Though I live alone, I was screaming, Come with me, come with me, hurry up! I opened the door, and looked out into the night, and felt the cold on my face, and listened. I waited by the door. I wasn't sure if I was waiting to run outside or if I was trying to lock something out.

* * *

The present of this story consists of these words—my ordering them in a way I have allowed myself to believe will make the tightness in my chest go away.

The tightness in my chest reminds me of the year, several years after my sister was gone, when I became afraid of the weather. I counted the seconds between lightning and thunder. I would not go outside when it rained. At the sound, or feel, of the slightest wind, I would ask my father, and then my mother, to close all the windows. No one closed the windows. No one told me the wind would not blow down our house, would not blow all of us away.

note to future self

My twin sister called me collect last week and told me that her boyfriend had been beating her for the past two years and that a few days earlier he had kicked her so many times in the face that she had to go to the hospital to have the cuts on her lips sewn shut. She was calling me because now her boyfriend had threatened to rip the stitches out of her lips. He pulled out all the phone cords in the house and went out to have a drink and to think about what he was going to do to her. He took the phone cords with him. My sister was calling from a pay phone down the street from where she lived. She didn't know what to do.

"That scumbag," I said. "I should fucking kill him, that animal. I should—"

Then I said: "You're calling me after two years of this?"

"You're my brother," she said.

"Jesus," I said. "What do you want me to do?"

My sister was calling from upstate, where her boyfriend made her move because he said he had work there. As far as I know, he stayed home while my sister worked, and it was his strong opinion that she didn't bring home enough money. The reason for the last beating, my sister told me, was that she, after three weeks of looking, had not found a second job.

My sister had not bought a new pair of socks in two years. Her boyfriend had control of her credit cards. This, and other things, I learned from my mother, who didn't know about the beatings but would call me every few weeks to say, "Listen to what he did to her now" or "This guy is just like your father" or "What did I tell you—this guy is no good."

Now my sister was crying into the phone. It was snowing, she told me. She wasn't wearing a coat. I could hear her starting to hyperventilate.

"Don't go back into the house," I told her. "Go to the bus station and take the next bus to the city."

"I don't know where the bus station is."

"Call information."

"I don't have a quarter."

"You don't need a quarter to call information."

"I don't want to take the bus," she said. "I'm afraid."

"What are you afraid of?"

"Strange men."

"Nothing will happen to you."

"The last time I was on a bus, a man put his hand on my leg. Every time I moved away, he kept putting his hand back on my leg. So finally I just . . . I let him keep his hand there, and—"

"Okay."

"I kept trying to move away, but where could I go? I was on a bus. Where was I supposed to go?"

"Okay, okay."

"I'm sorry."

"Jesus," I said. "Take it easy."

"I'm sorry," she said.

"Listen," I said. "If anyone tries to touch you, get up from your seat and go tell the driver."

"What would I say?"

"That some pervert is trying to touch you."

"I can't say that."

"Why not?"

"What if the guy hears me saying that about him?"

"Let him hear," I said. "And, besides, no one is going to touch you. Trust me. Just get on the next bus. I'll be waiting for you at the station. As soon as you step off the bus, I'll be right there."

"I don't have any money," she said.

"Go to a friend's house and borrow some money."

"I don't have any friends."

"Go to a neighbor's house."

"I don't know the neighbors," she said. "I'm not allowed to speak with anyone."

"For God's sake," I said, and then I thought about what to say next.

"Hello?" my sister said.

"Hello," I said. "I'm here."

"Hello?" she said. "Are you there?"

"I'm right here. Can you hear me?"

"Hello, can you hear me?"

"I'm right here. I can hear you."

"Hello?" she said. "Hello?"

"Jesus Christ," I said. "I can hear you. I'm right here."

"Where are you?" she said. "Are you there? Hello?"

"I'm right here!"

"What happened?" she said. "Where did you go?"

"I was here the whole time."

"I thought you hung up the phone."

"Now why would I hang up at a time like this?"

"I don't know," she said. "I'm just scared. There's no one else I can call."

"Listen to me," I said. "Go to the police and—"

"I won't go to the police."

"Just tell them you need to borrow some money."

"I'll have to tell them what the money is for."

"Of course you will."

"Then they'll go after him," she said. "They'll pick him up and bring him in."

"Good," I said. "That's what you want."

"Then what will I do?"

"Then you'll be able to get money from your checking account and get on a bus to the city."

"I don't have a bank card."

"Trust me," I said. "The police will get you on a bus to the city."

"Would you drive up here and pick me up?"

"You know I don't have a car."

"Maybe you can borrow someone's car."

"I don't want to go asking someone to borrow a car," I said. "I wouldn't know who to ask."

"Can you rent a car?"

"Listen," I said. "Just get on a bus to the city."

"I don't have any money!" she said. "Can't you please rent a car and drive up here and get me?"

"It's three hours at least," I said, "and by the time I rent a car . . ."

"Please," she said.

"It will be much quicker for you to get on a bus," I said. "Do you want him to rip the stitches out of your lips?"

"No," she said, and then she cried into the phone.

"Listen," I said. "You need to get your bearings here."

"I would feel much safer if you would come pick me up."

"It's three hours," I said. "And, besides, where would I pick you up?"

"I would be at the house."

"And where would he be?"

"He would be at the house with me."

"It's three hours!" I said. "Do you know what could happen to you in three hours?"

"I'll stay out of his way," she said.

"Jesus," I said. "In three hours he could . . . Jesus, I don't want to think about what he might do to you."

"Please," she said.

"What am I supposed to do when I get there?"

"Just knock on the door," she said, "and when I answer you can say that you know what's been going on and that you're taking me home."

"Wait a second," I said. "What if he pulls out a gun or goes into the kitchen and brings out a knife and tries to kill me or something?"

"He won't do that."

"He busted up your lips," I said, "and God knows what else he's done to you."

"It's been awful," she said.

"I don't want to know," I said.

"I don't think he owns a gun," she said.

"That's great," I said.

"Don't worry," she said. "As soon as you knock and say why you're here and that you're taking me home, I'll walk right out the door."

"He's not going to just let you go," I said. "I mean, we both know he's not the type of man to sit there and watch me take you away. He's likely to try something."

"Hello?" she said.

"Hello," I said.

"Are you still there?"

"Yes," I said. "Can you hear me?"

"Are you there?" she said. "Hello? Hello?"

"I'm right here."

"Say something," she said. "Say something so I know you're still there."

"I'm here," I said, and then the line went dead.

I waited five minutes then called my sister at home. There was no answer. I waited another five minutes and called again. There was still no answer. I waited ten more minutes and tried again. This time her boyfriend answered.

"Hello," he said.

"Who is this?" he said.

"Who the hell is this?" he said, and then I hung up.

I sat by the phone, angry with my sister for not listening to me. She was probably on her way back to the house. Her boyfriend was probably furious that she wasn't home, where she was supposed to be (I knew from my mother) every minute she wasn't working. I started imagining his fingers digging into my sister's lips, and I found myself becoming angrier with my sister for not listening to me.

I tried calling again. My sister's boyfriend answered. "Hello?" he said. "Who's there?"

I waited, hoping I might hear my sister's voice or some other noise that would indicate she was there.

"Who the fuck is this?" he said.

I stopped breathing and listened.

"If you call here one more time—" he said, and then I hung up.

I kept telling myself: She's going to be fine, she's perfectly safe, she's going to be fine, she's perfectly safe. I was able to convince myself that my sister had gone to the police, or had managed to get on the next bus to the city, or was home with her boyfriend and knew, as she said she did, how to stay out of his way.

But when a half-hour passed and I didn't hear from her, I dialed her number again. No one answered. I hung up and dialed again. Still no one answered. I waited ten minutes and tried again. I let the phone ring thirty, maybe forty, times.

Flashes in my head: My sister lying on the floor with blood on her lips and teeth, her eyes open. My sister's body dragged across the floor.

I dialed again and after each ring told myself that the next ring would be answered, and I was prepared, if my sister's boyfriend answered, to tell him that I knew what was going on and that I was coming to get my sister and that he had better not be there when I got there because I was going to rip his balls from his body and step on them, and I waited another ten rings, then another twenty or thirty, and then I decided I would give it another twenty rings, and I counted each one, and when I got to twenty I decided to give it one more ring, and when no one answered I hung up the phone.

I tried to think of where I might be able to get a car. None of my friends in the city owned a car. My mother had one, but she was the last person I wanted to involve. I didn't want to hear her say, "I told you so. What did I tell you about that guy—just like your father." The first car rental place I called was too expensive, the second was closed for the evening, and the last place had no cars available. "Are you sure?" I asked the woman who had answered the phone. "We're sorry, sir." "But aren't you supposed to always have cars?" "It's a very busy time of year." "Are you sure no one has canceled reservations?" "We're sorry, sir." I thought of explaining to her why I needed a car, but then she started what I knew—because I had heard it before—was a scripted speech about how I could get free maps and emergency road service and how I could save up to 20 percent in more than five hundred hotels nationwide, and so I thanked her—for what, I'm not sure—and hung up.

I dialed my sister's number. I counted forty rings. I told myself I was going to let the phone ring until someone answered—I would not move from where I was standing until I heard my sister's or my sister's boyfriend's voice—but after forty or fifty more rings I became angry at the predictable and very annoying sound in my ear and slammed down the receiver and, without intent, chipped off a piece of the phone, and then I was so furious that I had chipped the phone—and all because my sister would not listen to me and get on the next bus to the city—that I pulled the phone up from the table (what I intended to do with the phone, once in my hands, I can't recall) and in the process yanked the cord from the wall jack, and after I sat down for a moment to calm down I realized that at that very moment my sister may have been trying to call me, and so I tried to plug the cord back into the wall jack, and it was then that I discovered that the plastic piece that connects the cord to the wall jack had been broken when I pulled up the phone, and by this time I was beginning to panic at the thought that my sister may have been trying to call me, and was becoming even more furious that everything that can go wrong *will* go wrong at the exact moment you can least afford to have anything go wrong, and then I closed my eyes and breathed in through my nose and held each breath to the count of ten and thought good thoughts about things finally working out when you want them to work out, and once I had achieved some semblance of optimism I opened my eyes and looked through all the drawers and closets and cabinets in my apartment until I found (what little faith in the universe I had would have been destroyed had I not found it) a spare phone cord. I plugged the phone back in the wall and waited.

I closed my eyes and tried to envision my sister at the bus station. She was dialing my number. I could see her fingers pressing each button for each digit in my phone number. My phone was going to ring . . . *now.*

I concentrated. My sister in a bus station. Her fingers pushing the buttons. My phone was going to ring . . . right . . . *now.*

I dialed my sister's number and waited. Countless rings. No answer.

I put on my boots and coat and gloves (deep breath in, hold to ten, long exhale) and walked to the subway station. When the train arrived, I saw that most of the cars had only a few people inside. I sat far enough away from the other people so that no one would be tempted to speak to me. I tried to look angry, but then I felt silly that I was trying to make myself look angry, so I decided, instead, to close my eyes. I didn't feel safe with my eyes closed, so I opened them. Above the seats across from me were advertisements for wart removal cream, invisible braces, and a debt counselor. While my train was stopped in a station, a train passed going in the opposite direction. I could see people going home from work standing against one another. The looks on their faces (angry, tired, defeated, or a combination of all these) seemed directed at me. I closed my eyes. I put my hands over my face. The train I was on moved out of the station.

A man's voice on the train's intercom said, "Port Authority, transfers here to—," and the rest I didn't hear. I walked through the station and tried not to question what I was doing. This could be a fine trip, I decided. Sure, this could turn out to be a trip with a happy ending. "Everything is going to be fine," I said, and then worried that someone heard me say this. What was going to happen when I arrived where my sister lived might be something I'd remember for the rest of my life (I told myself) and could very well turn into a story I might tell—and with pride—to my children, if I ever have children. *Did I ever tell you about the time my sister called from upstate and told me her boyfriend had been beating her, and I took a bus all the way up there, three hours, and took her away from him? Sure, he tried to get tough with me. He said I wasn't taking her anywhere but over his dead body, and I stared at him with this look that said, Listen, I have news for you, my body isn't going to be the dead body, okay, and then—.* I looked up and realized I had been walking in the wrong direction. I turned around, and after a while (deep breaths) I saw the sign for the bus terminal. I checked the departure schedule and found that the universe was starting to work in my favor: A bus was leaving for where my sister lived within the hour.

I bought, from a vending machine, a bag of corn chips and a can of fruit juice. I read on the back of the bag that there were five chips per serving and approximately four servings in the bag, which meant there were, give or take, twenty chips. The bus was leaving in forty minutes. I ate a chip, took a sip of juice, then counted to 120 before eating the next chip and taking the next sip of juice, and in this way I was able to pass the forty minutes without thinking too much about what I was about to do. A man struggling to carry three bags, a boy and a girl walking behind him, asked if I knew when the bus to Providence was leaving and where from, and I told him I didn't know, that I was waiting for a bus going upstate, and he showed me his ticket and asked again if I knew, and I told him I had no idea, and while he was asking me all this one of his kids, the boy, had wandered off, and I pointed this out to him and felt good about doing so, but then the man ran after and caught his son playing in a garbage pail and pulled the boy away from the pail and smacked him twice across the face and pulled the boy by his hair back to where I was standing and with an angry look on his face said he was sorry, and then turned and yelled at his son, who was crying, to shut up, and then he asked again if I could look at his ticket and figure out where he was supposed to go, and I looked at his ticket and said no, I was sorry, I had no idea, and the man walked away with the boy and girl behind him, and this was why, when I boarded the bus, I still had a few chips left in my bag of chips and a few sips of juice left in my can of juice—because this man trying to go to Providence had taken up several minutes of the time I would have otherwise spent eating chips and sipping juice.

I sat near the front. The bus, with the exception of a few overhead reading lights, was dark. A kid with a Walkman sat next to me, his eyes closed, his head moving to the beat of his music. There were lights on the sides of the highway, but after a while there were no more lights. A piece of the moon was visible in the sky, and the rest of the moon (I reminded myself) was right there as well. For a while I stared out at the dark part of the moon and wondered if I was the only person in the world actually looking at that part of the moon no one could see, and thinking about this passed a little time. But staring too long at something I couldn't see made me feel sick to my stomach, so I stared instead at the seatback in front of me. It was difficult not to imagine a future me thinking back on the present me and saying, "Man, what the hell did you think you were doing that night? Did you think you were some kind of hero?" I hated my future self for saying this, and I hated my present self for not having the power of foresight. I was angry with myself for not having thought to buy another bag of chips and another can of juice to ration out during the ride. I closed my eyes and tried to think of something that would distract me from questioning what I was doing, but all I could think about were the two children and their father in the bus station. I spent the first hour of the ride creating elaborate fantasies about their lives, and for some time it was as if I were in a trance or watching a movie, but after a while I discovered that what I thought I was imagining I was not imagining at all: The two children were actually my sister and I, and the imagined father had become my father, and the slaps to the faces of those two children had become slaps to my face and to my sister's, and eventually my father slapping my sister's face turned into my sister's boyfriend slapping her face, and I found myself getting very angry that people smacked around other people, and even angrier that people allowed themselves to be smacked around, and to distract myself from these thoughts I ate one of the four chips left in my bag of chips and drank approximately one-fourth of the juice left in my can of juice and counted to eighteen hundred (there were, with luck, only two hours left on the trip), and did this three more times, and within thirty minutes after I ate my last chip and drank the last of my juice, the bus pulled into the station.

I called for a cab. The driver drove me through the town. I had never been there before, but it looked like what I had imagined up-state towns looked like: a few churches, a school, a grocery store, a row of bars, piles of snow along the curbside and a dusting on the streets. The driver stopped the car in front of a small blue house. "Is this it?" I said.

"This is it," he said. "That's why I stopped the car."

I said, "Could you do me a favor and leave me off at the corner?"

First, I walked past the house, as if I were just some person on my way somewhere else. I glanced at the house as I passed and saw that a light was on downstairs. When I reached the opposite corner I waited a few minutes (so as not to cause suspicion) before retracing my steps. This time I stopped in front of the house next door. I could see nothing I hadn't seen the time before—a light was on downstairs. I stepped closer to the house. *I'm afraid I have some terrible news for my sister. It's our mother. One of her neighbors found her in the hall-way. They're saying it was a heart attack. I wanted to give her the news in person, of course, and I didn't want her to travel down to the city alone.* The porch light came on, and I ran into the driveway. I waited to hear the door open, but it did not open. I stood where I had been crouching. Through a window I could see the living room. There was a couch and a coffee table and a television and two chairs, and in one of these, a bottle of beer in his hand, was my sister's boyfriend. Since the last time I had seen him, more than two years ago, he had put on some weight (I could see it in his face) and had shaved the hair on his head to a dark shadow. I saw his lips moving and assumed my sister must be home, but then I realized he was talking to himself. He stood, put on his coat, and walked to the door. He leaned his face into the door, said a few things to himself, then sat down with his coat on and talked to himself some more, and then he took off his coat and threw it on the floor. I went from window to window, looked into the kitchen and what might have been (had there been a table and chairs) the dining room, but didn't see my sister. There were no lights on upstairs.

I walked to what looked like the main street of this town, found a pay phone, and dialed my sister's number.

"Hello," my sister's boyfriend said.

"Who is this?" he said.

"Listen—" he said.

"Hello," I said.

"Who is this?"

"Hello?" I said.

"I said hello," he said.

"Is anyone there?" I said.

"What is this about?" he said.

"Your wife," I said.

"Yes?" he said.

"There has been an accident," I said. "Your wife—she must have fallen on the ice and hit her head, and we have her here at the hospital."

"What happened?" he said. I couldn't tell if he sounded worried or annoyed.

"We're not sure," I said. "It appears that she may have fallen on the ice and hit her head."

"What do you mean?" he said. "When did this happen?" His voice was beginning to shake.

"We're not entirely sure," I said. "What we know is that someone found your wife on the ground, unconscious, and saw that her head was bleeding and that her lips were split open, and this person called 9-1-1, and an ambulance brought her here to the hospital, and the doctors are running some tests as we speak."

"Where did she fall?"

"Again, we don't have all the details at this point," I said. "We only know that she busted her head open, most likely from a fall. Unless you have any other information you can give us."

"What do you mean?"

"Unless you can provide us with any other information concerning your wife's accident."

"What does that mean?"

"I'm talking about her medical history," I said. "Your wife has quite a few stitches on her lips. Since we don't have any medical records for your wife, and since she was brought in unconscious, we were wondering if you could tell us exactly what happened that she needed stitches in her lips."

"What is this about?"

"It's about your wife," I said. "We're interested in her medical history. For example, the stitches in her lips. We were wondering—does she fall often? And if she does, are her falls the result of seizures of some kind, or is there some other reason your wife has a tendency to fall?"

"My wife does not have a tendency to fall."

"We're not saying your wife has a tendency to fall," I said. "We're not saying that at all."

"What are you saying?"

"We're merely trying to get some information from you."

"Who is this?"

"I'm calling from the hospital."

"What hospital?"

"Sir, there's only one hospital in the area."

"Tell me the name of the hospital."

"Don't you know the name of the hospital?"

"I know the name, but I want you to tell me."

"Excuse me," I said.

"I want you to tell me your name and position, and then I want you to tell me exactly where the hospital is and give me directions how to get there."

"I'm having trouble hearing you," I said.

"I want to know your name," he said.

"Hello?" I said.

"Hello," he said.

"Hello?" I said. "Are you there?"

"I'm right here," he said.

"I think we must have a bad connection," I said.

"I can hear you just fine," he said.

"Sir?" I said. "Are you still there, sir?"

"I can hear you," he said.

"Sir, I can't hear you, and I think we may have been disconnected, but if you can still hear me, let me tell you again that we think your wife may have fallen on the ice and landed on her head, and the doctors are running tests, and it would be helpful if you could come over to the hospital right away."

"Tell me your name!" he said.

"Thank you, sir," I said. "I hope you heard what I just said."

"I know who you are," he said.

"Good-bye, sir," I said, and then I hung up.

I walked back to my sister's street and watched her house. Snow was falling on the snow and ice already on the ground; wind blew snow from the roofs of houses, from the hoods of cars, and up from the ground. My sister's boyfriend did not come out.

I started to walk through the town, looking for the police station, but when I found it I had no idea what I was supposed to do or say.

I'm trying to find my sister. Is she missing? *Yes . . . well, no, not exactly.* Why are you looking for her? *She called earlier this evening and told me her boyfriend, whom she lives with, has been beating her for the past two years, and she was afraid he was going to hurt her again, and I told her to get on the next bus to the city, where I live, but she didn't have any money, and she didn't know where the bus station was, and then we were disconnected, and then—.* Hold on, hold on, where is the boyfriend? *He's at home.* How do you know? *I called.* Give me the address. *What for?* We'll go over there and ask him a few questions. *I don't want you to do that.* Why not? *I don't want to get involved with him.* Why not? *I just want to find my sister.*

I waited outside the station for a half-hour then decided it was foolish to expect my sister, if she had gone to the police, to walk outside.

I found a pay phone and called for a cab. While waiting, I tried to distract myself by kicking my boot heel through the ice of a puddle, but I lost my footing and fell, and when I stood I couldn't keep my back straight without pain, and I found myself angry at my sister again for not getting on a bus when I told her to get on a bus, and when the pain in my back began to move down into my legs I knew I was going to be in for a rough three hours sitting on the bus to the city, and I was furious at my sister for not walking into the police station and telling them that her fuckhead boyfriend had been beating her and had threatened to rip the stitches out of her lips and that she wanted him arrested and wanted to be able to get money for a bus ticket from the checking account she worked every fucking day to earn money to put into, and this anger, coupled with the pain in my back and legs, led me to start punching the glass around the pay phone, not hard enough to break through but hard enough to start a crack in the glass and cut open my hand, and the harder I punched the glass the more I was able to forget the pain in my back and legs and the anger I was feeling toward my sister and toward everything that had ever happened, but then I heard a horn and saw that the driver was there, and I walked, not without pain, to the car, and told him to take me to the bus station.

The next bus to the city was leaving in a few hours. I sat on a bench and rubbed the cut on my hand so that I could feel the pain from the cut but very little else.

By the time I was on the bus and well into the ride back to the city, I had rubbed the cut to the point at which I got so used to the pain that it was no longer pain, and it was difficult then to keep from thinking about other things.

I was riding my bicycle down the street and saw a girl slap my sister's face and pull her hair, and there were other girls watching, and I stopped and watched, and the girl kept slapping my sister, and the other girls laughed, and my sister did nothing, and I wanted to run to my sister and shake her and say, "Why don't you do something? How can you stand there and take that?" A few minutes later there was another thought—the time a girl at school lit my sister's shorts on fire, and my sister stood there while her shorts burned and did not move to put the fire out, did not cry, did not jump or scream, did not react in any way, just looked down, until a teacher saw what was happening, ran over, pulled off my sister's shorts, and threw them in the bathroom sink. "What are you doing?" the teacher said to my sister. "What's going on here?" she said. "Who is responsible for this?" My sister said nothing. I shook this thought out of my head, but there was another memory right behind it—the time on our street when my sister and I were about thirteen and one of my friends kept squeezing my sister's breasts between his fingers, and all my other friends were watching and laughing and kept saying to me, "Hey, look, he's giving your sister a purple nurple, why aren't you looking, he's giving your sister a purple nurple, look at that, do you see what he's doing to your sister," and I looked at her and then looked away, and said nothing, and my sister did not flinch, did not back away, did not raise her hands in defense.

In the sky I could see the first glow from the sun. I couldn't sleep. Every time I closed my eyes I saw shapes in the dark under my eyelids.

The bus pulled into Port Authority. I walked through the station and waited for the train back to Queens, and I was grateful for all the people around me because I could look at them and wonder about their lives and create stories in my head about who they were and what they were like and everything that had happened to them, and in this way I was able, for a short while, to forget what I had remembered about my sister and to forget that I still didn't know where she was.

There was some hope, as I turned the corner and walked up my street, that my sister would be waiting for me outside the building where I lived, but she wasn't there. I went upstairs, changed clothes, made a cup of coffee, and turned on the television. I dialed my sister's number. There was no answer.

An hour later I dialed her number again and waited. Though I couldn't see it behind all the buildings, I knew the sun was up. In a few hours I would have to leave for work. I hung up the phone.

I took a shower. My sister was under my eyelids: Her hair was on fire, and her hands were at her sides.

When I turned off the water I thought I heard something. I stood where I was and listened. Then I heard it again. I went to the intercom and pressed the button. "Who is it?" I said.

"It's me," my sister said.

I waited with my finger on the button.

"Hello?" she said. "Are you there?"

"Is that you?" she said.

"Hello?" she said. "Is anyone there?"

"I'm looking for my brother," she said. "Is that you?"

"Hello?" she said.

"Would you please let me in?" she said.

"Are you still there?" she said. "Hello?" she said.

"It's cold out here," she said. "I'm tired."

"Will you please say something?" she said.

When my sister and I were fifteen, maybe sixteen, we made plans to meet in front of Macy's. We were shopping for Christmas gifts. I said, "Meet me right outside the main entrance, where they keep all the perfume." I waited and waited and waited, and after an hour had passed I started to become excited that my sister was late and that I had every reason, when and if she showed up, to scream at her, to make her feel like nothing, to unleash all the anger inside me, to tell her what a fuckup she was for always fucking up the simplest things, and with every minute that passed I grew more excited about being able to unleash all this anger on someone I knew would do or say nothing in her own defense, and after another half-hour passed I called home and asked my father if my sister had called, and he said no, and asked what was the matter, couldn't my sister and I do anything right, Jesus Christ, couldn't we just meet each other where we said we would meet each other, and I told my father it was my sister's fault, how at that very moment I was standing—and for the past hour and a half had been standing—in the exact spot where my sister and I had agreed to meet, and my father told me to call back if my sister didn't show up within the next half-hour, and when she didn't I called and my father said, "Jesus fucking Christ, this is typical, whenever the two of you make plans, you can bet someone is going to fuck up," and I explained how it was my sister who had fucked up and how I was exactly where I was supposed to be, and he said that now he was going to have to stop what he was doing and drive across the

Williamsburg Bridge to Manhattan and "probably kill myself with all those crazy drivers over there and probably circle the block two hundred times before I even find you or your sister," and I told him he didn't have to come, that I would take care of it, and my father told me there was nothing I could take care of, that if I was the type of person to take care of things I wouldn't be calling him with "all this bullshit about your sister being lost," and I told him again that he didn't have to come, and he said, "And then what? What will happen to you and your sister if I don't come?" Ten minutes later my sister showed up, crying, and said she had been at the main entrance near where they sell perfume, and when I didn't show up she started to worry and thought about looking for me, but then she remembered what I told her, that under no circumstances should she leave the main entrance near where they sell perfume, but after more than an hour had passed she went inside, just for a moment, to ask one of the women behind the counter if there was another part of the store that sold perfume, and the woman said yes, there were other perfume counters around the corner near the other entrance. My sister said, "I'm sorry, please say something. Would you please look at me? I swear, had I known there were two entrances where they sell perfume, I would have looked for you here much earlier." My sister stood next to me and cried, but I refused to look at her. Then I saw my father's car in the street, saw my father waving us over, and my sister followed me, and no one said anything on the drive home. When we got inside my father took off his coat and sat on the couch, and I sat on a chair, and my sister asked if my father wanted something to drink, and thanked him for coming to get us, and asked if she could get him anything. My father turned on the television and said nothing. My sister left the room, but a few minutes later she came back and asked if she could bring my father a sandwich, something to drink, anything, it was no problem, and when my father said nothing my sister thanked him again for coming to get us and offered to give him money for gas and tolls, and it was then that my father stood up and slapped her face, knocking her to the floor. He stood over her and said, "Everything is after the fact, everything is always after the fact," and then he sat back on the couch and looked at my sister and said, "It's not about the gas or the tolls. Jesus, if only once you could do something right and listen," and then I stood up and walked past my sister and out of the room.

"Hello?" she said, and I could tell she had been crying.

My finger was on the button. I was trying to breathe deeply. "Hello," I said.

"Where were you?" she said. "I got on the next bus, like you said, and I came here looking for you." She waited a moment and then said, "Are you there?"

"I'm here," I said.

"What's wrong?" she said.

"I don't feel well."

"Are you going to buzz me in?"

"No," I said.

"What do you mean?" she said.

"Don't move," I said. "Don't do anything. Just stay where you are," I said. "I'm coming down to get you."

I put on some clothes and walked down the stairs. I opened the door and let her inside. The stitches were still in her lips.

"I'm sorry," I said.

She walked up the stairs. I walked behind her.

the worst degree of unforgivable

The bedroom drapes must touch; we must beat dust from the drapes; we must wave our hands through the airborne dust; if the dust makes us sneeze, we must use a tissue from the tissue box on the nightstand; we must place the used tissue in the small garbage pail beside the toilet; if the garbage bag is filled, or almost filled, we must tie the bag, remove it from inside the pail (making sure to recover any stray garbage found in the pail under the bag), and place it inside a larger bag under the kitchen sink; if the bag under the kitchen sink is filled, or almost filled, we must tie that bag, remove it from under the sink, and place it in one of two garbage pails in the backyard; if both garbage pails are filled, or almost filled, or if it is Tuesday or Friday—pickup days—we must wheel the pails to the front of the house and place them at the curb; we must make sure the pails' lids are secured tightly enough that raccoons or stray dogs cannot easily knock the lids off and rip open the bags and scatter garbage along the sidewalk; we must position the pails close enough to the street so that sanitation workers may carry them the shortest possible distance from curbside to the back of the sanitation truck (thereby decreasing the chance that garbage might fall from the pails), but not so close to the street that the sanitation truck, when it passes, can possibly knock over and damage the pails; we must sweep any leaves and pollynoses that have collected in the spot in the yard where the garbage pails have been; before we step back into the house, we must wipe the bottoms of our shoes on the welcome mat outside the back door; we must place a fresh medium-sized garbage bag under the kitchen sink; we must place a fresh smallest-size garbage bag in the bathroom pail; we must make sure the tissue box on the nightstand beside the bed is in its proper place at the proper angle with exactly one tissue extending up through the hole in the top of the box; if while sneezing or blowing our noses we sit or lean on the bed, we must smooth the bedspread so there are no creases, so that the design embroidered onto the bedspread is symmetrical, with an equal number of butterflies and an equal number of flowers on each side of what we estimate is the center of the bed; if while smoothing and aligning the bedspread one or more of our fingers should touch the headboard, we must use the furniture polish and the furniture-polish rag stored under the bathroom sink to wipe away our fingerprints; we must rub the polish onto the headboard thoroughly so that there are no streaks; after using the rag to wipe any fingerprints from the furniture-polish can, and using the rag as a buffer between our hands and the can, we must place the can and rag in their proper positions under the bathroom sink; if when we sneeze we spray the bedroom mirror, we must use the glass cleaner and the glass-cleaner rag stored under the bathroom sink (next to the furniture polish and furniture-polish rag) to wipe away any moisture; we must rub the glass cleaner thoroughly onto the mirror to prevent streaks; we must wipe any fingerprints from the plastic glass-cleaner bottle and place the bottle in its proper place under the sink; we must fold the rag and place it in front of but not touching the bottle (if we forgot to fold the furniture-polish rag and place it in front of but not touching the furniture-polish can, we must do so now); if thoroughly rubbing glass cleaner on the mirror causes any earrings or pins or framed photographs on the dresser below to shift, we must move these items to their proper places; if our fingers leave marks on these items when we move them to their proper places, we must use the glass cleaner and glass-cleaner rag to clean the smudged glass fronts of picture frames, and the furniture polish and furniture-polish rag to clean any wood frames; we must place the furniture-polish can and glass-cleaner bottle in their proper places under the bathroom sink, making sure the rags are folded and placed in front of but not touching the appropriate bottle or can; if we touch the dresser top while making sure the items on the dresser are in their proper places, or while polishing or cleaning these fingerprinted items, we must use the furniture polish and furniture-polish rag to wipe away any smudges, making sure to rub in the polish thoroughly, and making sure to place the can and rag in their proper positions under the sink; if at any point we notice that the furniture-polish can or glass-cleaner bottle is empty, or close to empty, we must look in the hallway closet for an unopened bottle or can and place it under the sink; we must wrap the empty or almost-empty bottle or can in the rag that goes with it and place bottle or can and rag in the small garbage pail at the side of the toilet; we must take from the rag pile in the hallway closet a fresh rag and place it in front of but not touching the unopened bottle or can; we must return to the bedroom to shake the blankets; we must fold the blankets so that all the edges are aligned; if while shaking and folding the blankets we scatter lint and dust on top of the dresser or on the headboard or on the glass fronts or wood frames of the picture frames, we must use furniture polish and glass cleaner to wipe everything clean, making sure to rub thoroughly and making sure to return the bottle, the can, and the rags to their proper places; we must secure each pillow in its pillowcase (so that the tagged side of each pillow cannot be seen) and smooth each pillowcase so that there are no creases; we must pluck lint from the pillowcases; we must place the blankets in their proper order inside the pillows-and-blankets storage alcove in the hallway and place on top of the blankets, in their proper order, every pillow; we must balance the pillows on top of the blankets so there is no chance of their toppling if someone opens the storage alcove; the storage alcove door must be closed and the door's handle wiped clean; every drawer of every dresser must be closed and every drawer handle wiped clean; every piece of clothing must be folded neatly in a dresser drawer or hanging in a closet; pants must be clipped onto pants hangers, skirts onto skirt hangers; shirts must be hung from wire shirt hangers, jackets and coats from wood jacket-and-coat hangers; there must be uniform space between hangers so that each article of clothing touches the next but not so that the removal of one article of clothing disturbs the symmetry of articles hanging nearby; belts must hang from the metal hooks on the inside of the closet door; shoes and sneakers must be arranged in their proper order on the closet floor (laces inside, left shoe or sneaker to the left of the right shoe or sneaker); the top of every dresser in every room must be wiped with furniture polish and furniture-polish rag; every mirror and every glass front of every picture frame in every room must be wiped with glass cleaner and glass-cleaner rag; every framed picture or certificate on every wall in every room must hang straight; every light in every bedroom must be turned off; before cleaning the bathroom the bathroom light must be turned on; the bathroom floor must be dry; the rim and sides and faucets of the tub and sink must be wiped with tub-and-sink cleaner (found under the sink) and tub-and-sink sponge (found next to but not touching the soap in the soap holder on the inside rim of the tub), then rinsed with warm water, then dried with a fresh towel (found in the fresh-towels pile in the hallway closet); if any water spills onto the floor, the floor must be dried with a fresh towel (never with a used towel, which may have picked up stray hairs and soap scum); every used towel must be placed in the washing machine in the basement (making sure not to drip any water onto any part of the floor in any part of the house); the television in the living room must remain off (so that if someone touches the back of the television it will not be warm); the front door must remain double-locked; if someone knocks, the door is never to be opened; we are never to look through the small triangular stained-glass window in the wood door; if by mistake we look through the window in the wood door, we must use the glass cleaner and glass-cleaner rag to wipe away any nose or finger smudges, and then we must return the glass-cleaner bottle and rag to their proper places; the living room drapes must touch; we must never part the drapes to see who is knocking at the door or leaving a flyer in the mailbox; we must never answer the phone; if by mistake we answer the phone, we must say politely that our mother is busy at the moment and that if the person at the other end of the line would care to leave his number our mother would be happy to return the call; we may sit on the living room couch, but we must never lie on the couch or place our feet (and certainly never our sneakers or shoes, which are never to be worn in any part of the house, not even in the basement, where the floor is cold) on the coffee table in front of the couch; if by mistake we lie on the couch, we must realize our mistake and stand up; we must make sure all couch pillows are symmetrically spaced against the couch's long back cushion; we must smooth the couch's bottom cushions until no creases remain; if by mistake we place our feet (or God forbid our shoes or sneakers) on the coffee table, we must use the furniture polish and furniture-polish rag to wipe away any dirt and smudges (rubbing thoroughly) and return furniture-polish can and rag to the cabinet under the upstairs bathroom sink; we must never eat or drink on the couch; we must never eat or drink anywhere in the house but at the kitchen table, and always with plastic serving mats under our plates and coasters under our glasses; if by mistake we eat or drink anywhere in the house but at the kitchen table, we must make sure never to spill; if we spill dry food we must make sure to recover all crumbs or whole pieces of food, even taking the extra few minutes it takes to check under the couch and under the coffee table and around the entire room, even going so far as to vacuum the rug (making sure to wipe away with a damp rag any finger smudges on the vacuum handle, or sometimes using a damp rag as a buffer between the handle and our hands, and certainly making sure to return the vacuum to its proper place in the back of the dining room closet, and while returning the vacuum making sure not to disturb the symmetry of the clothes hanging in the closet); if by an act of the worst carelessness we spill a drink on the rug of any room, we must immediately wipe the spot with a damp rag with all the strength we have, even sometimes taking turns to maintain the maximum amount of pressure on the wet spot, for as long as it takes to eliminate any evidence that a drink has been spilled in a place a drink never should have been; if we rub the spot until the rag breaks apart, we must dampen another fresh rag and begin again; if we rub the spot until all four of our arms are sore to the point of unbearable pain, we must throw away the used rags (first making sure to wrap them in paper towels or aluminum foil or anything else that will prevent them from being seen should she glance into the kitchen garbage bag) and vacuum any remains of the rags from the rug (carefully returning the vacuum to its proper place in the dining room closet); if we discover, after sitting on the rug (holding hands) and watching the spot dry, that the spot has become a stain, we must do our best to stand up, compose ourselves, and move through the rest of our day without thinking too much about how carrying a drink where a drink never should be carried is one of the worst acts of carelessness; we must try not to hate ourselves; we carried a drink where a drink should never be carried; we lost our concentration for a fraction of a second; we committed an irreversible act of supreme carelessness; still, we must try not to hate ourselves; we must remember that, as terrible and unforgivable as one act of supreme carelessness is, two or three or twenty acts of carelessness can be worse, can be more unforgivable (if indeed there are degrees of unforgivable, as we believe there are); we must recover enough to remember to wipe the plastic serving mats with a fresh damp rag and dry them with a fresh dry rag and place them in their proper places in the pantry; we must wipe the insides and bottoms of the coasters and place them in the cabinet above the stove; we must stand on a chair to reach the cabinet above the stove; we must remember to wipe our fingerprints from the handle of the cabinet; we must remember to wipe from the leather cushions of the kitchen chairs any dirt and smudges caused by our feet (or, if we have not learned from past moments of carelessness, by our shoes or sneakers); the chairs must be spaced properly around the kitchen table; while arranging the chairs we must use every bit of our strength to lift rather than slide, so as to prevent the chair legs from scratching the floor; there is no recovery from scratching the floor; if by the worst sin of carelessness we scratch the floor, we must try immediately to forget about the scratches and not to concern ourselves with how the sun shining through the kitchen window may illuminate the scratches; we must close our eyes, breathe in through our noses, out through our mouths, concentrate every bit of our mental energy on slowing the beating of our hearts, count to five after every breath out and before every breath in, tense our fingers, turn our hands into fists, dig our nails into our palms until the skin turns white, relax our hands for a moment, pinch the skin on our thighs or on the undersides of our arms, clench our toes inside our socks, release, breathe, open our eyes, and remember: There are degrees of unforgivable; we must compose ourselves enough to remember to wash any utensils, plates, and drinking glasses we may have used; when walking slowly from table to sink, we must remember to cup our free hands under utensils, plates, and drinking glasses to prevent any morsels or condiments from falling or dripping onto the floor; should a fluid drop of anything fall or drip onto the floor, we must use a fresh damp rag to wipe away any evidence that one of us has committed an act of supreme carelessness; we must dry the wet spot on the floor with a dry rag; we must throw both used rags into the kitchen garbage bag; we must use hot water when washing utensils, plates, and drinking glasses; we must use a dab of dish soap when washing plates, making sure to wipe away with the soft side of the dishwashing sponge any traces of food (and remembering to wash the bottoms of the plates, which may have picked up crumbs); if any morsels of food are stuck to the plate, we must use the rough side of the dishwashing sponge; if these hardened morsels remain stuck to the plate, we must scrape them away with our fingernails; we must rinse each plate thoroughly with hot water; we must hold each plate up to the ceiling light (or, on sunny days, up to the sunlight coming through the window above and behind the sink) to make sure every hardened morsel is gone, every dish-soap streak gone; when washing forks we must make sure never to forget the food that sometimes gets caught between a fork's teeth; we must not forget the back of a spoon; we must be careful when washing the serrated edges of knives to avoid slicing the dishwashing sponge; if by an unforgivable lapse of concentration we slice the dishwashing sponge, we must wrap the sponge in aluminum foil and place it at the bottom of the kitchen garbage bag; we must find in the cabinet below the sink a fresh dishwashing sponge and place it in its proper place on the rim of the sink; we must remember to rinse the dish soap from the used dishwashing sponge and squeeze it dry before placing it on the rim of the sink; we must use only a dab of special glass-cleaning soap for each used drinking glass; we must use the drinking-glass sponge to scrub each glass, pushing the sponge into the glass vigorously enough to remove any remains of juice from the bottom and sides of the inside of the glass; we must fill each scrubbed drinking glass with the hottest water the kitchen tap can produce and allow this water to remove any remains of juice even our most vigorous scrubbing cannot remove; while the hot water is acting on the insides of the drinking glasses, we must use the dish-drying towel to dry the plates and utensils, making sure never to forget the handles of spoons or between the teeth of forks, making sure to concentrate when slowly drying the serrated edges of knives; we must place the sharp knives with the other sharp knives in the drawer between sink and stove; we must place large spoons with large spoons, small with small (making sure the back of each spoon rests inside the bowl of the spoon below); we must stack the forks so that all fork teeth are aligned; we must place the plates on top of similar plates in the cabinet above the stove; we must pour the now warm water from the drinking glasses and hold the glasses up to the ceiling light (or up to the sun on sunny days); we must wrap the dish-drying towel around our fingers and do our best to squeeze our fingers deep into each drinking glass to dry every inch of the bottom and sides; we must stand each dried drinking glass mouth down alongside other drinking glasses of its kind; we must use the sink-cleaning sponge and a dab of dish soap to clean the bottom and sides of the sink (remembering to clean the drain and to remove with a paper towel, or with our fingers, any pieces of food too large to pass through the holes in the drain); we must remember to clean the rim of the sink, making sure never to spill soapy water onto the floor; we must rinse the sink with the hottest water from the sink's spray hose; if one of us burns the other (and in the process sprays water onto the floor), we must try our best not to retaliate; we must not point fingers; we must not swear; we must not spit; we must not slam our hands on the kitchen counter; we must not smack or kick; we must not pull hair; we must not scratch the other's eye; we must not pull the other's lip or bend back the other's fingers; we must believe when the other says sorry sorry sorry, the spraying from the spray hose the hottest water the sink can produce must have been an accident, must not have been meant to harm; we must compose ourselves; we must close our eyes and take deep breaths; we must remember the degrees of unforgivable; we must forgive; we must work together; we must dry the faucet, the hot and cold knobs, the inside of the sink, the rim; we must dry the floor; if at any point, while drying the kitchen floor, or while dusting the basement coffee table and the top and sides of the basement television set and credenza (making sure not to disturb the glass knickknacks on the shelves inside the credenza) and stereo and bookcase (remembering the tops and bottoms of the four shelves of the bookcase), or while making sure the books on the basement bookcase are arranged in their proper order (the spine of each book dusted and any dust that falls dusted from where it falls), or while cleaning with a damp rag between the numbered buttons of the basement television remote control, or while making sure the pillows are symmetrically placed on the basement couch, or while making sure the zippered sides of the couch's bottom cushions cannot be seen, or while vacuuming the basement rug (remembering that the rug continues up the stairs to the main floor), or while cleaning the basement television screen and the glass front of the stereo and the glass front of the wall clock and the glass fronts of all picture frames, hanging or standing, with glass cleaner and glass-cleaner rag, or while returning glass-cleaner bottle and rag to their proper places, if at any point, while making sure the decorative towels hanging from the towel bar in the basement bathroom are not damp from use, or while drying any carelessly dampened decorative towels with the blow dryer stored in the upstairs hallway closet (making sure never to hold the blow dryer close enough to damage the towels), or while draping the dried towels symmetrically over the towel bar, or while returning the blow dryer (first wiping away any fingerprints with a damp rag) to its proper place in the upstairs hallway closet, or while making sure all dirty clothes and used towels are spread out evenly inside the washing machine (remembering, after closing the lid of the washing machine, to wipe away any fingerprints), or while making sure the drapes hanging from the three small basement windows touch, or while beating dust from the drapes, or while waving our hands through the airborne dust, if at any point, while cleaning the basement, or while waiting quietly in the living room, going through the mental checklist of all that must be done, if at any point our anger returns upon remembering the pain of the hottest water from the kitchen sink spray hose being sprayed on our face or neck or in our eyes, we must resist the urge to retaliate; we must resist the urge to point fingers or swear or spit or slam or smack or kick or bend fingers or scratch or pull hair; we must remember sorry; we must remember forgive; we must resist the temptation to threaten; if we cannot resist the temptation to threaten, and if upon threatening we see the familiar repulsive look of fear on the other's face, we must resist the urge to hate the other more than we already do; we must recognize that threatening one threatens both; we must use every bit of our mental energy to resist following through with our threat; we must not remove used tissues from the garbage and scatter them on the bedroom floor; we must not press our fingers against the bed's headboard and against the bathroom mirror and against every window in every room; we must not spray the mirrors with furniture cleaner and spray the tops of the coffee tables with glass cleaner; we must not place the furniture-cleaner rag in front of but not touching the glass-cleaner bottle and the glass-cleaner rag in front of but not touching the furniture-polish can; we must not use the decorative towels in the basement bathroom as rags; we must not hang pants from shirt hangers and skirts from jacket-and-coat hangers; we must resist the temptation to place shoe next to sneaker, left to the right of right; we must not eat or drink in the back of the pillow-and-blankets storage alcove; we must not rip open the outside garbage bags and scatter garbage on the street or roll around in the garbage for all the neighbors to see; we must not pull apart or tear down the drapes; we must not pull off the bedspread or burn the bedspread or throw the earrings and pins from the top of the bedroom dresser into the toilet; we must resist the urge to break the glass fronts of every picture frame or slam the blow dryer into the upstairs bathroom mirror; we must resist the growing urge to pull out our own hair, to pull out each other's hair, to place those hairs in the bathroom and kitchen sinks and along the rim of the tub; we must not stomp on the soap; we must not close the tub's drain and turn the hot-water knob and allow water to run over the sides of the tub and onto the floor, nor allow water to drip from the downstairs ceiling, nor allow water to pool on the downstairs rug, nor allow water to drip from the basement ceiling onto the basement rug; we must remember there is no turning back from the worst degree of unforgivable; we must not turn the kitchen chairs on their sides; we must not scratch the kitchen floor with unwashed knives; we must not tear open the rugs; we must resist the most powerful urge to rig the kitchen sink spray hose with a rubber band so that when she turns the hot-water knob her face will be sprayed with the hottest water the kitchen sink can produce; if we cannot resist the temptation to follow through with our threat, we must begin again; we must close our eyes and breathe deeply; we must compose ourselves; we must try to slow our hearts; we must tell ourselves that there is enough time, the day is only beginning, certainly there must be enough time before we hear a key in the front door, before we hear the doorknob turn, before we hear footsteps moving from one room to the next, before we wait, eyes closed, for the sound of her voice.

shift

Don't leave them sharp, he says. I want them smooth. That way I won't scratch myself.

His arm jabs near my face. I cannot hold his hand in place long enough to file his nails.

Have you seen the scratches on my legs? he says.

The closer his arm gets to my face the more his arm shakes. I tell myself I am not going to flinch. I would rather he hit me. I would rather he break my nose.

Your eyelids flutter like butterfly wings, he says. What happened? Did your mommy smack you around?

He looks at his wife in her chair. Do you see his eyelids? he asks her.

She opens her mouth wide, which means inside she's laughing, then she drools on her shirt. He tells me to wipe her chin.

Our little butterfly boy, he says.

She makes the noise I know means she wants something.

Do you want something to eat? Do you want the channel changed? Do you want to take a nap? Do you want to read? Do you want to be moved from your chair to the couch? (She raises her eyes and arches her neck, as if trying to look at the top of her head.)

With a clean towel I cover the bottom cushions of the couch; with a disposable pad I cover the towel. I prop the pillows the way she likes them propped. I lift her from the chair and lay her on the towel.

Is there something wrong with the towel? Something wrong with the pad? Did I hurt you? Are you uncomfortable? Are the pillows wrong? Do you want me to get the mail? Do you want me to check who's working the next shift? Do you want a clean pair of socks? Something to drink? Something to eat? Back in the chair? The channel changed? (Eyes raised.)

I find the remote control between the clean clothes in the laundry basket.

A channel from one to ten? From ten to twenty? Twenty to thirty? Above thirty? Below thirty?

Didn't you just say you wanted the channel changed?

She wants to be changed, he says.

Is that what you want?

I know what she wants, he says.

I carry her into the bathroom, making sure to keep one arm under her neck, the other arm under the bend in her knees. Her body is approximately four feet long and weighs less than sixty pounds. I make sure not to fold her body. I lay her body gently onto the plastic cushion of the shower bed. I watch that she does not roll off the shower bed and onto the floor. I make sure her leg does not spasm into the wall.

The rubber gloves are found in the glove box under the sink.

I pull up her skirt and pull down her underwear. I take off her diaper, fold it so that the wet parts are inside the dry parts, and drop it in the small trash can under the sink. I push the diaper to the bottom of the bag.

Do you want to be washed? (Eyes raised.)

I wait for the sink water to warm.

The washrags are stored in the washrag box on the shelf above the sink.

Is the water warm enough?

Better?

Too hot now? (Eyes raised.)

Better?

Now? (Eyes raised.)

I watch her face as I pull apart her palsied legs. When her face tells me I should stop, I stop. I wipe the insides of her thighs. When I release her legs, her legs snap together.

Do you want powder? (Eyes raised.)

The plastic powder bottle is stored in a bin under the sink. She does not like when the powder gets into her eyes or nose. I must make sure to turn the opening of the bottle away from her face as I squeeze the powder onto her legs. I watch her face as I pull apart her legs and as her legs snap together. Her toes curl into the bottoms of her feet.

Do you want clean underwear? (Eyes raised.) A specific pair? (Eyes raised.) Blue? (Eyes raised.) With flowers? (Eyes raised.)

Her underwear are kept in the underwear drawer, where I put them every day after washing and folding them. I look through the underwear drawer, then through the other drawers.

I can't find them, I tell her. Do you want a different pair?

They're out here in the laundry basket, he says.

She raises her eyes and arches her neck.

I take everything out of the laundry basket. I put everything back into the laundry basket.

I can't find them, I call to her.

He moves his chair closer to where I'm standing, so that the wheels stop just before my feet. He lifts the blue underwear with his unpalsied foot. I know where everything is, he says.

The diapers are stored in the diaper bin under the sink.

I roll her body toward me so that she is on her side. I open the diaper on the shower bed, then roll her onto the diaper. I pull the diaper around her hips. I tape the diaper, watching her face to make sure I have not taped her skin. I make sure the diaper is secure. I pull up her blue underwear, pull down her skirt. I throw away my gloves. I wash my hands with the soap I use only to wash my hands.

Ready? (Eyes raised.)

I make sure my arm is under her neck, the other arm under the bend in her knees. I carry her into the living room and lay her gently on the couch, making sure the diapered part of her body is above the pad, the pad above the towel. I prop her head and neck against the pillow the way she likes.

She frowns.

Are you uncomfortable? Do you want to go back in your chair? Did I not change you the right way? Are you still wet? Do you want me to start dinner? Do you want socks on your feet? Do you want your hair brushed away from your face? Would you like me to scratch an itch? Something to drink? Time for your pill? The channel changed? (Eyes raised.)

I find the remote control on top of the television.

A channel below thirty? Above thirty? (Eyes raised.) Above forty? (Frown.) Thirty-one, thirty-two, thirty-three, thirty-four, thirty-five, thirty-six, thirty-seven, thirty-eight (eyes raised).

Is the volume okay?

Too loud?

Louder? (Eyes raised.)

I watch her face to know when to stop.

I sit at the end of the couch to fold the laundry.

She makes the noise I know means she wants something. It sounds like the sound I've heard bear cubs make on the nature shows she likes to watch.

The wrong channel? More volume? Do you want pillows under your legs? (Eyes raised.)

I place two pillows under her legs the way I know she likes them.

I sit with the laundry. She makes a bear cub sound.

Something else? (Eyes raised.) An extra pillow under your legs? Too many pillows under your legs? Something to eat? Is the sun in your eyes? Do you want to order more books on tape?

Go get the mail, he says from his chair. She wants you to get the mail.

Is that what you want? (Eyes raised.)

I take my time fitting the key into the hallway mailbox. I count to one hundred after removing each envelope from the box.

I pretend not to hear him calling me. I light a cigarette. I count to one hundred after each drag from my cigarette. I stare at the ash at the end of the cigarette and watch it fall on the hallway rug. With the bottom of my shoe I rub the ash into the rug. When I finish the cigarette, I count to one hundred before going back inside.

He's trying to answer the phone with his unpalsied foot, the foot he uses to press the pedal that makes his chair move. He gives up on the phone and moves his chair closer to where I'm standing. One leg looks twice the size of the other.

The phone was ringing, he says. Ring ring ring, and then it stopped, and a few minutes later ring again.

I was getting the mail, I tell him.

Didn't you hear me calling you?

I was told to go get the mail.

You were smoking. I can smell it all over you.

I wasn't smoking.

You're going to start a fire, he says. The other tenants say they've seen you smoking where you're not supposed to be smoking.

Do you want me to open the mail?

He moves his chair closer. His arm spasms close to his face. Junk, he says. Throw it all away. It's all junk.

On the couch she raises her eyes.

I sit on the couch to fold the laundry. I hear her making the bear cub sound. I can see her raising her eyes, arching her neck.

I am trying to fold the shirts the way she likes them folded. Each sock must be kept with its matching sock. If a towel is not clean enough, it must be placed in the hamper in the bedroom where dirty laundry is stored.

I can hear her getting louder. Her head is all the way back.

She wants something, he says.

Do you want something? (Eyes raised.)

Are you uncomfortable? Do you need another pillow? Do you want your medication? Are you hungry?

She wants you to make dinner now, he says. (She raises her eyes.)

What do you want for dinner?

She can't answer that, he says. You have to give her choices.

Do you want to order out? Do you want steak? Chicken? Pasta? Fish? (Eyes raised.) With onions and butter? (Eyes raised.) Do you want me to cook? (Eyes raised.)

He turns his chair to face me. I want to cook dinner, he says.

Right now?

Now, he says. You can fold the clothes later.

I leave the laundry and follow him into the kitchen.

Open the refrigerator, he says. Get out of the way. Let me see what we have.

Take out the fish, he says.

Butter, he says.

Lemon, he says.

Not that one, he says. That one's too dry. Get a fresh lemon.

Throw the other one away, he says.

Onion, he says.

Get a better onion, he says. One without so many nicks.

Don't throw that one away, he says. Put it back in the bag.

Get a can of green beans.

In the other cabinet.

Chop the onion.

Make sure you chop it small enough.

Crybaby, he says. Run the water.

Melt some butter in a pan.

A lot of butter, he says. Use the big pan, the black one.

Enough.

Not so high, he says. Do you want to burn it?

I hear her making the bear cub sound. I continue to chop the onion.

Chop it smaller, he says.

The music that means a television show is ending. Her bear cub sound gets louder.

She wants something, he says.

I imagine slicing off the tip of one of my fingers and being rushed to the hospital. The butter in the pan begins to crackle.

Go see what she wants, he says.

As soon as I finish, I tell him.

She sounds like she needs something right away, he says.

I have onion on my fingers, I say.

She wants something now.

My eyes are burning, I tell him. I can't see anything.

Crybaby, he says. Breathe through your mouth.

What about the butter? I ask him.

I'll keep an eye on it, he says.

What if it starts to burn?

Go see what she wants, he says.

I'll be there in a minute, I call. She gets louder. I walk into the living room and show her the knife. I'm chopping an onion for your dinner, I tell her slowly. I have onion on my fingers, and my eyes are burning. It's very difficult to see. Could you please wait until I finish one thing before you ask me to do another?

Her cries get louder; she frowns and looks at the television.

You'll have to wait a few minutes before I can change the channel, I tell her. Her lips curl into a frown I know means she wants me to do it now.

Do you want me to finish making dinner, or do you want me to change the channel?

Change the channel if that's what she wants, he says in the kitchen.

Okay, I say. If you want the remote control to smell like onion.

I love the smell of onion, he says.

Channel thirty or higher? Lower?

That's all the channels, I tell her. You need to make up your mind.

Maybe she needs to look up a program, he says, and she raises her eyes.

Look it up in the newspaper, he says. It's over on the table with yesterday's mail.

I find the listings in the back of the newspaper. I hold the page in front of her face and point the knife blade at the first program listed. I slowly move the blade down the page so that it passes over every program listed at seven o'clock.

Do you see the show you want to watch?

Is it on later? (Eyes raised.)

Do you know what you want to watch now? (Eyes raised.)

I throw the newspaper across the room and onto the table where I found it. She frowns, and her arms shake; she makes the bear cub sound.

Do you want me to change the channel now?

She wants to find her show in the paper, he says.

Do you know what time the show is on?

You want me to go through every page until you find it? (Eyes raised.)

I bring her the paper from where I threw it. I turn to the page that begins with the program listings for seven-thirty. I watch her eyes. Bits of onion are falling from the knife onto the floor. She looks at the knife and frowns. I'll pick it up later, I tell her. Do you want the page turned? (Eyes raised.)

I turn the page and watch her eyes.

The butter, he says in the kitchen. Hurry up and turn off the heat.

I'll be there in a second, I tell him.

Hurry up before it ruins! he says.

I drop the newspaper on her chest, the knife on the newspaper.

With his foot he is trying to turn the knob that controls the heat. His leg shakes and the pan falls from the stove.

Her cries in the other room are louder. She is going to die. If right now the channel is not changed to the channel she wants, and if right now she does not find the program she wants to find in the newspaper television listings, and if the increasing volume and intensity of her cries are any indication of what is going to happen in the next few minutes, then certainly she is going to die.

Fuck fuck fuck fuck, he says.

I place the pan in the sink and run water to make the pan steam. I use a towel to wipe melted butter from the floor, then a wet rag to clean the floor, then a dry rag to dry the floor, and when I am finished I place the towel and used rags in the bedroom hamper.

Melt some more butter, he says.

Use the same pan.

That's too much butter.

I turn up the heat under the pan.

That's too high! What do you want to do—burn it again?

I twist the knob so that there is only a flicker of blue flame. She has not stopped making her noise in the living room.

Come back, he says. That's not going to melt it.

She is watching the knife on the newspaper on her chest. I turn to the last page she was looking at. Her eyes reach the bottom. I turn to the next page. Her eyes reach the bottom. I turn to the next page. I am willing to turn every page in every newspaper. I will not feed her her dinner, nor give her her medication, nor prepare her for bed, nor will I run into the kitchen to save him from being burned by hot melted butter, nor will I pull down his pants and hold in place the plastic container he urinates into, nor will I leave this apartment, until she finds the television program she has been trying to find.

Look out for the butter! I hear him saying.

She makes her bear cub sound and looks toward the kitchen.

Have you found your program?

Do you want me to stay here until you find it? (Eyes raised.)

We're going to have a fire, he says. The butter is coming over the top.

Do you want me to stay here until you find the program? (Eyes raised.) Can you hear your husband in the kitchen? (Eyes raised.) Would you like to see your husband burn himself? Can you smell the burning smell? (Eyes raised.) Do you want the building to burn down? Do you want every person in this building to die?

Would you like to explain to everyone why your finding the television program you want to find is more important than the lives of the people in this building?

Go ahead and explain. I want to hear why.

Tell me why your finding the day and time and channel of this television program is so important that you're willing to risk hot butter falling on your husband and maybe a fire burning this entire building and all the people in it down to nothing.

Go ahead and tell me. I'm waiting.

Hurry up and get in here, he calls to me.

I'm not going to move from this spot until you explain why your television program is more important than everything else in the world.

I look into her eyes until she looks away.

Now, I'll ask you one more time. Would you like me to stay here until you find the program?

Do you want me to go into the kitchen and turn down the heat? (Eyes raised.)

Are you sure? (Eyes raised.)

Hurry, he says. Where are you?

The program that's on the television now—is it good enough for you? (Eyes raised.)

Good. I'll let you know when dinner is ready.

I've been calling, he says. Take it off the heat.

I run water over the pan. Steam rises into my face. I find another pan in the cabinet under the sink and set it on the stove.

No more butter, he says. Use vegetable oil.

Finish chopping the onion.

Put the onion in the oil.

Add some black pepper.

More.

That's enough.

Stir the onion. Use the wood spoon.

Write that we need more butter.

Butter, I write on the shopping list held to the refrigerator by a magnet.

Keep stirring, he says, and I then I hear her making her noise.

Skin the fish, he says. Make sure you get all the bones. I almost choked on a fish bone the other night.

Watch the onion, he says. It's starting to brown.

Get all the skin. Use the sharp knife. The smaller one. In this drawer, he says, and points with his foot.

I run the water to drown out her cries. I run it so hard that it bounces off the burned pan and sprays onto the floor.

Turn that down, he says.

Not that knife. The smaller one.

Watch the onion, he says.

I can hear her through the water and the sound of his talking. I walk into the living room with the smaller, sharper knife. I turn the volume knob on the television as far as it can be turned, then I turn it back the other way. Her mouth is open, her eyes closed. I can see her eyes moving beneath her eyelids, her neck arching, as if she is trying to see the top of her head—that part of her head just below the skin of her scalp, below the hair I wash every morning with two kinds of shampoos. I see the wet of her teeth. I see the clump of her eyelashes. I see the wrinkles under the powder on her face, the hairs at the openings of her nostrils, the lipstick I wipe from her lips before she eats.

Watch out for the sink, he says. It's about to overflow. You've got the drain blocked with the dirty pan.

Where are you? he says.

Where were you? he says.

I lift the pan, and the water disappears. I set the pan on the counter on top of a dish towel.

You better put the fish on, he says. The onion is ready.

Get off that last bit of skin.

Right there where your left hand is.

You've got the knife pointed right at it.

Right there.

Over here, he says, and points with his foot.

Hurry up and get the fish in the pan.

First more oil.

A little more.

Stop stop stop. That's too much.

Dump some out into the sink.

Never mind. Leave it alone. Get the fish in there.

Watch that you don't pin the onion underneath. Make sure the fish is on the bottom. That's it. Make sure the onion gets all over the fish.

Watch that the fish doesn't burn. Only a minute on each side.

She's calling me, I tell him.

Don't leave the fish.

It must be an emergency for her to be calling me like that, I say.

Flip before you go.

Look out that it doesn't break.

Careful!

Get the onion all around.

Don't go yet.

But she must be having an emergency, I say.

Cut the lemon in half.

Squeeze it over the pan.

Watch the seeds.

Squeeze harder. Get it all in there.

Now the other half.

Get the seed that fell into the pan.

Right there, on top of the fish.

Right where you've got your finger.

Watch out that it doesn't fall into the juice. Someone could choke on that.

I really should see what she wants, I say.

Get the seed out of there. Do you want someone to choke?

From the way she's carrying on, I tell him, it sounds like it could be life or death.

It's right where your hand is.

I'm sorry, I tell him. I don't see it.

Just pick it out and throw it away.

I really should check on her before it's too late.

Take the fish out of the pan first.

From the way she's carrying on in the other room, I explain to him, it really does sound like it could be a literal case of life or death. I really think it must be something much more important than a piece of fish.

Just take it out of the pan. It will take five seconds.

I don't want to break it up, I tell him.

Then at least turn the heat off.

Now take it off the burner.

I'm sorry for not getting here sooner, I tell her, but I was busy frying the fish. Do you need me to call 9-1-1? Are you choking? Are you having trouble breathing? Chest pain? A pain in your side? In your head? In your neck? A pain somewhere else? A cramp? Something in your eyes? A burning sensation?

Come back in here, he says. The fish is sticking to the pan.

Let me ask you again, I tell her. I know it must be something life or death. Are you choking? Trouble breathing? Chest pain? A pain in your side? In your head? Your neck? Somewhere else? A severe cramp? An excruciating burning pain in your eyes, or somewhere else? Should I take out the medical emergency book and go through it page by page? That way you can raise your eyes when we come to whatever life-or-death emergency you're going through that made you call me and carry on the way you did when I was busy frying the fish, and squeezing lemon over the fish, and trying to find a seed that dropped into the pan.

Should I get the book?

Do you want something else? (Eyes raised.)

Do you want the channel changed?

Don't be afraid to tell me. Is that what you want? (Eyes raised.)

Let me do that right away for you, since it must be an emergency. A channel above thirty? Below thirty? (Eyes raised.) Below twenty? (Eyes raised.) Below ten? (Eyes raised.) One, two, three, four, five, six (eyes raised).

Is this what you want? The end of the news? (Eyes raised.)

This fish is no good, he says.

That's okay, I tell him. We're out here watching the weather report. Something about tomorrow's weather is life or death. Maybe you should forget the fish and come in here.

If you take it out of the pan now, he says, we can still eat it.

Let me turn up the volume, I tell her.

I turn the volume knob as far as it can be turned.

Turn that down! he says. What do you want to do—bust my eardrums?

I can see in the shape of her open mouth the sound that means she wants something.

Turn it down! he says. Someone is going to call the cops that's so loud.

This is very important, I say. We really should hear this.

My ears, he says. I'm going to call the cops if you don't turn that down.

I watch him try to press the speaker phone button with his foot.

Tonight will be a good night for stars. Tomorrow will be hot and humid. The record high for tomorrow's date, set more than forty years ago, may be broken. Tomorrow will be an unbearable day for anyone with allergies. The air will be heavy. A 50 percent chance of an evening shower. Tomorrow night the sun will set one minute earlier than tonight.

Get the phone cord out from around my foot, he says.

Do you want me to help you call the police?

I want you to turn down the volume, he says.

Is that better?

Lower.

Lower?

Turn it off, he says. My ears are ringing.

Now my foot.

Watch out for the phone.

Now you'll have to make something else for dinner, he says. He presses the pedal that makes his chair move into the kitchen.

Open the refrigerator.

I hear her making the noise that means life or death. I leave the refrigerator door open and go into the living room. I ask her does she want to be moved, does she need to be changed, does she want the television on, does she want a window open, does she want the hair brushed from her face, does she want the fan moved closer, does she need more pillows under her legs, more pillows behind her head, a clean pair of socks, an itch scratched, something about dinner (eyes raised.)

You know what you want to eat? (Eyes raised.)

Something in the refrigerator? Something in the cupboards? Do you want to order out?

What else is there?

She wants the fish, he says in the kitchen.

Is that what you want? (Eyes raised.)

Do you want it in the food processor? (Eyes raised.)

Extra black pepper? (Eyes raised.)

Is the fish okay with you? I ask him.

If that's what she wants, he says.

I divide the fish into two portions, his slightly larger than hers. I pour some of the sauce onto his fish—carefully, so none runs off his plate and onto the counter, and off the counter and onto the floor. I empty the can of green beans into a small bowl and cover the bowl with plastic wrap. The microwave timer must be set for two minutes. I blend her portion of fish to the consistency of oatmeal. I cover her fish with the rest of the sauce.

The microwave makes the sound that means two minutes have elapsed. I touch the green beans to make sure, then divide them into two portions, his slightly larger than hers. His green beans must be placed next to but never on top of his fish, and both fish and green beans must be topped with a generous amount of salt. I blend her green beans to the consistency of split pea soup; her green beans must be placed in a bowl that is not the bowl holding her fish. She likes her fish and her green beans topped with a generous amount of black pepper.

In the living room I position a snack table between where her chair is and where his chair will be. I set his plate and her bowls carefully on the snack table. I cover the seat of her chair with a pad. I make sure to lift her gently—one hand under her head, the other hand under the bend of her knees—and place her into her chair. I bend her legs and arms the way she likes. I make sure her head is secure in the headrest that extends from the top of the chair back. I fasten a clean towel around her neck with a safety pin so that the towel drapes across her chest. I drape a second towel over the first. I drape a pad over the towels. With a wet paper towel, I wipe the lipstick from her lips.

After he moves into the living room, I make sure the snack table is equidistant from his chair and her chair. I fill his plastic cup with cold water and insert a fresh straw into the straw hole in the top of the cup. I fill her plastic cup half with ginger ale and half with cranberry juice. Her cup must be covered with a special cap that has a tiny opening to prevent liquids from flowing too quickly. I tie a bib around his neck so that it drapes over his shirt.

I feed her a spoonful of processed fish. I feed him a forkful of fish. I hold the next piece of fish at his lips until he stops chewing and opens his mouth. When she opens her mouth and raises her eyes, I feed her more. I wipe the sauce from his chin. He asks for more salt; she asks for more pepper. I wipe the corners of her eyes.

Don't give her so much at one time, he says. What, are you trying to kill her?

Give her a rest, he says. She can't take so much.

She moves her mouth and arches her neck, and I wipe the tears from the corners of her eyes.

Give her some more, he says.

Not so much!

Take that away from me, he says. I don't want any more. The fish is too dry.

The beans are no good, he says. Throw them away.

If she coughs food onto her chin and onto her chair and onto her ankles and onto the television screen, her chin and her chair and her ankles and the television screen must be wiped clean.

I worry every time she eats, he says. One of these days—who knows?

Give her small bites, he says.

If I give her only small bites, I tell him, it could take an hour, maybe two, to finish eating.

She loves eating, he says.

If it takes an hour to finish eating, I explain to her, I won't be able to get you into bed in time to finish everything else I have to do.

She opens her mouth.

I place a spoonful of fish in the back of her mouth. I use the roof of her mouth to help scrape the fish from the spoon. Some of the fish falls out of her mouth and onto her chin. I spoon the fish back into her mouth.

Her neck arches, her eyes roll back. Her face turns redder than the red it already is. She is trying to look at the top of her head.

I'm sorry, I tell her. Was that too much?

Her mouth makes the silence I know means she is choking.

Is she okay? he says.

Are you okay? he says to her.

Make sure she's breathing!

She asked you not to give her so much!

His voice fades; the room becomes quiet. I stare at her mouth, then her neck. Through the skin of her neck I can see the food clogging her windpipe. Then the windpipe is gone, and I can only see the clump of food.

Through the disposable pad and the two towels on her chest, and through her blouse and through the skin of her chest, and through the tissue and bone below the skin of her chest, I can see her heart beating. I can see bits of food on the shiny parts of her teeth. I can see the rough part of the back of her tongue. Below his shirt, and below the skin and tissue and bone of his chest—his own heart. Below my own, my own. As if everything else in the world has been erased, I see three hearts suspended in the air, beating.

Do something, he tells me. Get behind her chair and pump her stomach.

She's going to stop choking, I say.

This is worse than usual, he says. Reach your fingers into her mouth.

What are you doing just standing there? he says. Make her breathe.

She's going to breathe, I tell him.

Call for an ambulance! he says.

Give her a minute, I say.

Use your fingers, he says. Go get a rubber glove if you want.

She's going to be fine, I tell him.

He tries to press the speaker phone button with his foot. The phone cord wraps around his foot. His leg spasms and pulls the phone to the floor.

She's going to be okay, I keep saying, and I'm watching the three hearts suspended in the air.

You're crazy, he says. Crazy crazy crazy.

She's going to cough it up, I say.

Now the hearts are gone, and I see only her windpipe suspended in the air above where her chair used to be, above where the floor beneath her chair used to be. I see the processed fish trying to fight its way up through her windpipe.

She's going to die, he says.

It's only been a minute, I hear myself saying. This is going to be fine. Everything is going to be fine.

The food shoots up through the opening at the top of her windpipe and lands on the floor. Above the floor is her chair, and sitting in her chair is her body. There are three heads in the room. Six eyes, six arms, six legs, six lungs. Six lips, three upper and three lower. There are three hearts. There is skin covering the three hearts.

Is she okay? he says. Ask her is she okay!

Are you okay? he asks.

Would you like something to drink? I ask her.

Do you want anything else to eat?

So I can start the dishes, and then get you ready for bed? (Eyes raised.)

Good, I say. Now I can finish everything I need to finish before I leave.

Crazy, he says.

Get my foot loose from this cord, he says.

Pick up the phone. Put it back where it belongs.

Through the aftersounds of her choking, I hear her making the sound I know means she wants something.

Give me my pill, he says.

Pills are stored inside a locked metal box in the kitchen. Even if the sounds of her carrying on increase in volume and intensity so as to indicate a life-or-death situation, and even though neither he nor she is physically capable of opening the metal box or unscrewing the cap of a pill bottle, I may never leave the unlocked metal box unattended. I push his pill through the foil backing and into a tiny paper cup, making sure the pill does not touch my hands, making sure it does not come into contact with any food or any other medications, making sure it does not fall onto the floor, or even touch the kitchen counter. I log the pill as taken in the medication logbook. I push another pill into my hand and put the pill into my pocket. I log this pill as contaminated and disposed of, with the date and time of disposal written clearly. I count the remaining pills and write the total in the appropriate place with my initials under the number.

Did you drop another pill? he says.

What do you mean another?

You're always dropping pills.

When was the last time?

I know you, he says.

I think someone hit you on the head too many times.

They did, he says. The workers over at the state home. They gave it to me all the time. I would ask them for something, maybe a cracker, or a drink of water, or for them to take me to the pot, and they would ask me what, what, what, and then they would beat me.

Do you want your pill?

I think *you* want my pill, he says.

Do you want it with water?

Why don't *you* have it? he says. It will stop you from shaking.

I'm not shaking.

Sometimes I see you shaking, he says.

Open your mouth.

I hold the cup steady and make sure the pill drops into his mouth. I hold the straw where his mouth can grab it. When it appears that he cannot swallow any more water without taking a breath, the straw must be pulled from his mouth. If the straw is not pulled from his mouth, he will cough water onto his shirt.

Through the last traces of the sounds of her choking, I hear her making the sound I know means she wants something.

He coughs water onto his shirt; his palsied leg kicks.

Did you swallow it?

His hands spasm with each cough. Water spills from the corner of his mouth onto his chin. I wipe his chin and wait.

Did you swallow? Or do you need more water?

I got it, he says through his choking.

Do you want more water?

No more, he says. Go see what she wants.

Do you want the television turned on? Are you in an uncomfortable position? Do you need your head moved? Your arms? Do you want something to drink? A pain in your chest? Do you need to make a phone call? Do you want to be changed? Do you want me to clean you up? (Eyes raised.)

I remove the pad from her chest and use it to wipe spilled and coughed-up food from her cheeks, lips, chin, and clothes. I use the first towel to wipe any food not wiped by the disposable pad, the second towel to wipe any food not wiped by the first. I carry his plate and her bowls, his cup and her cup, his fork and her spoon, to the kitchen sink, where they must soak in hot water.

She wants something else, he says.

I hear her, I tell him. Do you think I don't hear her?

I was just making sure, he says.

I'm not made of rubber, I tell him.

He's not made of rubber, I hear him telling her.

Through the sound of running water, I hear him say to her, He's our little butterfly boy.

I spoon her leftover processed fish and mashed green beans into the garbage disposal and watch everything sucked down into the hole. I stopper the drain. I squeeze dish soap into the empty sink. I fill the sink with hot water. I place one of her bowls under the water and count to one hundred. Her other bowl under the water, and count to one hundred. His plate under the water. One hundred. After dropping each fork and spoon and knife and plastic cup into the sink, one hundred. I put my hand into the cloudy water; I can feel the soap working its way into my skin. I lower my face to the water, press my lips to the surface, then push my lips, then my nose and eyes, then the rest of my face down into the water, and then my ears. I tell myself I am going to count to one hundred. I make myself count slowly. I hear ten in my head. Twenty. I imagine him sitting in his chair behind me, telling me I will not—cannot—keep my head under the water for one hundred seconds. I hear forty—the water pressing against my eyelids. Fifty. I imagine everything sucked down into the disposal, the bowls cracked into pieces, the plate broken, the cups melted and sucked down (sixty), the spoon and fork and knives sucked down, my hair and eyelashes and eyebrows and nose and lips and ears and the skin of my scalp and the tissue and bone under my skin (seventy), all of it broken apart from me and sucked down into the disposal, until my eyeballs are alone (eighty) floating in the cloudy water (ninety).

Bring her to bed, I hear him saying.

I rub the soap from my eyes and use the dish towel hanging from the refrigerator door handle to dry my hair, my face, and inside my ears.

She wants to listen to her book before going to sleep, he says.

Where are you? he says.

Are you alive in there?

Where were you? he says. I've been calling. She wants to listen to her book.

Does she ever listen to any other book?

She wrote the book; why shouldn't she listen to it?

She didn't write it.

I saw her write it, he says. Five years it took her to write that book.

She had a ghostwriter.

Shut your mouth, he says. What do you know?

I know enough to know that—

Take her to bed, he says.

Wash her good, he says. Between her fingers.

Her hands won't open, I tell him.

Don't be lazy, he says. Pull them open.

Don't pull too hard, he says.

And make sure she listens to whatever book she wants to listen to, he says.

I carry her with one arm under her head, the other under the bend of her knees. I lay her on the shower bed. I pull off her socks, then pull apart her legs and pull down her underwear, then I unbuckle her belt and pull down her skirt, then I pull her blouse over her head, then her slip over her head, then I remove her earrings, then I place rubber gloves on my hands, then I unwrap her diaper and slide the diaper out from under her. I remove the pin from her blouse and place the pin in the pin box in the bedroom. I remove the belt from her skirt and hang the belt from one of the hooks in her closet. I bring her socks and underwear and skirt and blouse and slip to the hamper in the bedroom.

I use a warm wet cloth to wipe near her eyes. I wipe her nose and around her mouth. I wipe her lips. I squeeze the wet of the cloth into the sink and wet the cloth again with warm water. I wash her neck and chest and stomach and under her arms. I pull open her hands and wash between her fingers. I wash her legs and feet and between her toes. I squeeze out the wet of the cloth and wet the cloth again. I wash between her legs. I roll her body toward me and reach around to wash her back. I roll her body away from me. I place a towel over her face and spray deodorant under her arms.

My lungs feel heavy. The skin of my face is pulling. I touch the pill in my pocket. I crouch, then press my finger against the side of my nose. I count to one hundred before standing.

I remove the cloth from her face.

I wrap a clean diaper around her hips. I watch her face to make sure I do not tape her skin. I wait for the water to warm, and then I wash my hands with the soap I use only to wash my hands.

Do you want your favorite nightgown? (Eyes raised.) Is it clean? (Eyes raised.)

I find her favorite nightgown folded on the bed. I fit her head through the bottom of the nightgown, then through the hole on top. I pull the nightgown down. I bend her arms into the sleeves. I carry her to her chair and lock the chair in place. I brush her teeth with her tiny toothbrush. With a wet cloth, I wipe her lips and where the toothpaste has run out of her mouth. I show her her face in the mirror.

I wheel her chair into the bedroom and leave the chair at the foot of the bed. I lift her with one arm below her head, the other below the bend of her knees. I cover her side of the bed with a pad and lay her on the pad. I prop her head and neck against the pillows the way she likes.

She makes her bear cub sound. I make sure the tape of her book is still inside the player.

Is it on the right side? (Eyes raised.)

Do you want the volume higher?

Something else? (Eyes raised.)

Are you hot? Are you cold? Do you want socks on your feet? Do you need another pillow behind your neck? Too many pillows? Do you want to be under the blanket? Do you want the window opened? The fan pointed at your face? Something about the tape? (Eyes raised.)

A different tape?

You want me to listen? (Eyes raised.)

I have to fold the laundry, I tell her, and then I have to wash the dishes.

I carry the laundry basket from the living room into the bedroom. She is making the bear cub sound.

I know you want me to listen, I tell her. But I have to fold the laundry.

She frowns to mean she is disappointed, to mean if she does not get what she wants—if I do not hear what she wants me to hear—she will not stop making the sound I know means she wants something.

I'll listen while I fold, I tell her.

Nights, I became aware of sounds coming through the ceiling, a woman's voice on the tape says. *Screaming, crying, moaning. Human animal sounds.*

Each sock must be stuffed into its matching sock; each pair must be placed in the sock drawer.

The food was tasteless. They shoved it into my mouth. When the food fell from my mouth, they said I was difficult. They smacked me and shoved more food into my mouth. Poor little bird, the nice ones called me.

She makes a sound I know means she wants me to listen.

I fold his shorts, then his pants, and put them in his dresser. I button the top buttons of his shirts and hang them in the closet.

There was a woman hunchback, and a girl who slammed her head into walls, and two girls who wouldn't stop reaching inside their diapers, and a girl who had to be put into a straitjacket, and two girls who had to have boxing gloves put on their hands, and a girl who would not stop screaming, and then there was me. I had braces on my legs. I raised my eyes to say yes, and people said, "Poor bird" or "Poor little idiot girl."

Hurry up, I hear him calling from the living room.

I'll be there in a minute.

Hurry up!

I'll be there in a minute.

I blocked out the human animal sounds by thinking of the names and voices of everyone I had ever known. We were allowed one hour every day to listen to the radio.

I have to go, he yells from the other room.

I'll be there in a minute.

Hurry hurry hurry, he says.

This woman used to wrap her legs around her neck. She tied herself up into knots. They called her "Monkey."

I'm going to have an accident!

Give me one minute.

Fluid had enlarged her head to several times its normal size. She looked at me from her bed, and I raised my eyes.

I dump the rest of the laundry onto the floor. I sit on the floor. I press my finger against the side of my nose. I count to one hundred. I make sure the towels are clean, and then I fold them.

I'm about to have an accident!

I could see snow outside the window. My parents used to wheel my chair out into the snow. I used to like cold on my nose.

I only have to fold a few more things, I call to him.

I don't want to have an accident!

The girl who slept in the next bed understood. One night we heard footsteps, and I looked at her and raised my eyes. She knew what that meant. It meant: Here he comes. Here comes Stony Hands.

You're going to have to clean up the mess!

I wanted to talk about my baby brother. How much I missed him. I wondered what he was doing that very moment at home with my mother and father. I looked at her teddy bear and raised my eyes. I tried to raise the pitch of my voice to make it more like a baby sound. She understood. She knew I was talking about my brother.

Can I lower the volume?

Not even a little bit?

I hear his chair slamming against the bathroom door.

I'm going to break it down, he says. Do you hear me? I'm going to break it down.

On Thanksgiving I was allowed one small piece of turkey and some cranberry sauce.

Where have you been? he says. Didn't you hear me calling?

I was taking care of something.

Get me on the pot, he says. I'm about to have an accident.

I had dreams of running and skating. I had dreams of playing with dolls.

I close the bedroom door. Through the door I hear the sound I know means she wants something. I hear, faintly, the voice of the woman on the tape.

I position his special bathroom chair over the toilet seat. I move his wheelchair in front of and facing the toilet. I lock the wheels and unfasten his seatbelt.

Hurry, he says. I pull his pants to his ankles; I pull his underwear to his ankles. Jesus Christ, he says.

I lift him with my hands under his arms, my face pressed against his chest. I make sure to bend my knees. In one quick motion I pull him up from his wheelchair, turn him around, and drop him onto the seat of his bathroom chair. He leans into the wall beside the toilet. His palsied leg kicks at me.

Stop flinching, he says. My leg isn't going to hurt you.

I strap him into his bathroom chair then push his wheelchair out of the room.

Take off my pants and my underwear, he says. I'll have a shower right after this.

I bring his pants and his underwear to the hamper in the bedroom.

One of the girls fractured her skull. They gave her a helmet. "Let me out of here!" she used to yell at me. "I'm cracking up! Let me out of—

Let me know when you're finished in there, I tell him.

Through the bathroom door I can hear him groaning. I can hear his body thrashing against the chair, the chair smacking against the wall. Through the bedroom door I can hear her bear cub noise.

In the living room I sit in the chair I usually sit in—the chair I have never witnessed anyone have an accident on. I touch the pill in my pocket. I close my eyes and begin counting to one hundred.

Hey, I hear him calling. I'm ready now.

I'm all finished, I hear him say.

Hello out there. Where are you? Are you out there?

Later: Hey, I'm calling you. I'm ready now. I'm all finished on the pot.

Hey, he says. Hey hey hey hey hey.

Where the hell are you? Hey, Butterfly Boy! Where are you? Do you hear what I'm saying in here? I'm calling you!

Later: What the hell is going on out there?

Where are you?

I'm just sitting in here.

What do you think I'm doing in here?

I know you hear me calling you!

I'm going to tell how you like to drop pills!

Do you hear me?

Do you hear what I'm going to tell?

Later: Come on!

What are you doing?

I'm going to have sores on my bottom!

Do you know what you're doing to me?

Please, he says.

I stand up from the chair. I open the apartment door and slam it shut. I knock on the bathroom door.

Are you finished in there yet?

I'm just sitting here!

Are you finished?

Yes yes yes. Of course I'm finished. I've been calling you.

I open the door and see him leaning against the wall. There is a crack in the seat of his bathroom chair.

What took you so long? I ask him.

I've been calling!

I couldn't hear. I was out in the hallway. I was putting the second load of wash into the dryer.

My bottom is sore, he says.

Do you want me to wipe you? Or do you want to just take a shower?

Wipe me first.

No no no no no. That's too sore. Use the wet wipes.

No, he says. It's too sore. Put me in the shower.

You broke your chair.

I know, he says. You'll have to wrap some tape around it.

I pull his shirt over his head. I pull off his socks. I place his shirt and socks in the hamper in the bedroom.

I loved her because of that. She was the only one to look at me that way. She would sit next to me on my bed and watch me raise my eyes.

I remove his glasses and put them on his dresser.

She would ask me yes-or-no questions. She had been married twice, and she had been to Florida, and she sat with me and told me things.

I pull the shower bed from the shower area; I wheel his special chair into the shower area.

I brush his teeth and watch him spit the paste on his chest. I pour mouthwash into his mouth and wait for him to spit on himself. I turn on the water. I hold my hand under the shower spray hose.

Too cold, he says, and his leg kicks out at me.

How about now?

Jesus, that's too damn hot!

Now?

That's nice, he says. That's how I like it.

I place rubber gloves on my hands and squeeze shampoo onto one of the gloves.

Rub, he says.

Through the closed bathroom door and the closed bedroom door I hear her making her life-or-death sound.

Rub it in good, he says.

Not so hard! he says. You're hurting my neck!

Take it easy! he says.

She's calling me, I tell him. Do you hear her?

Rinse, he says.

I'm going to see what she wants, I tell him.

Rinse first, he says. Don't leave me like this.

Listen to her, I tell him. That could mean something serious.

Rinse my hair, he says. She probably wants her tape turned to the other side.

Maybe I should check on her, I tell him. I wouldn't want her to hurt herself carrying on like that.

Get it out of my eyes! he says. Hurry up and wash it out!

Right after I go turn over her tape.

It's burning my eyes! he says. Where are you going?

Water drips from the gloves onto the floor. Water on the bedroom doorknob.

Do you want the other side? (Eyes raised.)

Water on the tape player and then on the tape.

Water on the play button.

I always received an honest answer when I looked into her eyes. I never cried when she fed me. She was like a miracle to me. All the time we used to have laughter episodes. We used to tell each other—

Jesus Christ, he says. My eyes!

Look up, I tell him. Keep your eyes open.

Don't walk away like that anymore!

She didn't write that book, I tell him.

Sure she did, he says.

Just like you cook your own dinner, and do your own laundry, and wipe your own ass.

I did so cook dinner tonight!

Then I guess you ruined it, I say.

Don't be late tomorrow, he says.

What?

Don't be late, he says. This morning you had us waiting twenty minutes.

It wasn't twenty minutes, I say.

Wash me, he says.

Under my arms, he says.

Inside my ears.

Between my legs.

Save my bottom for last.

I know, I tell him.

Don't forget between my fingers, he says.

I know, I know.

I know, I know, I know, he says.

Easy on my bottom, he says.

Watch it! he says. That's too hard.

She wrote that book, he says.

She sat in her chair and made noises, and someone else wrote it.

Rinse, he says.

You're all rinsed.

Rinse it good, he says.

I dry his hair, then his body. I spray deodorant under his arms. I move him from his bathroom chair into his wheelchair.

I find his pajama bottoms in the pajama bottoms drawer (*I was fifteen at the time, and I wanted to prove I possessed a personality*), his socks in the socks drawer (*like a well-trained dog doing tricks*), his bed shirt in the bed shirts drawer (*through the window I watched a squirrel run across the grass, and I was sad*).

I put clean socks on his feet. He leans forward, and I pull his bed shirt down over his head. He pushes with his good leg and holds up his body long enough for me to pull his pajama bottoms up to his waist.

I find his glasses where I put them on his dresser (*from the wink she gave me, and from the way I raised my eyes, we knew we didn't have to worry*), clean them with glass cleaner, and put them on his face.

I push his wheelchair into the living room. I wash and dry his bathroom chair. I wash and dry the toilet seat. I flush the toilet. I dry the shampoo bottle, and the floor, and the plastic cover of the shower bed. I bring the used washcloth to the bedroom hamper (*he said "I do," and I raised my eyes*). I spray the bathroom. I bring the used towels to the hamper (*after so many bad days, that was one of the best days of my life*).

I would like to write something, he says. Maybe my own book. I would like to write about all the terrible things I've gone through.

She is making the sound I know means she wants something. The walls have disappeared, and I can see her heart pumping in the bed.

Maybe I would write about you in my book, he says. About how you don't come right away when I call.

Maybe I'll write something about you, I tell him.

What would you write?

I would write how your body shakes.

I would write about your eyelids, he says.

I would write about the way you groan when you're on the pot.

I would write how you like to drop pills, he says.

You're not going to write anything, I tell him.

Neither are you, he says.

Then he says: What would you really write about me?

I would write how you like salt on your food, I tell him.

What would you really write about me? I ask him.

I would write how you like to drop pills, he says.

When was the last time you wiped my ass? I ask him.

That's not nice, he says. Sometimes you're not a nice person.

I'm sorry.

I would wipe your ass if I could, he says. I would do a lot of things.

I said I was sorry.

I just remembered, he said. You never finished filing my nails. You can finish them now, he says.

Don't look that way, he says. It will be easy. They're nice and soft from the shower.

Get a file from the bathroom, he says. In the cabinet above the sink.

What are you waiting for?

Don't look at me that way, he says. I never did anything to you.

In the bathroom I look into the mirror.

I turn the knob of the sink.

I reach into my pocket.

What are you doing in there? he says. How long does it take to find a nail file?

I know what you're doing in there, he says. I know you. I know.

I cup my hands under the water.

the usual human disabilities

The incident with the van happened a few months after his wife choked to death. She didn't die on my shift, as I imagined she would. I used to have nightmares about it. I would wake hearing the choking sound she made when she ate. Every time I put a spoonful of anything in her mouth she would tilt her head back and most of the food would spill onto her chin and neck and the rest she would swallow not as if swallowing but more as if breathing, and she would cough and her eyes would get wet and a noise so terrible would come from her chest that I was sure the food had gone directly into her lungs. I would stand there watching her face turn red, and her husband, Henry—who, unlike his wife, could speak—would say, "She's okay, she's okay, give her some more." Even when I wasn't working, even if I was doing something I like, like smoking a cigarette or watching a quiz show on television, I would hear her choking sound in my head just as clear as if she were sitting on my lap, and I would think, *She's going to go on my shift, I know it, that's just how my luck goes, it's only a matter of time.*

But like I said, she didn't go on my shift—she went on the shift after my shift. I set her up on the couch with a towel and a pad under her and turned the television to the news program she watched every evening before dinner, and I even made the chicken she would choke to death on and blended it the way I knew she liked it blended

—enough so that she could get it down, but not so much that she couldn't taste it. Then my shift ended, which is when I washed my hands, literally and figuratively. From what I was told, it was only a half-hour later that she started choking. The woman working the shift after mine called 9-1-1, but it was too late. They stuck tubes down her throat and rushed her to the hospital, but she was dead before they got there. Again, this is what I heard from the woman who worked the shift after mine, and I would understand if her version might not be exactly the way it happened—you know the way people slant their stories sometimes to make things seem more in their favor.

It didn't surprise me that Henry started pointing fingers at me, even though I wasn't there. "He was the one who made the chicken," he said. "I think he wanted her dead. I saw the way he used to look at her when she asked him to change her."

People asked me questions for the incident report. I told them exactly what happened: I made the chicken, blended it like I usually blended it, washed my hands, and left.

The way Henry looked at me after his wife died, you would think I poisoned her or something. What I had been doing for the last two years of her life was wake her, wash her, dress her, brush her hair, feed her, carry her, wash her clothes, open and read her mail, give her her medication, change her diaper, wipe her ass, brush her teeth, change the television station, wheel her to the store, wheel her home, carry her to bed. For Henry I did the same, except I didn't have to carry him and I didn't have to change diapers. Henry I had to lift onto a special bathroom chair and strap him down so he didn't fall when he was straining to go, but when he was finished I had to wipe him just like I had to wipe her.

But I should get back to the incident with the van. Two months after his wife died, on the day I'm talking about, Henry decided he wanted to have his best friend, Casper, over. They were going to watch the ball game, he said—the Sox and the Yankees. I assumed that Casper was like me—you know, a regular walking, talking guy, not someone in a wheelchair with cerebral palsy. I'm not sure why I assumed this—maybe because most of Henry's friends I had met had nothing wrong with them—not that having cerebral palsy is having something wrong with you, I only mean that these other friends weren't disabled in any way, unless you count the usual human disabilities like not knowing how to be nice or being a little too funny for your own good or having bad breath or not thinking before you act—those kinds of things—but what I'm trying to say here is that none of them had cerebral palsy, which is why I was surprised when I answered the door and saw this man in a wheelchair, and I was even more surprised, when he spoke, that his voice sounded just like Henry's—garbled so much I had to ask him to repeat himself two or three times before I got what he was saying.

But there's no good reason I should be surprised by anything anymore. Case in point:

"Where is your personal care attendant, Casper?"

"He dropped me off."

"What do you mean he dropped you off?"

"He'll be back later to pick me up. I told him whoever was taking care of Henry would take care of me."

"Why did you tell him that?"

"Because that's what Henry told me to tell him. My guy is pretty stiff—he doesn't even let me have a beer once in a while or nothing."

Casper had a young face, but his hair was white. Even his eyebrows and eyelashes were white. I knew Casper had to be a nickname—nobody names a kid Casper, not even if he's in a wheelchair and speaks with a garbled tongue, not even if every hair on his body is white. I'm not making fun, I'm just being honest about the name Casper.

He didn't have a power chair, like Henry did, so I had to go outside and wheel him in.

As soon as I had him inside, he asked for a sandwich.

"I'm not making you a sandwich."

"Make him a sandwich," Henry said.

"I'm not being paid to make him anything."

"Then make *me* a sandwich," Henry said.

"What do you want?"

"I want what I always want," he said. "Peanut butter and butter."

I made the sandwich like I always made it—with about half a jar of peanut butter and half a stick of butter. Henry was almost seventy, but he had the body of someone maybe thirty or forty—lean from all the shaking he'd been doing his whole life. I liked to load his food with as much fat as possible to see if he would ever get a belly like the one I had. It got to be a game—I wanted to see how much he could eat and stay thin. I would put so much butter on his toast I was sure he would say something, but he just ate and ate—anything I gave him, he ate. One time I dumped so much salt on his eggs I thought he would hop out of his chair when he took his first bite, but instead he told me the eggs were too dry. But my favorite was to see him struggle with peanut butter—he would have to chew a single bite so many times I thought his jaw was going to lock on him. Sometimes I used to imagine his jaw locking, and I would have to walk out of the room just to laugh. I don't mean any of this in a mean way, and I don't want to give the impression that I wanted him to choke or anything—it's just that he had a sharp tongue and was always picking on me for not doing things right—don't put the food in the garbage, put it in the garbage disposal, what do you think we have a garbage disposal for, what are you some kind of dummy, didn't you make it past the third grade—that sort of thing. Not to mention the fact that he made me make him a sandwich just so he could say "I'm not hungry" and give it to Casper, who had the nerve then to ask me to cut the sandwich in fours.

When Casper finished the sandwich he said, "Let's go for a walk downtown."

I said, "I'm not going downtown."

"Why not?" Henry said.

"Listen," I said. "I'm not lugging you guys through the street."

"I want to see some fireworks," Casper said.

"Have your own attendant take you somewhere on the Fourth," I said.

"He doesn't like to do anything."

"Does he wipe your ass and cook your breakfast?"

"That's his job."

"Well, then don't say he doesn't do anything."

"I'm just saying I want to see fireworks."

"I have to finish the laundry," I said.

"I have to go to the pot," Henry said.

"Now?"

"Hurry," he said.

I strapped him into his bathroom chair and waited outside. I could hear him thrashing around in there: I knew, because I had seen it before, that his arm was smacking against the wall near the toilet, the skin of his face was pulled tight, and his glasses were crooked on his face. When the thrashing stopped, I went in and wiped him.

But get this: As soon as I came out of the bathroom, Casper said he had to go.

"Go where?"

"To the bathroom."

"That's not my responsibility."

"Come on," he said. "I have to go."

"Your guy should be here for that."

"He can use my cup," Henry said.

"I don't need the cup," Casper said. "I have to sit."

"I'm not wiping your ass," I said.

"What's the difference? You wipe Henry's ass."

"I get paid to wipe his ass—that's a choice I make. Here is eight dollars an hour, now go wipe that man's ass—that's how it works. But I don't get paid to wipe your ass. If you want a sandwich, that's one thing—"

"You wouldn't even do that."

"If you want a sandwich, that's one thing. If you want to watch the ball game, that's fine. If you need me to tie your shoelace, okay. But wiping your ass is where I draw the line."

"What do you want me to do?"

"Hold it in."

"I can't."

"You can."

"I'm telling you I can't."

"I'm going to report you," Henry said.

"For what?"

"For being abusive," he said.

"Hold on," I said.

"You're always being abusive," he said.

"You're the one who's abusive," I said.

"How can a man in a wheelchair be abusive?"

"I'm really going to go in my pants," Casper said.

"If you let him go in his pants," Henry said.

"You can't even imagine what it's like to mess your pants," Casper said.

"You're right—I can't."

"It's humiliating," he said. "And then you have to sit in it the rest of the day. I don't have a change of clothes."

"All right."

"I'm not a walking closet. I don't bring an extra pair of pants when I go out. I just assume if I need to go to the bathroom I'll be able to go. I never thought someone, another human being, would say, Listen, man, you're going to have to go in your pants."

"All right."

"If you can just get me on the pot, even that would be better than messing my pants—I mean, I'd have to pull my pants up without wiping—that would be terrible, it would be very uncomfortable, I don't even like to think about it—but at least I wouldn't have the whole mess in my pants."

"For Christ's sake—I said all right."

"You wouldn't have to wipe."

"I'm reporting this," I said to Henry.

"Report what—that a man in a wheelchair asked for your help?"

"This is unacceptable."

"Remember," Casper said. "You don't have to wipe if you don't want to."

"Jesus—I'll wipe."

"You don't have to."

"I said I'll wipe."

"I'm just going on record as saying that you don't have to."

"I heard him," Henry said. "I'm a witness—he said you don't have to."

I lifted Casper onto Henry's bathroom chair. As soon as I had him over the toilet I could hear him going. "Hold on," I said. "At least wait until I have you strapped in."

"I couldn't help it."

"Well, just let me get out of here."

"I'm sorry," he said.

I went into the other room and wouldn't look at Henry. He asked me to change the lightbulb over the stove, but I just sat where I was. I lit a cigarette, even though I wasn't allowed to smoke in the apartment.

"Hey," Henry said, but then he stopped himself. He must have figured that I didn't care anymore, that no matter what kind of a stink he put up I was going to smoke my cigarette down to the filter.

Then I heard Casper in the bathroom. "I'm ready for you to pull my pants up now, if that's what you've decided you want to do."

I went in there with the cigarette in my mouth and didn't care where I breathed the smoke. At that point I wanted everyone around me to choke—I wanted to give everyone lung cancer, including myself. I put two rubber gloves on each hand and wrapped the gloves in toilet paper. I reached between the bathroom chair and the toilet seat and wiped, hoping it would be a dry wipe, but I could tell without looking that it was messy, so I wadded more toilet paper and wiped again, and Casper was sort of mumbling "Thank you" in this way that made me furious—it was the way he was so half-assed about it, like he didn't know if saying "Thank you" after every wipe would make me think, *You better do more than thank me for this, buddy.* If I leaned forward, the lit end of my cigarette would have burned his thigh, and I'm not ashamed to say that I thought about it—I told myself I could make an easy case that it was an accident, and Jesus, I don't want you to take what I'm saying—what I'm being honest about, for Christ's sake—you know, the real things real people think about doing—I don't want you to hear what I'm saying and think, *Man, this guy is a cruel bastard—this guy really did want to see Henry's wife die—maybe he really did blend the chicken a little bit less than usual.* All I'm saying is that I had been at this job too long, and now I was wiping this guy Casper's ass for free—that's how I looked at it; wiping his ass wasn't part of my eight bucks an hour—and the lit end of my cigarette was maybe an inch away from his thigh. But let's not forget that I didn't burn him, didn't move my face even though I knew I could have gotten away with it. The point I want to get to here is that I was "rewarded" for making the "right" decision by getting shit on my wrist. I really do believe that moment was a turning point for me—I mean, something in my head went *snap.* I pulled his pants up—I didn't even care if he was clean—and washed my wrist for about ten minutes with three different kinds of antibacterial soap—and Jesus, I'm not saying it was the guy's fault—that's exactly what I'm *not* saying—all the guy wanted to do was take a dump, it's not like he purposefully got shit on my wrist—and this is what I mean when I say turning point—I started thinking that it wasn't anyone else's fault that I had shit on my wrist, it was *my* fault—who else could I blame that I had this job and that I was making this guy peanut butter-and-butter sandwiches and that I was wiping his ass for free and that I was the kind of guy who gets rewarded for not burning a disabled man's leg by getting shit on his wrist? I must have been doing something wrong, I told myself, and once I realized that, something in my head snapped and I thought, *Oh man, I'm going to kill these guys with kindness, I'm going to pull down Casper's pants and make sure he's clean,* and that's what I did. And not only that—I rubbed some lotion on his ass and asked him if he wanted another sandwich (he did), and then I changed the lightbulb over the stove, and when Henry said the bulb wasn't bright enough I was perfectly gracious about digging through the drawers until I found a sixty-watt bulb rather than a forty, and when that was done I said to them, "Men, how about a few beers?" and at that moment, if they could have high-fived each other, they would have, and I said to myself, *What can I do for these guys to really blow their minds, what can I do to make this the best fucking day of their lives,* and I kept thinking about this while I went back and forth—a sip of beer for Henry, one for Casper, then another beer, back and forth—and I looked at Henry's Yankees shirt and I said, "Men, you're not going to watch the game on TV tonight," and Henry turned his chair toward me and almost whacked me in the shin, and then I said, "I'm going to throw you guys in the back of the van, and we're going to head to the stadium—we'll sit in the bleachers with all the nutjobs, and I'll get you good and drunk, and I'll even get each of you a pennant or something."

I don't think I've ever felt like I did at that moment. It was this fucked-up feeling of wanting to squeeze each of them until they couldn't breathe—it would be violent and loving at the same time—I'd squeeze them *almost* to death. I was absolutely manic with emotion for these guys. I wanted to throw them off the Brooklyn Bridge and watch them flap around in the water and then jump in and save them. I wanted to kiss them on the lips—not in a gay sort of way but in a *Jesus, I'm so fucking happy right now I could kiss you on the lips* sort of way. Like I said, something in my head went *snap,* and now I was prepared to just go—anywhere, it didn't matter. There was nothing I wouldn't have done. At that moment death meant nothing. I wanted to save everyone who needed saving.

I gave Henry the pill that makes him shake less, and then I gave myself one, and then I washed it down with a beer, and then I went back into the medicine box and took another pill. I lit a cigarette and breathed smoke near Henry's face, and then I asked if he wanted a drag and he said sure, so I put the cigarette between his lips and he was shaking so much he almost sucked the cigarette into his mouth, so I held it for him while he breathed in. "I used to smoke two packs a day," he said, and I said, "Get out of here," and he said, "I'm telling you," and I said, "Get out of here," and he said, "When they had me in the state hospital, all I had to look forward to was the next cigarette," and I said, "I know that feeling," and he said, "Give me some more," and I took a drag and then held the cigarette between his lips, and sure enough he smoked like an old pro—he took a nice deep drag and breathed out through his nose.

Casper said we should bring some beers for the ride, and I said, "Now you're talking," and I grabbed a six-pack and a bottle opener and a few clean straws for Henry and Casper.

The sun was low in the sky, and I could hear fireworks in the distance. The sun was huge—the largest it had ever seemed to me. I swear I was taking deeper breaths than I had ever taken. The fact that I was sweating amazed me—for several minutes I could think of nothing else but how strange it was that my skin was wet. I looked at a tree and thought that it was alive—I mean alive with thoughts and feelings like humans have—and I actually spoke to it, "Hey, thanks for helping me breathe"—something (looking back on it now, that is) only a nutcase, or a person who didn't care anymore, would say.

I strapped their chairs in the back of the van—Henry's in his usual spot, Casper's where Henry's wife's chair used to go. I could hear them garbling to each other back there—something about how good it was to have a few beers.

While driving I started having this fantasy about how we would keep going and maybe never stop. It was as if we had no destination—there was no ball game—*fuck the ball game*—and we were setting out on some crazy adventure with no fear of what might happen. I wanted these guys to remember this night—to remember *me*—for the rest of their lives. I had this image in my head of Henry choking to death—just like his wife did, only he would choke on peanut butter. Just before blacking out, he would think about this night. Some poor sucker like me would be pounding on Henry's back, giving him the Heimlich, reaching into his mouth, and Henry would be thinking, *Best fucking night of my life,* and then he would go under and die happy, which is something I could only hope for myself, and *Jesus, who the fuck knows,* I was thinking, *maybe when I go under this will be my best night too—sure, there had been lots of nights of drinking and drugging and getting laid and getting into trouble, but right now I can't remember one of them as separate from the rest, they're all one long night, and where are all those people now—no, this is going to be my best night too—me and a couple of guys in wheelchairs who can't speak right and who need their asses wiped and who need someone like me to cook their food and wash between their toes and give them a few beers and give them for once in their lives a happy fucking memory.*

When we hit the expressway, I turned up the radio. I scanned the stations until I heard Roger Daltrey wailing, and Pete Townshend was no doubt breaking a guitar, and I swear if there was something in the van to break I would have pulled over and broken it—Jesus, this was better than being high at a concert—the sun was setting and Henry and Casper were in the back trying to sing with The Who; they sounded like a couple of coyotes, but it was more beautiful than singing, and I actually pulled off the highway just to slow things down and listen to these two guys; I opened a few beers and made sure they were getting nice and drunk, and I took a swig and my bottom lip was starting to get numb, and I tried to remember how many pills I took before we left but wasn't sure, and I heard Roger scream and then I screamed, which at first scared the shit out of Henry, whose head snapped back, and this made me laugh, made me almost piss myself, and then we all started screaming together, a bunch of coyotes howling at the moon, which I could see above the city in the distance, and I thought, *Why not scream, why the fuck not, from now on we're going to scream all the time, these guys need to go out and scream a little bit, they need to get laid for Christ's sake,* and then I thought, *Fuck the game, these guys are getting laid,* and I finished the beers I had opened and pissed on the side of the highway and got back in the van and drove.

On the bridge Henry said, "Where are we going?" and I said, "Trust me," and he said, "Do you know where we're going?" and I said, "Just trust me," and Casper said, "I want another beer," and I said, "Don't worry, I'm going to give you something better than beer," and Henry said, "Are we going to smoke some weed?" and Casper said, "I don't want any weed, I want another beer," and I said, "Hold your horses, men," and Henry said, "I have to pee," and I screamed, only this time they didn't scream with me. Henry said, "Cut that out, you're breaking my eardrums," and I said, "It's good to scream once in a while," and when we got off the bridge Casper said, "Is this the way to the stadium?" and I said, "Fuck the stadium."

There was a strip joint I had been to a few times—I'm talking the kind of place where you can get a "private lap dance" in a back room, which everyone knows is more than a lap dance—only now my mind was fuzzy and I couldn't quite remember where it was, so I drove all the way up one avenue and then all the way down the next. I ran a red light and almost got us smashed up, and Casper started talking about getting to the game, and I said, "Jesus, are you dense—we're not going to the game—this is going to be better than a stupid ball game," and Henry said, "We could be watching the game at home," and I said, "Just sit tight," which made me laugh since they were strapped into their chairs and their chairs were strapped to the inside of the van.

I drove downtown, turned west somewhere in the twenties, and when I reached Ninth Avenue I saw a joint on the corner that looked good enough—flashing red *X*'s, a fat guy standing at the door. The place looked a little scummy, which means you don't know what the ladies will be like—some clubs have ladies like the ones you might see on the cover of *Playboy;* other clubs have, you know, regular everyday ladies who live down the street and have three or four kids and whose stomachs might not be so flat, maybe a little extra flesh on their asses, which some guys like—but this wasn't for me, okay, this was for the two coyotes in the back who, let's face it, were in no position to be picky—I mean, when I said I was planning to get these guys laid, I didn't *literally* mean laid—as far as I know, I don't think they can do that—you know, I don't think they can control that part of their bodies, and I'm not saying that as a negative thing, just as a fact—as far as I know, I mean. What I meant by *getting these guys laid* was something like a lap dance—a few tits in their faces, a bare ass, some dirty talk—something to make them feel like regular guys—not that they're not regular guys the way they are, but you know what I mean.

I left them in the van garbling about where are we, what are we doing, where are you going, you're not supposed to leave us alone, and I almost stopped and shouted at them, *There's no such thing anymore as supposed-to, boys, or not-supposed-to, tonight is about want, do, want, take, okay,* but I said screw it, let them stew for a while in the back of the van, let them curse me all they want, let them garble about missing the game, because I knew this night was going to be better than that, way better than anything that had ever happened to them, or to me.

The bouncer asked me for the ten-dollar cover, and I said, "Hold on, I know people here, I'm one of your best customers," and he said, "I don't care who you are," and I said, "I just want to go in for a second and have a word with a few of the girls," and he said, "What girls?" and I said, "You know—the girls—I don't know their names," and he said, "Ten dollars," and I said, "Listen, I've got a couple of guys in that van right there, maybe you can see them thrashing around in the back, and it's very important that I—" and he said, "Are you going to give me ten dollars or what?" and I said, "Okay, let's play it your way, fine, ten bucks, here you go," and he stepped aside and let me in.

You could tell the ladies dancing on stage were regular ladies who had other jobs and maybe husbands and kids, which made them in a strange way a little sexier—you know, knowing they were actual people you might pass in the grocery store with one kid yapping in the basket and the other whining about his feet being tired. But they weren't *too* regular, which would have ruined things—you know, too much of a belly and stretch marks from giving birth and cottage cheese on the skin of their thighs, not that there's anything wrong with women with imperfections like that, I'm only talking about what a guy might want to look at in a club after paying ten bucks to a goon outside and after paying eight-fifty to a goon inside who won't leave you alone and keeps asking if you want a drink, would you like to order a drink, sir, are you sure you wouldn't like to order a drink, and he gives you this look like it's some kind of crime to pay ten bucks to a goon outside for absolutely nothing and then not order a drink, so I stood there and drank my drink and felt my legs loosen a little bit, which I knew was from the pills and beer.

I looked around the club and saw a lady standing near the back wearing a white robe with the belt untied, not much underneath, so I assumed she worked there. As I walked closer to her, I kept saying "Jesus, Jesus" because she was one of the tallest ladies I'd ever seen—I mean, she was a giant of a lady, but nice—you know, a nice body; she looked exactly like a normal lady only she was incredibly tall. Her hair was pulled back tight like a ballerina might pull it; her eyelids sparkled with glittery blue eye shadow.

"Excuse me, but I'd like to make you an offer."

"You have to talk to Burt."

"You don't understand—this isn't for me."

"Everything goes through Burt."

"Listen," I said. "I'll give you two hundred dollars if you come outside for ten minutes—that's twenty bucks a minute—and give two guys in wheelchairs lap dances."

"Where outside?"

"Right out front. They're in the back of the van."

"No vans," she said, and I said, "They can't even move," and she said, "What about you?" and I said, "I'm harmless," and she said, "No way," and I said, "I swear, I'm just a regular guy," and she said, "I'm not getting kidnapped and raped and chopped into forty pieces."

"I'm telling you," I said, "these guys couldn't swat a fly on their noses."

"What's the catch?"

"No catch—just a lap dance for each of them, you know, tits in the face, that kind of thing."

"No touching."

"They won't touch. If they touch it will be by accident—you know, if they have a spasm or something."

"No funny business."

"What funny business? Listen," I said, "these guys have had hard lives. One was in the state hospital for twenty years. It was brutal—piss on the sheets, slapped around by the workers, the whole nine yards—they thought he was a retard. The other one is an albino on top of being disabled, so you can imagine what it's like for him. They need someone to cook for them, clean for them, wipe their asses, do everything. I'm telling you—this would make their *lives.*"

"All right, all right, I never said I wouldn't do it, I only said no funny business, and I get to hold the keys."

When I got outside I could see through the van window that their mouths were open, probably howling about the ball game, which I didn't want to hear. I leaned against the van and smoked a cigarette. I could feel the vibrations of their garbling. Spit was flying out of their mouths; if they could have, they would have pounded on the windows. I turned around and mouthed into the window, "Keep. Your. Pants. On."

When she came out, she whispered something to the goon at the door, probably about keeping an eye on me. Beneath her open robe she was wearing black sweatpants, a white T-shirt, heels. I said to her, "What's with the jogging suit?" and she said, "You didn't say striptease, you said lap dance," and I said, "You're taking those off, right?" and she said, "The top comes off, the panties stay on, and any touching and I'm out of there," and I said, "Didn't you listen to me when I told you this is for a couple of guys in wheelchairs?" and she said, "I'm just saying," and I said, "Don't worry," and she said, "I get the two hundred now," and I said, "This is practically my entire paycheck, you know," and she held out her hand and I gave her the money.

"I'm not doing it right here," she said.

"Where do you think you're doing it?"

"At least pull around to a side street."

"What difference does it make?"

"I don't want a crowd standing next to the van watching."

"What are you talking about?" I said. "You dance in front of a crowd every night."

"Those people are paying customers."

"All right," I said, and I opened the door for her.

"I'll meet you around the corner," she said.

"What's the matter?"

"I already told you—I don't get into vans when someone else has the keys."

"I just gave you two hundred bucks."

"So."

"So what if I drive around the corner and you disappear?"

"I won't do that."

"How do I know?"

"I just won't."

"Give me the two hundred."

"What for?"

"You'll get it when you meet me around the corner."

"Jesus," she said, and then she gave me the money.

"Where around the corner?" I said.

"Right around the corner, only ten or twenty yards from the avenue. If you're too far up the street, I won't get into the van."

"Make up your mind," I said. "Do you want to be around people or away from people?"

"I don't want people watching," she said, "but I don't want to be found two weeks from now chopped into forty pieces."

"Take a look in the back of the van," I said. "Look at those guys."

"So," she said. "A couple of guys in wheelchairs."

"Do you think these coyotes are capable of chopping you up? Trust me, they can't even chop an onion."

"I'm just saying," she said.

As soon as I opened the door, I could hear them yelling in the back, but they were so worked up I couldn't tell what they were saying. Henry was thrashing around in his chair, and his face was tight; the veins in his neck were bulging; his glasses were sliding off his face. "Take it easy," I said, and Henry, from what I could make out, was saying something about a dog, so I said, "What dog?" and his mouth kept trying to make the sounds he had in his head, and Casper looked like he was falling asleep, and I said, "What's this about a dog?" and finally, as I was pulling around the corner, I was able to make out that Henry was saying, "Not even for a dog," so I said, "What dog are we talking about?" and Casper said, "It's illegal to keep a dog locked up in a car in the summer," and I said, "So," and he said, "So you've had us tied up back here for almost a half-hour," and I said, "It hasn't been a half-hour," and Henry almost fell out of his chair he was thrashing so much, and he said, "It has too been a half-hour," and I said, "You're crazy," and Henry said, "Don't tell me I'm crazy, that's what they used to say in the state hospital," and I said, "Sorry."

I parked two buildings from the corner, in front of a closed bread shop, and I thought, *Man, who the hell gets their bread here, you've got to be crazy to—*

"Don't call me that," Henry said. "Don't ever call me that."
"Call you what?"
"You know what."
"I said I was sorry."
"It's hot back here—we can't breathe."
"I think I'm going to be sick on myself," Casper said.
"Take a deep breath," I said.
"Where the hell are we?" Henry said.
"Just around the corner from where we were before."
"Where were we before?"
"Right around the corner."
"Where is around the corner?"
"I don't know," I said. "Somewhere in the twenties."
"Yankee Stadium is all the way up in the Bronx."
"I'm going to be sick," Casper said.
"Maybe he has heatstroke," Henry said.
"No one gets heatstroke in the back of a van at night."
"I have low blood sugar," Casper said.
"Jesus," I said. "You just had a peanut butter-and-butter sandwich."
"That was hours ago."
"It was an hour ago, tops."
"At least two."
"You're crazy."
"Son of a bitch," Henry said.
"I wasn't talking to you," I said. "I didn't say you were crazy. I was talking to him."
"I don't care who you were talking to," Henry said. "It's not nice."
"It's just an expression."
"Tell him it was at least two hours," Casper said to Henry.
"Okay," I said. "Listen, I don't want to fight about this. It was two hours—whatever you say."
"You don't mean that."
"Jesus, I mean it. I just said it was two hours ago."
"You didn't say it like you mean it."
"For Christ's sake, I mean it—it was two hours ago!"

"At least," Casper said.

"Where the fuck is she?" I said, and Henry said, "Who?" and I said, "Never mind," and Henry said, "Are you meeting one of your girlfriends or something?" and I said, "This is for *you,*" and he said, "I don't want this, I never asked for this," and I said, "Sometimes you don't know what you want—what you really want—until someone gives it to you," and he said, "I want to go home, the game is probably over by now," and then I heard Casper getting sick.

I found a rag on the floor that someone must have used to check the oil and which seemed the only thing I could use to clean up Casper's mess, so I got out and opened the back doors. Casper had puke on his lap, on his hands, on his shirt, on his shoes, and I said, "Jesus, I'm sorry," and he opened his mouth like he wasn't finished, so I backed away and waited, but it was a false alarm, dry heaves, and now the back of the van smelled like a subway station, and here comes Miss Two Hundred Bucks sticking her hand out, "Where's my money?" then, "God, what's that smell?" then, "No way, I'm not giving him a lap dance."

"Fine," I said, "but you're giving him a dance—some kind of dance—anything."

"I need an extra hundred for the smell."

"Come on," I said.

"That's terrible," she said. "*You* get in there and dance for ten minutes."

"Don't you have a fucking heart?" I said. "Don't you ever just want to do something nice for someone who's maybe had it rougher than you have?"

"You don't know my life," she said. "How do you know I haven't had it rough? For your information, Buster, my father—"

"Okay, okay, I don't need to hear this."

"Don't get me started," she said.

"I don't have any more money," I said.

"I want to go home and watch the game," Henry said.

"In a few minutes," I said.

"I didn't ask for this," he said.

"Give me a few minutes."

"How do you know what we want?"

"I said give me a few fucking minutes, okay?"

"Listen to them," she said. "They don't even want this."

"Trust me—they want it."

"I'm reporting this," Casper said.

"I don't care what you report," I said, "as long as she dances for you."

"I don't want anyone to dance for me," he said.

"You want this," I said. "You *need* it."

"We're not you," Henry said, and I said, "What did you say?" and he said, "You think we're you, but we're not you."

With the rag I wiped Casper's hands.

I gave the lady from the club the two hundred dollars. "I don't want this," she said, and I said, "Just take it," and she said, "For what?" and I said, "I have to give somebody something," and she said, "How about I take fifty and we pretend this never happened?" and I said, "Take whatever you want, just leave me something for the tolls," and she took fifty and gave me her robe and said, "You're going to need this," and I said, "I'm sorry," and she walked away.

With the robe I cleaned Casper's shoes, and then I laid the robe over the puke on his lap.

As I was about to close the back doors, Henry said, "Hey, what about my glasses?"

"Higher up," he said. "It pinches my nose that way."

"It still pinches," he said. "I need new tape on the bridge."

"Well, we don't have any tape," I said. "Do you think I walk around with tape for the bridge of your glasses in my back pocket?"

"I'm just saying," he said.

"Well, I'm just saying we don't have any tape at the moment."

"All right, all right," he said.

"Anything else before we head back?"

"No."

"Anything else for you?" I said to Casper.

"No," he said.

Before I closed the back doors I said to Henry, "You know, I didn't kill your wife," but he said nothing. "Listen," I said, "I blended that chicken just like I always blended it."

I waited, I kept waiting, but he said nothing.

When we got back to Henry's apartment, the police were waiting for us.

But that's not the end of this story—the end is what happened the other day that made me want to try to figure this out—you know, why regular everyday people like me do the things we do. I was sitting in front of the Laundromat, waiting for my clothes to dry, when I saw some guy, clean-cut, glasses, button-down shirt, wheeling Henry down the street. They were coming right toward me. I hadn't seen Henry since a week after the incident with the van when I went to pick up my check and almost got arrested for being near him when I wasn't supposed to go near him. At first I got scared and tried to sneak back in the Laundromat, pretend I'd never seen him, but then I said, *Screw this, I'm not going near him, he's coming near me, that's not my fault,* and besides, I was curious what, if anything, he'd want to say to me.

I stood in the path of the wheelchair and said, "Hey, Henry, what's going on?"

"Hi," he said, very friendly.

"So how's your life?" I said.

"Terrible," he said. "Did you hear my wife died?"

"Of course," I said.

"Choked to death," he said. "This crazy guy who used to work for me—he didn't blend the chicken the way it was supposed to be blended, and by the time they came it was too late."

"I'm sorry to hear about that," I said. By this time I figured out that he didn't remember me; maybe he was going senile or something.

"So this guy who used to work for you," I said. "Are you sure he—"

"He was crazy," he said. "Listen to this," he said. "One night he took me and one of my friends on a wild-goose chase. He drove us into the city, into a bad neighborhood, and locked us in the back of the van in the summer heat, and we couldn't breathe, and he tried to get this lady to dance for us."

"You're kidding," I said.

"I swear," he said, and I shook my head as if to say, *Some people,* and the guy pushing Henry's wheelchair nodded his head as if in agreement.

"So what happened to this guy?" I said.

"Fired," Henry said. "When we got back, the police were waiting. They took him away, and then we fired him."

"That serves him right," I said.

"Crazy," he said.

"Hey, buddy," I said. "Could you do me a favor?"

"Sure," he said.

"Could you tell me more about this guy?"

"What do you want to know?"

"I want to know everything you know about him."

"Like what?"

"Like what he was like—what he looked like, what he talked like, any strange mannerisms, what kinds of things he talked to you about, what he did for you, what he did for your wife, was there anything he was particularly good at, was there anything especially nice he ever did for you, do you think that deep down, despite his craziness, he could have been a nice guy—like I said, I want to know everything."

"Trust me," he said. "You don't want to know this guy."

"No," I said. "I *do* want to know him. I'm very interested in what kind of person would do some of the things you're telling me he's done."

"So you want to know everything," he said.

"Everything," I said. "Don't leave anything out."

the other man

They stabbed her to death on the street below our apartment. There were three of us then. My father watched from behind a third-floor window. He called for help. She was a young woman on her way home from work. They took her purse and looked inside. When they did not find any money, and after she reached for the purse in order to show them where the money was hidden, one of the men stabbed her while the other watched. She was stabbed seven times, twice through her neck. The police arrived too late, the ambulance arrived too late. The police asked my father questions. The body was placed inside a body bag and taken to the coroner. Five days later the body was laid out in a funeral home, and two days after that it was lowered into the ground. My father followed the story on the news. It was said on the news that there was a witness who did nothing to help. Reporters came to the apartment, wanting to know my father's version of the story. What my father wanted to tell them, what he told me the day after the young woman was buried, was that there was another man. There was another man watching from behind a window across the street.

It has been ten years since this woman was killed, and this is the first time I am telling her story. But no, I am not telling her story. I am telling my father's story. But how do you tell a true story about your father? Perhaps it would be best to invent a character who resembles your father but who, when the story is complete, turns out to be someone else entirely. You can change his name. You can conceal the fact that you are writing about your father. People will read your story and assume that it is fiction and that the father of the story is not quite your own. If you are lucky, your family will read your story, but they will not recognize themselves in it. Years later, if you are very lucky, they will recognize themselves, but they will know that the story was written with love. This—what I am writing here—is not a story. This is not a fiction in the way short stories are fictions. This should be called something else. My father's name is Nicholas, and in this—what I am writing—his name is also Nicholas. My father and I share the same name. If you look at the cover of this book, you will see my name. I am pulling away the curtain and telling you something that is not a fiction. I am giving to you my father. Forget for a moment about the rest—those fathers I have invented before this moment, those fathers I have used to disguise my own. Those fathers—though each contains a bit of my own—are only a getting to this point, a means of making my way, slowly, to the father here, the real one, the one who before this moment has remained behind the curtain I have placed in front of him.

Here is the most important thing I can say about my father—more important than the color of his hair or his height or his name: He became convinced, in late-middle age, several years after the murder, that he was no longer human.

He called me and tried to explain. "I feel like I'm outside my body looking at myself, and what I see is crazy. Nothing is right," he said. "I feel like I don't belong here." And then he was quiet, he had nothing else to say except that he was afraid of dying—not someday, but now, in the middle of this confusion. He asked if I could come home for a few days, and so I drove from Massachusetts to Queens. During the drive I kept drifting out of my lane; I very well may have crashed into the divider if it weren't for the grated pavement between the road and the shoulder. I drove most of the way in the slow lane, gripping the wheel tightly, trying my best to concentrate on the road, but my mind kept wandering to my father and what he might look like when I saw him. I had not seen him in almost six months.

He looked weaker, much older than the fifty-something he was, pouches of wrinkled flesh under his eyes. He was nervous, rubbing his chest.

"I've been saved," was the first thing he said to me. And here he was speaking literally. He was almost killed three weeks earlier, he explained, when a young man robbed him at gunpoint. "There was a car," he told me. "A young woman driving. She drove the car onto the sidewalk and hit the man holding the gun."

"Why didn't you tell me?"

"It doesn't matter."

"No wonder you haven't been feeling well," I said. "You're still shaken up."

"No," he said. "It's much more than that. Sometimes I stop breathing. My chest tightens and my skin starts to tingle, and then I realize that my body is forgetting to breathe."

"Have you seen a doctor?"

"They won't find anything," he said.

They followed her home from work and out of the subway. My father watched them stab her, and then he called for help, which arrived too late. She was stabbed seven times, twice through the neck. The body was placed inside a bag and then into the ground. The police asked my father questions. What exactly did you see? Two men grabbing a woman's purse. And then what? One of the men got angry. And then? One of them stabbed her. How many men were there? Two. Did you get a good look at their faces? No, it was too dark. Did you try to help her? I didn't know what to do. Didn't you think to make a noise or scream out the window that you were calling the cops? It happened much too quickly. How much time passed from the moment you saw them grab her purse to the moment they stabbed her? I don't know, maybe a few minutes. And you didn't think to yell something out the window or go down there to help her? I didn't know what to do. Did you wake your wife and tell her what was happening? No. Why not? I don't know. Did you wake your son and tell him what was happening? No. How old is your son? Seventeen. What did you do after you called for help? I sat by the window. And what did you see? I saw her lying on the ground. And you didn't go down to see if she was alive? I didn't know if they were still there. Did you see them at all after you called for help? No. So it was just her body lying on the sidewalk? Yes.

My father was afraid of dying—not someday, as we all must, but now, in the middle of this confusion. "I'm afraid of an animal death," he told me. "Do you understand?"

"No. I don't think so."

"When you feel like this, what are you left with?" he said. "You're left with nothing but your body and eventually, in the end, an animal death."

"I think maybe you're still in shock," I said.

"That's true," he said. "I'm in shock. There's no doubting that. I keep thinking about my insides. The guts and organs and all that business," he said. "At least once every minute I'm thinking about that. I'm imagining all of it just hanging there inside me."

"You're going through some sort of crisis," I said. "It's okay to go through something like this. Especially now, in your fifties. This is normal."

"This is something else," he said.

Some things my father knew, and the rest he pieced together. He read the papers. He watched the news. He did research until he had a story in his head, and it was this story he asked me to write. She was a young woman on her way home from work, the two-to-ten shift in the perfume section of a department store. They followed her into the subway and stood next to her on the platform and one of them asked if she knew what time it was and she said ten after ten, and after they had waited five minutes more for the train one of them asked her if she had a light and she reached into her coat pocket even though she knew she did not have a lighter or a book of matches, who knows why we do these things, and then she said no, and then the train came and they sat across from her and looked at her when they thought she was not looking, and by this time she was thinking about these two men. This is what we do when strangers ask us questions and sit across from us, especially this late in the city. We do not know what she thought about them, though it would not be surprising to discover that she considered moving to another car or that she hoped a police officer would step onto this car at the next stop or that these men would prove to be harmless, on their way home from a hard day of work. Perhaps they were factory workers; their clothes were worn, their hands dirty with the kind of dirt that gets into your skin and does not go away no matter how many times you scrub, and perhaps for a moment this young woman felt safe. These men were workers going home to their beds, maybe to their wives and children. These men were more like her than not, they were all three of them on the same side of the fence, hard workers not afraid to get dirty, proud of a paycheck, or, in her case, since she had time to go to the bank that afternoon during her break, proud of the cash that came from a paycheck, though now she was regretting her decision to cash her check, it is very easy to second-guess every decision we make. There were about a dozen people on this car, and she looked at each of them closely. Two older women, older in this case meaning old enough that they would be of no use in a struggle, and here, as often happens, her mind wandered a bit and she imagined a struggle, one of the men pointing a gun at her face, and these older women would scream, clutch themselves, faint. And there were a few older men, and again she imagined a gun pointed at her face, and these men would move away from her. That is something we do when there is danger, we move away from it, it is our instinct to do so. There were other people with her on the car, younger people, but by this time she had decided that people, young or old, moved away from danger, people saved themselves first and then they thought about saving someone else. She would do the same if she saw another person in trouble, a gun pointed at someone else's face, she would move away and take cover, she would save herself and then figure a way to help, and if there was no way to help the other person she would feel terrible, she would not be able to sleep, but she would have no regrets. What good are two dead people? She saw now that the two men sitting across from her were whispering to each other, and she felt her chest tighten, and then she remembered something a friend told her years ago, something about the best-laid plans, how if you imagine something the way you want it to be, an event or a party or a date, it is almost impossible that it will turn out that way, for we cannot imagine the future exactly as it will happen, we cannot get every detail correct, and so by imagining a perfect future we can guarantee that our future will not be perfect, and this young woman remembered now what she said to her friend in reply, that the opposite was also true, by imagining a disaster, a future filled with horror and heartache, we can guarantee that it will not happen, or at least not in the way we imagined, and this thought alleviated some of her fear, even though the men were staring at her now. She was the one making sure not to make eye contact, and now she set her plan into motion—this is just a phrase we use, there was no motion to speak of except the one inside her head—and she imagined these men following her off the car and cornering her in the station and shoving her face against a cold wall and pressing a gun against the side of her head. Give me your money. It's in my purse, take the whole thing, take everything. She could not help imagining herself brave, but there is no way to know how we will react in the face of such danger. She imagined the men shooting her and walking away with her money. She saw her body on the ground and the men shooting it and the body jerking as each bullet entered, but this was just a movie in her head, she could not know what it felt like to be shot, and as the train pulled into her station she stood with confidence, knowing at the very least that she would not be shot in the way she had imagined it. But there was much worse she had not imagined, there is not enough time in a year to imagine all the terrible things that can happen to a person, and then they followed her out of the subway car and past the token booth and up to the street.

* * *

I had trouble sleeping the night I stayed with my father. The evening had been quiet—my father and I sitting in the same dark room, the television light flashing off and on. Several times my father asked me to place my hand on his chest. He was frightened about his heart—that it was beating too quickly. I could feel his heart fluttering then skipping beats. "It sounds normal," I told him. "Maybe a little fast, that's all." An hour later he asked me again. Was I certain? Try putting your ear against my chest. It sounds normal. Listen to it for a full minute and see if you can hear it. I'm sorry, I don't hear anything. And then later he said, "It's happening again. Something doesn't feel right." But what was I supposed to say? Did he want me to take him to a doctor? Or did he simply want me to tell him he was going to be okay?

It was no surprise that I dreamed about my father. He was chasing me through the street with blood in his mouth and on his hands. His skin was pale, and he appeared to be both dead and alive. And then I saw, sitting on a tree branch, a smaller version of my father: He looked as he did now, but he was the size of an infant. He was calling for my help, but I ran past him. I heard him screaming, but I was too afraid to look back. And then I woke to find him standing over me.

"I need to find the other man," he said.

He was speaking of the man he saw watching from the other window. He knew the man's name and where he lived. "He lives upstate," he said. "About three hours by car." He stood above me, breathing slowly. He was rubbing his chest. "I'm sorry," he said. "I never spoke to him about what happened. I need you to drive."

I lay there looking up at him, still trying to shake the dream from my mind. "When do you want to do this?" I said.

"As soon as possible," he said. "Tomorrow."

But how should I say it? How do you tell a true story about your father? Perhaps it is best to move away from what actually happened. The truth may not be enough for a compelling story. If you state only what happened and what you feel and that you are a writer writing a story about your father and that you are writing this story because you love him, because he had a breakdown from which he has not recovered and may never recover, then the reader may not care. Perhaps it is best to make things up so that the reader will care. Perhaps you should not say that you are a writer writing a story. Perhaps you should conceal yourself, or if you must be yourself you should not use your real name or your father's real name. If you live in Massachusetts, perhaps your narrator should live somewhere else. If your father lives in Queens, perhaps the narrator's father should live somewhere else. How should I say it? Is it enough to say that I woke several hours later and again my father was standing above me? Is it enough to say that I opened my eyes and he said nothing, and that I closed my eyes and pretended I had not seen him, and eventually he went away? Does the truth do justice to my father's confusion or my own fear? Should I say he was crying when really he was not? When writing a story about a man who had a nervous breakdown, perhaps it is best to show him, at least once, in a mental hospital. It may be a good idea to include some of the colorful characters from inside the mental hospital. It may make for a compelling story if you create a dramatic situation such that one of the colorful characters in the mental hospital forges a friendship with your father and together they make it through their problems, or perhaps only one of them makes it through his breakdown and the other becomes worse, making for what some people call a bittersweet ending. Or perhaps the son plays an important role in bringing his father back to health. The son visits the father every day for a year at the hospital, he brings old family pictures, he takes his father to a Mets game, he lets his father drive the car, even though he is not supposed to. There are any number of dramatic scenes that may be used, and if you cannot think of one you may borrow one from any number of books written on the subject. Should I give my father some mannerisms so that the reader knows he is having a breakdown? Does he talk to himself? Sure he does. Does his eye twitch? Of course it does. If you include only those things your real father did, the reader may not care: If you say that your father no longer thought himself a human being, or that his body stopped breathing on him, or that he could not stop thinking about his insides, or that he was afraid of dying an animal death, or that you have also had these thoughts, or that you are afraid you will also have a breakdown from which you will never recover, or that this story about your father, such a kind and loving son to write about his father, is really about you. People may not want to read about a selfish young man worrying about himself. They want to read about a caring young man and his sick father: Will he make it or won't he?

There were three of us then. My mother had been sleeping. I was not asleep, as my father told the police. I was awake in bed, listening to music from my Walkman. If my father had come into my room and told me there was a woman on the street bleeding to death, I do not know what I would have done. I do not know because that did not happen. My father did not come into my room and tell me, and that is the only way to know what I would have done. I have thought about this often, but I can only bring myself so far. I can see myself getting out of bed and going to the window first to see if it was true, if there was a woman bleeding on the street below, and then I can see myself going downstairs, carefully, opening the hallway door and standing in the vestibule next to the mailboxes and looking out into the street and listening and waiting and trying to convince myself to walk outside, don't worry, the people who did this are no longer here, certainly they have fled, you will not die, you should help this woman. But what if you risk your life for someone who turns out to be a terrible person, what if this woman bleeding on the street beats her children? But that does not matter, this is a life and you should try to save it, this is a moment that will define your own life, there is no more honorable way to die than in an attempt to save another, and of course the men who did this are gone by now. Every second you think about this is another second she moves closer to death, and here, in my imaginings, the ambulance arrives and discovers that the woman is dead. I have not made it past the final door, every time it goes this way, and I must remind myself that I am not my father.

* * *

Have I been saying it right? Perhaps I have been much too slow in getting to the other man.

Should I tell you that it was snowing during our drive to Albany? Should I tell you that my father was quiet with his head resting against the window? Should I tell you that he asked me to pull the car to the side of the road and that he got out and sat in the brown grass and tried to breathe? Should I tell you that he stayed there in the grass for twenty minutes and that he sat for the rest of the trip in the backseat? Do I need to build suspense about the other man? Should I tell you that we could not find him at the address my father had, and that we had to knock on doors and ask questions, and that it made me feel like I was a kid playing detective, and that I was very sad when I remembered I was not a child?

But please let me say a few things first:

(1) This is not a simple story about a man traumatized by a murder he witnessed. It is not about a man burdened by guilt. It is never that simple.

(2) Reporters asked my father questions. His name was mentioned in the papers. My mother, a woman very concerned with what others think, left us less than a year after the murder. This story is not about her leaving. This story is about a man who had a nervous breakdown from which he has not recovered. And so I will say that my mother's leaving caused a small pop inside my father's head. And his being saved years later by a woman who drove her car onto the sidewalk—another pop.

(3) For years I have been looking at my father's body—his growing belly, his crooked back. I have been looking at his body and then at my own. A few years ago I slipped a disc in my back and someone said, "That's just like your father. You're going to have a back just like your father's."

(4) I would love to look inside my father's head.

(5) This story is about a son who loves his father. But it is never that simple.

* * *

Now let me tell you, finally, about the other man.

We found him in a small apartment, living alone, and it was an effort to get him to open the door. He was older than my father, perhaps in his late sixties, and he did not smile. His body was thin in a healthy way. You could see the veins in his neck and in his arms.

My father said nothing at first. I told the man who we were, that we used to be neighbors and that my father had come a long way to speak with him.

His brows came together, which is a cliché for describing someone who looks disturbed, but should I say something else when really his brows came together?

He did not welcome us into his apartment.

I looked at my father and waited. "I don't know what to say," I told him. "You'll have to say it yourself."

He struggled through it, losing his breath every few minutes, and I am proud of him for that. I will not attempt to quote my father directly, for that would be misleading: There were too many pauses that cannot be accurately reproduced. There were so many pauses that the man, when he saw that this was going to take a while, asked us to come inside. He did not offer us a sandwich or a cup of hot tea—he was not that type of man, you could see that much by looking at him—but he let us sit on his sofa.

Here are indirect quotes of what my father said:

Tell me what you saw that night. Tell me everything.

How many times have you thought about her since then?

Where is your family? Do you have a wife or children? Where are they? What do they feel about this?

How do you breathe at night? How do you sleep?

Reporters came to my house. My name was mentioned in the papers.

I saw you behind your window. I protected you!

I'm sorry for what I'm saying. I've been very afraid lately. Do you want to know the truth of it? Do you want me to scare you? Do you want me to tell you what a human being can feel?

At least I called for help!

Why have I come to you but you have never come to me?

Tell me your version of the story. Tell me she never had a chance. Tell me the first wound was the one that killed her. Tell me that she fell to the ground and her eyes were open and she was gone.

How can you live your life every day and not think about it? You're lying when you say that. You must be lying.

"I live a happy life," said the man. "I'm sorry you feel the way you do, but I'm not going to lie to you. I'm very happy. I get up every day and eat a big breakfast. I watch television. I walk to the store. At night, sometimes, I see a movie with a friend."

My father could hear no more of this. "I'm sorry to have bothered you," he said.

The man led us out into the hallway. "There was nothing you could do for that woman," he said, but already my father was walking down the stairs to the first floor. "Listen to me," the man called. "You're alive. Look at yourself. Look at your son." He came down a few steps. "Don't you see the gift you've been given?" he said. "You're alive. Who can argue against that? Here you are, years later, and you're very alive."

We walked out into the cold air. The storm was over but didn't feel over. Sure enough, when I looked up into the streetlights, I could see the last flakes falling, or perhaps they were the first flakes of a new storm. My father sat in the backseat. I started the car and drove away.

I'm sorry. Do you want something from the mental hospital? Here. A visit after one week. "Can you come back some other time?" said my father. "I don't love you right now. I feel so sick for myself that I can't love anyone right now." I went back every day after that, and every day I heard the same thing. Not today. I can't love you today. What did you expect? There were no puzzles or blocks or coloring books or anything else you may have seen in the movies. There was not a single person talking to himself. There were very sad people. Confused and lonely and terrified people.

Perhaps the true story is not good enough. What actually happened may not make for a compelling story. If you state only what happened and what you feel and that you are a young man falling apart and you do not know why, then the reader may not care. Perhaps it is best to make things up and let the reader figure out the true story. But at the end you may say whatever you want: The worst that can happen then is the reader will say it was a bad story, the writer was false. But now I am telling you the truth. My father was confused and lonely and terrified, yes, but there was no mental hospital. He was afraid of dying an animal death. He was afraid people would not understand what he meant by that. He was falling apart. Is that not enough? But here is more of the truth: This story is not just about my father. This story is not just about a son who loves his father. This story is not just about the author of this story. The author of this story is different from the young man who jumps awake in my bed at night, or the one who breathes through one nostril at a time, or the one who is afraid to close his eyes in the shower. This story is about a young man falling apart, a young man afraid of dying an animal death. This story is about being afraid to say that you are falling apart. This is about fear—fear that you will tell a true story and people may not care.

Listen. Everything else has been a means of getting to this point. Here is what I want to say:

One night I woke to the sound of my heart. It was beating so rapidly I thought it would break through my chest. I tried to slow it, but I could do nothing. It existed beyond me. It was stronger than I was. Several people came and placed me on a stretcher. They attached wires to my chest and carried me out of my apartment. They brought me down to the street and lifted the stretcher into the back of an ambulance. A doctor examined me. There was nothing wrong, he said. A nurse jabbed a needle into my hip. I was given a prescription for pills. And since that night the world has not been the same. The prescription has been renewed. I have waked many times to the sound of my heart. Place your hand on my chest. Try putting your ear against my chest. Listen to my heart for a full minute and see if you can hear it.

* * *

So now it is your turn to hold up your end:
(Should I ask?)
Do you care? Are you worried about me? If we knew each other, would you tell me it's going to be okay?
Did I not say it right?

the november fifteen

They took fifteen of us away, but fewer than half came back.

They rounded us up one night in our homes and drove us blindfolded in several vans for an hour or more to what looked—when they removed the blindfolds—like an abandoned factory. I cannot speak for the other men, but I did not know why they had come for me. In any case, once we were in the factory and the doors had been locked and they began interrogating us, why they had come for us and what we knew and didn't know no longer mattered. One's life outside—as terrifying as it was the first few days imagining never returning to it—eventually fell away into a kind of dream or myth. The only reality we knew—the only one that mattered—was what was happening to us and to our bodies inside the mostly empty and therefore echoing rooms of the factory.

When they were not interrogating us, they kept us—sometimes blindfolded, more often not—in the main room of the factory, which looked like an airplane hangar, though much larger. From there we could hear the pleadings and screams of whomever they were questioning in one of the many side rooms. Our hands were almost always tied behind our backs, and we were made to spend most of the day, and sometimes the night, on our knees, side by side, and were not permitted to look at one another or speak or try to communicate in any way. We were not told these rules; we learned them by witnessing what happened to someone who broke one of these rules he didn't even know about in the first place. The first one of us who looked to his side was hit across his kneecaps with a lead pipe. The first who turned to look at the man who had been struck was himself struck. The first of us to speak—he said something innocent to me like, "Nice accommodations they have here," something intended not as the beginning of some insurrection but, rather, as an attempt at humor in the face of grim and certainly absurd circumstances—this man's knees were broken in front of us (we did not have to turn to see), and he was left there crying, much like my then-ten-year-old daughter cried when she burned her hand on an iron. If you have ever banged your knee on the bottom of your desk and know what that pain feels like and how it can bring you to tears and send you into a tantrum of swearing, still you have no idea—I didn't then, but soon would—what it feels like to have your knees broken. You are a baby; you keep crying for your mommy, and you don't care who hears you. You curse the person who gave you such pain, and besides, you know—or think you know—that that person can't possibly give you more pain than the pain you already have, and you further reason that perhaps if you curse him and his family enough, he might put a gun to your head and pull the trigger and put you out of your misery. But the man who gave you this pain does nothing, does not even respond to your curses with another whack with the pipe; he just sits where he has been trained to sit and does not even look at you but, rather, at the wall behind you. He has been trained not to know your face—the color and shape of your eyes, the hook of your nose, the acne scars near your temple—because to know your face might be to remember that you are human. Even as you vomit and scream and bang your head on the cement floor with the hope that the pain in your head will momentarily distract you from the pain in your knees, he lights another cigarette, picks his nose, farts. That he cares nothing for your suffering is why he is good at what he does and why you have every reason to fear what he is capable of doing to you. The same was true of the others: They were machines. You were not human; the skin they burned not human skin, the bones they broke not human bones but twigs they were being paid to snap so those twigs could more easily be disposed of.

I would be less than honest, though, if I did not say that, despite my hatred of them, there was something in the Zenlike way they operated that I admired. They were so focused; they seemed swept clean of everything but what they were doing. There wasn't a single sign of weakness in any of them. We looked for, but didn't see, one look that betrayed feeling: They never flinched upon striking or turned away upon seeing blood, never pulled back a punch or kick, never offered or even threw at us a handkerchief. The tone of their voices never changed; they did not scream and certainly were never soft-spoken, but were always neutral and cold. This was business. We were objects to be manipulated, nothing more; our bodies were to be made to feel pain until that pain was enough to make us tell them what they wanted to know. I did not know what they wanted to know, but I told them everything. It did not matter what I told them as long as I told them something: I said yes when I thought yes was what I was supposed to say, no when I thought they wanted no. When they asked if I knew the whereabouts of a man named Greg November, I told them I had no idea who he was. After they beat me to the point of almost being unconscious—volleys of punches and kicks to every part of my body—they asked again if I knew the whereabouts of this Greg November, but I was too delirious even to make something up, so they beat me again, this time into unconsciousness, and when I woke they asked me, as matter-of-factly as one would ask the time, "Where is Greg November?"

It is unlikely that you have ever been beaten to the extent that I was beaten, but perhaps, in the course of this telling, you have imagined yourself subjected to some of the tortures I have only begun to describe; perhaps you have imagined yourself, though in terrible pain, brave; perhaps you have imagined spitting in your captors' faces (as a few of us, all of whom did not make it home, did). But what you should imagine, if you want to be somewhat realistic, is you blubbering, you pleading, you kissing the shoes of the men causing your pain, all of which I am not ashamed to say I did. I told them I had a wife and daughter whom I loved and wanted to see again, though by this point neither my daughter nor my wife nor my ever seeing them again concerned me. What concerned me was only that my body would feel no more pain, and I swore to God and on the souls of my dead parents and on the lives of my wife and daughter that I had no idea who Greg November was and that I would even join them and do whatever I could to help them find him, would even beat and torture the other men, if necessary. After the delirium of a series of beatings, when I was left with bruises so sensitive even my clothing against them was enough to make me willing to sell my soul and the souls of my family for just one minute of relief, I was filled with a rage unlike any I had known before or have known since—not for the men beating me but for Greg November.

I have spent much time in the three years since my release making lists. The worst physical tortures. The worst psychological tortures. What's worse—hunger or thirst? What's more terrifying—suffocation with a plastic bag, or having one's head held under water until one blacks out ten or more times in a row, or the moment just before one's genitals are burned? The possibilities are endless; one can consider such questions with oneself or with others indefinitely and never become tired of the debate. There is no telling how many times I have revised my lists. I might wake in the night in a sweat and remember some torture I had forgotten and add it to my list, or I might remember just how terrible a torture low on my list was and move it up. I play games with the lists: Sometimes I will not look at a list for several months and will then try to rewrite it from memory, to see if I come up with the same order. Other times I give a list out of order to someone I know, or more often to a stranger, and ask him to order it based on his assumptions and speculations about pain.

They were pros: They had what they did to us down to a science.

They had no intention of obtaining information from the three men they sacrificed, but used them to better their chances of obtaining information from the rest of us. The first two were the man whose kneecap they broke and the man who turned to look at him. These men were given no warning, nor were they asked any questions. They were given pain to give the rest of us something to think about; they lay on the floor in front of us, crying and cursing, for almost a week, and they were brought no food and only enough water to be kept alive. The third man sacrificed was the only one brave—some might say foolish—enough to try to give food to the first two men. He was taken away to one of the side rooms, where, for three days, at varying intervals, we heard him screaming. I used to consider the worst part of those three days the time between screams (the only sound was of water dripping from a pipe somewhere behind us); the waiting would rattle my nerves to the point at which my hands began to shake. (They still do, though now I am proud to show them shaking and to tell people why they shake and to know that I know things these people afraid to look at me will never know.) Upon hearing the next scream—sometimes six or eight hours would pass between screams—I would jump (some of the men alongside me would cry out) and for a few minutes would shake violently—my hands, my head—and eventually would settle back to what, by that time, had become my usual amount of shaking. Only later was I able to see that waiting for this man's next scream was not half as terrible as waiting for his next scream and knowing it would never come. What you should understand, or pretend to, is that our waiting for his scream continues today. I do not intend this, or any part of what I am writing, to sound melodramatic, nor is it my intention—as I believe it was the intention of the TV stations that covered our return to the factory—to elicit in you, who do not know me, some kind of neatly packaged pseudo-grief, but, rather, it is my intention to help you see that you too are not alive, and if you see this, if you know it, *then* you will grieve.

I was one of the last interrogated and so was able to hear in the sounds the others made just what they had in store for me. Some of their screams sounded so fake, so much like the screams early film heroines made, that thinking about them now almost makes me break out in laughter. Some men came back to the main room shaking, some were crying, some had to be dragged back; no one was carried. Some did not come back; some came back, but when they fell and did not move, not even when poked or slapped, they were dragged away and never seen again.

I do not know why I lived and some of the others did not. Most of the time I attribute it to luck, which isn't the right word but the only word I can think of close to what I mean. I don't necessarily mean *good* luck, just luck. I will say about myself without shame that I have a low threshold for discomfort and without pride that I have a very high threshold for pain: I did not cry when they drove a nail into my heel, but I cried when I was not allowed to wipe my running nose; I did not cry when they burned my back, nor when they gathered around to beat and kick me, but their not letting me sleep broke me. After this, everything made me cry equally: their dunking my head under water dozens of times or their making me sit in my own shit or their breaking my knee. (For a long time knee-breaking was number one on my Most Physically Painful list, until recently, when I moved sleep deprivation to number one, where it remains as of this writing.) If you are not allowed to sleep for long periods of time—part of me hopes you will never know what this feels like, but another part of me *wants* you to know—you can think of nothing else. You will do or say anything to sleep; you will give up your children just to be able to close your eyes for a few minutes. They kept me awake for five days. If I closed my eyes, they beat me. After a while, I wanted them to beat me unconscious, but they knew to beat me only so much, or sometimes they burned my back or my genitals or broke one of my fingers. Life became a choice between pains: I could either experience the pain of not sleeping, or I could experience the pain of not sleeping *with* the pain from burns and broken bones. So I tried to stop closing my eyes. The last two days I spent on the floor; they kept propping me against a wall. They threw cold water on me, they boxed my ears, they made loud noises. I hated them, and then I was too weak to hate them, and then I loved them. What made me love them was that they were the only ones who could take away my pain, and when they did, when they allowed me to close my eyes, they became gods.

When I woke, I was both penitent and grateful: I stopped saying I was sorry only to say thank you for their having given me sleep, which I saw not as a right but as a gift. I trusted and loved them and would have done anything for them. It did not matter that they were the same people who had beaten me and burned me and kept me awake.

I had been awake for no more than five minutes before they asked me again, "Where is Greg November?"

I said, "For God's sake, I don't know."

They looked down at me on the floor; they gathered around me.

I kept saying, "I don't know why I'm here. I swear, I don't know."

"What is your name?"

"I don't know."

"Where are you?"

"I don't know."

"Where do you live?"

"I don't remember."

"Do you know the whereabouts of Greg November?"

"No."

"Do you know anyone who knows or has any information that might lead us to the whereabouts of Greg November?"

"No, I swear, I don't know who he is."

Then with a pipe they broke my kneecap.

Why they released those of us who had survived, I'm not sure. My theory is that they knew we would say nothing. Though some *did* go to the police; some spoke of Greg November. I did not go to the police; the police came for me. But before I get to what the police did, let me first say that upon my arrival home (I was left, kneecap and nose broken, near the garbage pails my wife had set curbside the night before), my wife and daughter were strangers to me. But no, that's not quite accurate: They were not strangers but were simply *strange.* Unrecognizable is what I mean to say. Two things, one smaller than the other, walking on legs, water running from their eyes, sounds coming from holes in their faces. They took me to a hospital where my cuts were cleaned, my burns wrapped, my leg put in a cast. A very short doctor with dark skin, who would not look directly at me except to treat me, packed gauze into my crooked nose and strapped over my face a plastic mask, which my daughter kept asking me if she could wear. When the nurses and doctors asked what had happened to me, I told them I had gotten into a fight; it was obvious I was lying, but I didn't care. I could see on my wife's face that she wanted me to tell the truth. But what had happened was suddenly something I wanted to keep to myself, not out of shame but out of possessiveness: It was mine, and I did not want these people who could never know what I was talking about to try to make what had happened to me their own, to try to make my pain their pain. But this turned out to be wishful thinking. Even before I had come back, they had taken it from me. The wives and neighbors and friends and coworkers and aunts and uncles and second cousins twice removed of those of us who had been taken from our homes—anyone who could claim grief—had sounded the alarm. The police had been involved since the day after we were abducted; there was an ongoing investigation. In the relatively short time we had been gone—perhaps it was two weeks, though my sense of time while I was in the factory was suspect—there had been daily prayer vigils and candle lightings at the churches those of us who attended church belonged to, a special assembly at my daughter's school, and three bake sales to help pay for a private investigator. Someone made posters with tiny pictures of our faces lined up in neat rows, and dozens of people went out after work and taped the posters to trees and telephone poles and in subway stations and to the sides of bus-stop shells. Every night search parties made up of friends and neighbors and even strangers searched the city and up to a one hundred–mile radius beyond the city. Everyone, my wife told me, wanted to be involved. The outpouring of support was, in her words, inspiring, and a sign that, despite the suffering I had endured, there was goodness in the world. Even more wonderful, it was pointed out to me, was that these people—many of them strangers who had volunteered in some capacity to help find me—took it upon themselves to visit me at home, where my nose and knee were healing, to tell me how happy they were that I was alive and safe and to wish me a speedy recovery and to tell me in great detail everything they had done for me while I was missing, to which I suppose I was expected to say—but could not say—thank you.

A young man running for city council paid for a parade to celebrate our safe return home. High school marching bands played, and there was a float in the shape of a ship, and lip-synching on the deck was an old man I was told was a crooner semifamous in Brooklyn in the 1950s, who now performed mostly at Italian weddings, and people tried to climb onto the float to touch him or get his autograph. When the parade reached its destination, a men-and-boys choir from Queens sang "Amazing Grace" and "Ave Maria," the latter of which made some people cry, and then the man running for city council gave a speech about our bravery and how what he was seeing that day—the outpouring of emotion and support from "the good people of New York City"—made him proud to be running for city council, and he hoped they would give him their votes so he could have an opportunity to "serve such fine people in the greatest city in the history of God's great earth." Cameras flashed as he shook our hands. I saw a reporter asking my wife questions; someone asked my daughter to be on a talk show about the children of survivors of torture. A man gave me his card and said a calendar was in the works and said not to worry, if I wanted to keep my shirt on, I could keep my shirt on, and 10 percent of the proceeds would go directly into an international fund to help victims of torture.

Someone was wearing a T-shirt with my face on the front and HOME WHERE YOU BELONG. WE MISSED YOU on the back. They needed something to call us, some catch phrase that could evoke any number of emotions. Since we had been taken from our homes in November, they called us—including those who did not make it home—the November Fifteen. A company in New Jersey trademarked the phrase and its numerical shorthand, 11/15. Baseball hats were made, which months later a local minor league team, the Brooklyn Cyclones, wore on opening day. The national anthem was sung by the daughter of one of the men killed, and after she finished, it was announced that she had recently won a scholarship to a school for the performing arts and "Let's give her an extra round of applause" and "We're sure her father is looking down upon her right now, smiling." Whenever I saw or heard the words "November Fifteen" or "11/15"—not just on hats or T-shirts but even on the clock on the table beside my bed—I was overcome first with a deep hatred for Greg November and then with what I can only describe as a sickness beginning in my stomach, then making its way into my lungs, then into my head, and eventually I would be felled by an exhaustion that kept me in bed sometimes for days.

Because my hands shook so much, I could not return to my job (I designed furniture for a company that specialized in "making the new look antique"), so they moved me to their main office and gave me a new title and a private bathroom. Men would knock on my door and ask how I was getting along and tell me I was doing a great job, even though I had done nothing, and they would bring me to meetings, during which people would come up with ideas about how to make the company more money ("It doesn't have to *be* antique to *look* antique"), and after which—though I had said nothing—people would talk about these ideas as if they had been mine and would pat my back and say, "Nice work, glad to have you on board," and so on. I sat in this office the better part of a year and revised my lists. And then one day I did not go to work. I sat in the park across the street from the office and ate a corn muffin, as I did each morning, but when an older man sat next to me to feed the birds (he put bread crumbs and seeds in the brim of his hat and the birds sat on his shoulders and ate), I was overcome, at the same time, with a terrible sadness and a joy so unlike anything I had ever felt that I feared I could not hold it inside me. I was very happy for this man, for what I took to be the life he had set up for himself in this park, his feeding the birds and their coming to him—yes, part of it was the way they came to him. But it was also that this man seemed not to care about his importance to these birds. He sat there and closed his eyes, and he was no more than a statue. But no, to them he was *not* a statue, and this was what made me sad—that I had become, to others, a statue, a memorial.

Even after I stopped going to work, I continued to receive a monthly paycheck, and every so often someone I did not know but who seemed to know me would come to my home, dress me in a suit, and take me to some company function or other at which bigwigs would give speeches during which I was made to stand and everyone would look at me and applaud, and then they, too, would stand, and everyone would raise their glasses to me, but by this point I would lose my hearing. I would see their mouths moving and their hands clapping but could hear no sounds.

I became quiet. Reclusive, some said. I spoke very little to the people I knew, including my wife and daughter, and tried to avoid those who—because they had heard about me on the news—believed they knew me. I felt most comfortable around people who, because they must not have watched TV or listened to radio or read newspapers or magazines, had heard nothing about the November Fifteen. (Even now it pains me to write this phrase.)

It was around this time, too, that laughter began to kill me. My daughter, then almost twelve, would be watching one of her favorite TV shows—a show, from what I could tell, about a group of girls in boarding school going through all sorts of dramas, most of which involved boys—and every half-minute or so I would hear something that sounded like what someone coughing inside your head might sound like. I would look up from my lists and see my daughter sitting on the floor, very close to the TV, and her smile seemed frozen on her face. She never asked what I was writing; I never showed her. Sometimes—I am almost too ashamed to admit this—I left my lists where I thought she would find them; I wanted her to know what I knew. I looked for my daughter's finger smudges—sweat or the chocolate syrup she liked to put on the ice cream she liked to eat every day after school—but the lists never seemed to have been touched. I began to have the feeling that I was slipping away from things, that the distance between me and my daughter and my wife—between me and everything, really—was becoming too great to return from. I did not know where I was slipping away to, but it felt like I was slipping away to death, or something close to death. Once, I tried to engage my daughter in a discussion about her favorite TV show, even though just thinking about this show caused me great anxiety: I asked which was her favorite character (*I guess this season I like Josie*) and why (*She's just so cool, plus she has the best hair*) and what was happening to Josie lately (*Her boyfriend broke up with her even though he loves her*) and what did she think of the laugh track? (*The what?*) What did she think of the fact that no one was really laughing at the show; it was just a recording of people laughing at something else? (*So what.*) Didn't it bother her that the laughter was fake? (*No, why should I care, and besides, there's another show about the first girls in what used to be an all-boys high school, and the show is pretty funny, but they don't use the laugh thing, and the show's not as funny.*)

"I'm sorry," I said, and she said, "What for?" and I said, "I don't know. I guess I haven't been feeling so well lately, and maybe I shouldn't be—"

"Okay," she said, "show's back on."

My daughter was watching this show when the police came to get me, and though she showed some concern, she could not help glancing at the TV as they questioned me.

They wanted to know what I knew about Greg November. They told me it was in my best interest to cooperate. "Tell them what they want to know," my wife said. No one seemed to hear or understand me when I said, "I don't know anything," which was the answer I gave to most questions they asked.

"We're going to have to bring you in," they told me.

"What for?"

"We need to ask you some questions."

"But you just asked me questions."

"Please come with us, sir."

"Are you arresting me?"

"No, we don't want to have to do that."

"Why would you do that?"

"If you would just come with us."

"Where are you taking me?"

"We'll have you back as soon as you answer our questions."

"I told you, I don't know anything."

"Maybe you should go with them," my wife said. "The information you have might save someone else's life."

"Yes," I said, "and then we can have a parade in my honor."

"Honey," my wife said.

My daughter said, "I don't want you to be arrested—what if my friends see you with handcuffs around your wrists?"

"Please, sir," one of the officers said, and so I went with them.

They took me to the police station and then to a desk where one man sat with me and asked questions—where and when I was born, the names of my parents, where I was employed, was I married, did I have any children—and then to a room way in the back of the station with a cage in the corner and bars over the windows and a mirror I knew was really a window on the other side through which they could watch me.

A man came in and sat across from me and smoked a cigarette and kept fingering his gray mustache and said nothing, and then he left.

A few hours later a different man—this one younger and with hair combed back and wet as if he had just taken a shower—came in and sat across from me and looked at me until I looked away. I was given neither food nor water, nor was I asked if I wanted anything or if I needed to use the bathroom.

Late that night—it had been dark outside for quite some time—the two men came back and stood behind me. The older man asked me if I thought I was special.

"Excuse me."

"Do you think you're some kind of hero?"

"No," I said.

"Do you think you can refuse to cooperate with us just because someone gave you a parade?"

"I'm not sure what you want from me."

"Tell us what you know about Greg November."

"I don't know anything about him."

"Why are you protecting him?" the younger man said. "What does he have on you?"

"I'd like to sleep," I said.

"Tell us what you know," the older man said.

I put my arms on the table in front of me and laid my head on my arms. The younger man pulled up my head. I put my head on my arms again. The older man turned over the table and kicked it to the corner of the room. I lay on my back on the floor and closed my eyes. They pulled me to my feet and walked me to the window. They handcuffed my wrists behind my back and then handcuffed the handcuffs to the bars over the window so that it was impossible for me to lie on the floor or even squat. The pain was so excruciating, I was sure my arms would break.

They left the room and did not come back for what must have been two hours. I know they were watching me from the other side of the mirror.

When they returned, the older man stood very close to me and said, "Tell us what you know about Greg November."

"He's a man everyone wants to find for some reason."

They left me and did not come back until morning. During the hours I was alone, I was not sure which pain was worse—the pain of my arms handcuffed and raised behind me or the pain of having to relieve myself. When one pain became too much, I would try to concentrate on the other, and for the better part of four hours I moved my focus back and forth, and had I had just one hand free I would have created some third pain to help take my mind off the other two. By the time they came back into the room, there was only the pain in my arms. My pants were wet, and there was a puddle at my feet. I could feel the beginning of a rash between my legs.

The older man said, "Tell us what you know about Greg November."

"He's a butcher in Bay Ridge," I said.

After a few minutes passed I said, "I'm sorry. I was lying. He's not a butcher. He works for the sanitation department. He lives with his sister in Kew Gardens. He goes by the name of Jon Richmond."

Later I said, "Okay, do you want the truth? Here's the truth: He doesn't live in Kew Gardens. He lives alone in the country and doesn't have a phone. He plays tennis and meditates twice a day."

Even when they left me alone again, I kept talking. I said, "He has three children, ages ten, seven, and two. He lost the pinkie finger on his left hand in a fishing accident when he was fifteen. He has agoraphobia and holds his fork with his left hand."

When the officers released me, and when I walked through the streets and into the subway station, I had to fight the urge to stop someone—a stranger, anyone—and ask for help, or even just to ask what day it was, what year, where I was, and could they see me, was I alive, would they look into my wallet (I was afraid to) and tell me my name.

I became more reclusive. Everything frightened me: bugs, cats, anything alive, my wife, my daughter, anything that spoke, anything that grew, my own fingernails, my daughter's hair, the sound and movement of clocks, the sound of leaves blowing through streets, the pressure of my feet against the floor, of my body against my bed.

It was around this time, too, that my dreams about Greg November changed.

For the first year after my abduction, I had recurring dreams of finding him and doing to him exactly what had been done to me, but I was much too frightened even to search for him. I always felt that I was being watched by the men who had taken me away, that if I made inquiries about Greg November or looked in the phone book for his name, they would find out and would assume I had known something about him and would come to take me away again. But now, in my dreams, upon finding him, rather than beating him and dragging him through the streets, I instead began weeping and embraced him as one would embrace a friend not seen for many years. (I dreamed that he was tall and thin and handsome and had a beard and looked like Jesus Christ.) We would hold each other for a long time, and in some of these dreams I would take his face in my hands and kiss his lips fiercely, and it was not like a kiss at all but more like an attempt to press my closed mouth into and through his.

I no longer care to know what Greg November did to make so many people want to find him. It has been written about in the papers and is still being talked about on the news and on radio talk shows: Greg November was found six months ago hanging from a ceiling fan in a small house in a Spanish village of fewer than one hundred people, where for ten years he had been pretending to be—and I suppose, after that long, *was*—a sculptor named Dan Havel. The initial conclusion was that his death—Havel's—was a suicide, but several people in the village, when questioned, said there was something strange about Havel: He seemed not to trust anyone; he went out only to buy food or art supplies and never allowed anyone inside his home; no one had seen his sculptures, each of which he was rumored to have destroyed upon completion. (In his home, at the time of his death, were dozens of unfinished works, some made from his own fingernail trimmings, others made from his hair, which he cut himself.) Even during the annual Spring Festival, to which everyone in the village brings food or wine, and during which, for three consecutive days, there is music and dancing and even some praying, and which is the event most people in the village spend all year looking forward to, to raise their spirits, they say, during long days of work or when life's misfortunes find them—even during this festival, Havel, as they knew him, refused to participate. Some of the villagers—after noticing that Havel had not been to the festival his first two years living among them—went to his home and offered to accompany him, but Havel said he was not feeling up to it, which was what he said the next year and the next, and eventually people no longer asked him to attend. In general, he became someone not to be bothered with, which went against the all-inclusiveness the village prided itself on. What the villagers told the police supported the initial report of Havel's death having been a suicide: He was a depressed eccentric—such seemed the logical conclusion. But there must have been something in what the villagers said that aroused suspicion or at least intrigue, or perhaps it was that the police found no identification on his person or in his home and could not locate any relatives or anyone who knew a Dan Havel who fit his description. A full autopsy was ordered, upon which there were discovered bruises on Havel's head, behind his ear, and on his hand. The possibility arose that Havel's death could have been a murder rather than a suicide. Someone could have knocked him unconscious and put the rope around his neck and hanged him from the ceiling fan. Everyone in the village was questioned, especially those who had been most put off by Havel's isolation, but no one could provide any information about Havel other than that he was, in their opinion, odd, and no one was named an official suspect. Perhaps most crucial to tracing Dan Havel back to Greg November, however, was a bookmark found inside one of the few books he owned. Written on the bookmark was: 312 E. 10th St., $400/month, 1 room, K. Steiner, 233-5141, 12/19/88. It turned out that Karen Steiner, whom the police were able to reach at the number on the bookmark, had never rented the room on East Tenth Street to a Dan Havel and could not remember ever having met someone by that name. But fortunately for the investigation she happened to be a person, as are many people, addicted to nostalgia and sentimentality. She had been saving all her calendars and appointment books for over twenty years and liked to begin each day by looking back at what she had done exactly ten years earlier. Even seemingly mundane memories—coffee with a friend now living far away or dead, or even something not as pleasant, such as a visit to the dentist—could make rise in her a swell of emotion so intense that some days it brought her to tears. In her 1988 calendar, she turned to December 19 and saw that she had met with three people that day—two women, whose faces she could not recall, and the man she ended up renting to, though only briefly, whose name was Greg November, and whom she described as . . . But I stopped reading at this point, as I do at any point in any article when I fear I am about to read information I do not want.

But do you see how I still suffer for Greg November? Do you see how easily the story of *my* death becomes the story of *his?*

Let me finish the story of my death and why I am no longer afraid.

Our return to the factory several weeks ago was arranged by a TV reporter and a congressional candidate. It was determined that Greg November's death had been a murder and that the men responsible were involved with a wide range of criminal activities and were linked to the torture of dozens of people, including the November Fifteen in an abandoned factory a few hours north of the city.

A young man and woman came to my house early in the morning. The man washed and trimmed my hair; the woman did my makeup. The man dressed me in a shirt and tie and gray pants and then said black pants would be better, and the woman said, "Yes, it will give off more of a funereal vibe," and the man gave me a darker tie, too, and the woman said, "Perfect." With gels and creams, the man sculpted my hair to look messy, and then he did my eyebrows, while the woman filed my fingernails. It was as if I really were a statue: I could not speak, and I moved only when they moved me—he to shave my neck, she to add more color to my cheeks.

They put me in front of a mirror and held a mirror behind me so I could see me from behind, and my wife said, "You look wonderful," and then said to the man and woman, "He hasn't looked so alive in months. He's been under the weather." My daughter came into the room and said, "Dad, your hair doesn't look like your hair," and began to cry, and that was when I knew there was hope for her.

They gave my wife a red dress, my daughter a blue skirt and blue blouse and black boots; the man did their hair, the woman their makeup.

A limousine came to pick us up. Inside were a cameraman and the TV reporter whose idea all this was and the assistant to the congressional candidate who financed the memorial they were driving me to. The reporter asked me questions, but I did not answer her, and my wife said, "I think he's too moved to speak right now." The reporter asked my daughter how she felt, and my daughter replied that she liked her new boots and asked could she keep them when the day was over. The assistant to the congressional candidate, a young man wearing a bowtie, kept smiling at me. When his cell phone rang, he would be angry and curt with whom I assume were his assistants and chipper and apologetic ("Yes, sir, of course, I'm sorry, yes, right away, of course") with whom I assume was the man running for Congress, whose name only later I found out was Ed Coronado.

The outside of the factory—because I had never seen it before now—brought back no memories; it was a nondescript rectangular building that elicited in me no more depression than any other building of its kind would. What made my hands shake more than they normally do was the familiar sound of the limousine's tires rolling over the gravel path leading from the main road to the factory. A banner at the end of the gravel path read: THE NOVEMBER FIFTEEN—SO THAT WE MAY NEVER FORGET. Past the banner, closer to the factory, were tables upon which were programs for the day's events and a narrative beginning with our abduction two years earlier and concluding with the death of Greg November and the findings of the subsequent investigation. Also on the tables were individually signed photographs of each of the November Fifteen (I later discovered that there was a signed photograph of me, though I had never signed any such photograph) and calendars with special pullout sections in November to mark the anniversary of our torture. Standing behind the tables were men in suits and women in skirts passing out programs and making sure everyone received complimentary buttons and bumper stickers that read THE NOV 15 LOVE ED CORONADO. At the main entrance to the factory was a plaque bearing the names of the November Fifteen followed by WERE BROUGHT TO THIS SPOT TO ENDURE SUFFERINGS NO HUMAN BEING CREATED IN THE LIKENESS OF GOD SHOULD EVER SUFFER AND WHICH THIS MEMORIAL WILL ENSURE WILL NEVER BE FORGOTTEN. Coronado's assistant moved me next to the plaque, and someone took my picture. Once I was inside the factory, my memories of having been there did not come back as I suspected they would; it no longer looked the same. The broken windows had been replaced with larger ones that allowed in more light, so that people could better see the many plaques memorializing the places where members of the November Fifteen had been tortured and killed. ON THIS SPOT WILLIAM RUDDIN ENDURED AN ORDEAL THAT CONSISTED OF REPEATEDLY DUNKING HIS HEAD UNDER WATER TO THE POINT OF ALMOST DROWNING HIM, A METHOD DEVISED IN . . . ON THIS SPOT MATTHEW DALUISO BREATHED HIS LAST . . . , et cetera. There were hundreds of people walking around the main room of the factory, some taking pictures of their families in front of the plaques; children played hide-and-seek in the side rooms. Somehow I had lost my wife and daughter, who were whisked away from me for a ceremony involving the families of the survivors, which included a photo op with Ed Coronado. I remember shaking many hands and even touching the heads of small children. People spoke to me, but I did not hear them. I must have spoken back to them, but I don't remember anything I said. There was wine and cheese and fruit, candy for the children, the buzz of people talking and laughing. Through loudspeakers along the walls of the main room, I could hear the theme music that news programs had been using for anything to do with the November Fifteen; it started with the percussive beat of something dire and ended with the sad pull of strings. Then there was a hush, and Ed Coronado began his speech. I never actually saw him; I looked where the other people were looking, but they were looking at the speakers from which his voice was coming. His speech, though I don't remember much of the content, was filled with peaks and valleys of inflection—a somber tone followed by a more passionate call to action followed by a tone of serious reflection followed by more passion followed by a moment of silence followed by a rousing conclusion, after which people applauded and then began clapping in unison to the more upbeat music playing through the speakers. Some people were dancing; I think I saw my daughter dancing. And then the crowd, still clapping, formed a circle around something covered with tarp. Slowly the circumference closed in on what was covered. I was ushered inside the circle along with the other survivors. Breathing was no longer involuntary. I kept having flashes of what I might see when the tarp was removed, though, as in the first moments after waking from a dream, what I saw in my mind was hazy, just beyond the reach of my knowing what it was. After a countdown from ten, the tarp was pulled up, and I saw then what I had had in my mind. We were all there, even Greg November was there; we would live forever. I caught a glimpse of me among the sixteen statues. I wanted to turn away but could not. I was more afraid than I had ever been, but I knew that from that moment forward I would be afraid of nothing. The people kept pressing in on me; I felt that I would be crushed by them. I closed my eyes and waited, but nothing happened. When I opened my eyes, they had passed me; they had not even seen me. People stood near the statues, which were on a platform, with their hands over their mouths. The music ended, then started again. Children stood on their toes and reached; the statues were too high. One child who had lost her parents—a girl, maybe mine, I could not be sure at that point—pointed to the statue of me, pulled on my pants, and said, "Mister, excuse me. Mister, can I sit on your shoulders, please, just for a little bit, so I can touch?"

the beginning of grief

There was an artist some years back whose most famous work was his being shot in the arm at close range. He staged and filmed the shooting, which played in museums around the country and which earned him his reputation for doing things no one else would do. The artist, a young man with short dark hair and a crooked nose, stands in a field of brown grass, a defiantly bored expression on his face: We wait three minutes, four, five, but nothing happens, it's just the young man in a field of brown grass. But we are not bored: We've heard from our friends, or have read in the paper, what we'll see if we keep waiting. Then—there is no way to anticipate it even though we know it will come—there is the shock of a gun firing, an explosion so loud it hurts our teeth, and immediately the artist, who is wearing ripped jeans and a sleeveless white shirt, is on the ground, where he is holding the meaty part of his arm, near his shoulder. We see blood on the hand he had been holding his arm with; then he stands, walks closer to the camera, and holds up his wound for us to see. Slowly the camera pans from his arm to his face, his expression just as defiantly bored as before, then the screen goes black. We say nothing, we simply wait for the video to begin again—brown grass, a young man's face, the shock of a gun firing, the wound—it's the same every time, yet somehow it's new: We notice the hole in his arm is a perfect circle, no, the shape of a star; there is a fleck of blood on his cheek we didn't see before. Eventually, we see ourselves, which is why we watch in the first place.

By now the artist, or rather his vision, has been culturally appropriated, and there are quite a few places you can go to be shot. It's a business now, as are most things—a way for someone to make money. The less cynical might call it a service, and I suppose, at least when I consider my own reasons for going, I would agree. Depending on where you go, it can cost up to one thousand dollars to be shot. Some people believe the best places are the safest, with the most accurate marksmen and a team of doctors standing by; others say the best places are those where they are willing to shoot any part of your body that won't obviously kill you and where there is no doctor on hand—they simply give you directions to the closest hospital. The young go because it has become somewhat hip to say one has been shot, in the way it used to be hip to have one's nose or nipples pierced or one's neck or face tattooed. Artists and writers go as a form of research or for inspiration or simply for the sake of knowledge. I've heard of couples who have gone in an attempt to save their marriage—perhaps seeing one's spouse with a hole in his or her arm might make one realize how precious life is, et cetera. I went for a different reason entirely—for a reason I felt but could not, at the time, name. This was a year ago, when I was in the early stages of the breakdown I'm in the later stages of now.

I found a wounding range in Philadelphia, where I live, but I wanted my experience to be a journey, literal as well as figurative, so I went, instead, to a place I had heard about in New Hampshire. I wanted those six hours in the car to think about what I was about to do, and when it was over, I wanted the drive home, not to think about what I'd done but to *feel* what I'd done—to poke at the wound, if I wanted. When one arrives at a wounding range, and especially after one sees people walking out with bandages around their arms or legs or feet, one might naturally conclude that such places and practices are barbaric, yet as the staff went over the process and had me sign the necessary legal paperwork, I found myself wondering why humans took so long to come up with this idea. I signed the papers without reading them—it really didn't matter to me what they said. Probably something about the range not being responsible for the wounds I was willingly contracting to receive, or for any medical complications resulting therefrom, or for my death, accidental or otherwise, that day or any day thereafter.

A doctor came into the room, took my medical history—was I anemic, did I have high blood pressure or heart disease, any allergies—then gave me a quick physical—checked my pressure, looked into my eyes, knocked my knees, listened to my heart.

"Good luck," he said. "Enjoy your experience."

Two men—one wearing a gray suit, the other wearing jeans and a baseball hat—led me to a field behind the building; the field was divided into rectangular sections, each section walled off. The man in the suit, whose name was Jacobs, explained that, though there may be ten or more clients in the range at any one time, each client has his or her own section, and no two people are shot at the same time—in fact, it was part of his job to witness every shooting and to make sure every client received the full benefit of his or her experience. The man wearing the baseball hat was busy making sure his gun was properly loaded. I saw him take out and put back into one of his eyes what I assume was a contact lens. I must admit I was anxious about being shot—not about the pain I'd feel and certainly not about the gun misfiring or the shooter missing the target I'd chosen but, rather, about it being over too quickly.

"I need to confirm the target," Jacobs said. "We understand you've chosen your right shoulder—is that correct?"

"Yes," I said.

"And we would also like to confirm that you've selected a full-impact wound, rather than our grazing option—is that correct?"

"That's right."

"Very well," he said, "I'm just going to make sure our marksman has the correct data, and then we'll be ready. What will happen," he said, "is that the marksman will take his place and give you a thumbs-up—you need to return his thumbs-up or he will not shoot. Is that clear?"

"Yes," I said.

"Very important, also," he said, "is that once you give the thumbs-up, you must not move. We pride ourselves on being a range that does not restrict our clients in any way—we do not tie our clients to posts, as do some of our competitors, nor do we tie our clients' wrists or ankles together. We prefer the wounding experience to be, let us say, raw—just you standing here while someone—not from close range, mind you—shoots you. So is that clear—you are not to move?"

"Yes," I said.

"Finally," he said, "I want you to remember that our marksman may shoot at *any* point after you give him a thumbs-up. What this means is that he may shoot immediately or he may shoot two or ten minutes later. You did request an element of surprise, did you not?"

"Yes, I did."

"Very well," he said. "Best of luck—we have a doctor just outside the shooting area who will attend to your wounds."

"Great," I said, "thank you."

Jacobs conferred with the marksman, who nodded his head and took his position about ten yards away, a gun in his hand at his side. He didn't wait very long before giving me the thumbs-up, but I wasn't ready. My hesitation had nothing to do with second thoughts; it was more that I wanted time to remember what the cab driver said about her—I wanted to get his words exactly right. "I don't know what happened," he had said. "She was in the back seat, nothing unusual, and then I heard what sounded like her breathing in—you know, like she was about to sneeze, but there was no sneeze, and when I looked back I saw her eyes were closed and her face against the window. When I dropped her off, I said, 'Okay, here we are,' but she didn't open her eyes. Like I said, I thought she was asleep. I said again, 'Okay, Miss, we're here,' but she didn't move. So I figured maybe she had too much to drink, what do I know, so I got out and knocked on the window, but still nothing. Finally, I opened the door, and that was when she came falling out. By then I knew she wasn't just sleeping. Right away I dialed 9-1-1. I feel terrible," he said. "I've never had something like this happen before. My wife's aunt had a brain aneurysm a few years ago, but they got her to the hospital in time. She was never the same after that happened—she had one of those facial tics, and she was always forgetting things."

I gave the thumbs-up and, surprising myself, for I had imagined it otherwise, decided to close my eyes. I didn't want to know a bullet was coming at me—I wanted to believe it could be anything—there are many things sudden and powerful enough to knock you down—I wanted it to be all those things—a strong wind, a wave breaking, a fist, bad news. I tried to hear her sudden intake of breath—exactly the way the cab driver described it—the beginning of a sneeze that never came. I tried to keep this sound in my head. I had heard it before—whenever she woke startled from her recurring dream about losing me. The cab driver said nothing about her crying out or doing anything else that might indicate she was in pain, yet I could not imagine there not being at least some pain. But this wasn't really about her pain or what her last moments were like, it was more about—

Only after I was on my back on the ground, listening to myself breathe, did I hear the echo of a gun fired. My eyes teared without my wanting them to. I could see blood on my hands, on my pants, on my shoes. I grabbed my shoulder, just as I had watched the young artist do years earlier. My legs were heavy, and the grass below me was soft, and I remember thinking that I wouldn't mind staying exactly where I was. I stared at the wound and tried to describe it in my mind with words, as if taking notes for a story I knew I would want to tell one day. Not what I'd call a hole at all, a very jagged opening, chunks of flesh missing, my shoulder burning. Every part of my body but my shoulder seemed heavy and sleeping. I checked for an exit wound but could not find one. I thought: *Right now the bullet is in your body—remember to ask for the bullet.*

"Mr. Holden, Dr. Sachs is going to examine you now, if you'd take your hand away from your shoulder please."

"It didn't go through," the doctor said. "We'll need to take him to the procedure room right away."

"I want the bullet," I said.

"I'm sorry," Jacobs said, "but it's extra if you wish to keep the bullet."

"Whatever it is, I'm sure I'll pay it."

"We can discuss that upon your discharge," Jacobs said.

"His vitals are stable," the doctor said.

"Do you hear that, Mr. Holden—you're going to be just fine."

"It didn't even hurt," I said.

"It must have hurt just a little bit," Jacobs said, and I said, "No, it really didn't," by which I meant, "It didn't hurt enough."

On the drive home it was impossible not to think about her, which is precisely what I wanted to avoid. I had the bullet in my shirt pocket, and once in a while I would take it out and look at it or put it on the seat between my legs. I kept poking at the bandage on my shoulder, then pressing and holding. At one point—I think I was in New Jersey—I pulled to the side of the road, unwrapped the bandage, peeled off the gauze, and moved my finger around in the clotting blood on my arm. Then I did my best to bandage the wound and continued driving. The closer I got to Philadelphia, the sicker I felt.

I did not take pain medication—in fact, I threw away the prescription. Days I spent lying in bed, getting up only to eat—if I *had* something to eat—or to walk to the park, where I would sit hoping I might see something that would interest me, or if not interest me, then make me feel something. I could see my grief sitting next to me on the park bench only as an idea, just as the wound in my shoulder soon became not much more than an idea. What physical pain there was—I suppose one might call it pain—was not enough to consume me, and I wanted a pain that would consume me, that would allow nothing else in.

What I mean is, I wanted a *new* pain to consume me.

Yes, this is about someone I loved dying, but the catch is that no one we knew—not even relatives or close friends—knew we loved each other, and so, after she died, there was no one I felt I could talk to or fall apart in the presence of. We met in Prague, where I was spending my faculty leave, writing a book of short stories, and where she was teaching sculpture. The ways human beings fall in love, stay in love, and sometimes lose love have been written about so many times I fear there is nothing I can write that would not sound maudlin. Suffice to say we believed, as all lovers should, that no love in the history of the universe was like ours. I am not concerned as much with our falling in love—that period of courtship during which one wants always to be in the other's presence, when one's every moment is consumed with thoughts of the other—as I am with our *being* in love. A description of her lips or her eyes or the quiet way she cried would matter very little to you—such details would be much too specific to mean anything to anyone other than me. So let me say, in more general terms, with the hope that we might begin to speak the same language, that we each brought joy and hope to the other's life and enabled the other, usually, to live in the present, and we worked through any bumps we had with kindness and grace and in a way that allowed us both to grow, and we imagined—and joked about—still loving the other just as much when the other was old or fat or in sickness, and we were certain, after only three months, that our being together was, as we called it, permanent.

Do you see how this risks becoming sentimental?

For years I have been unforgiving with my students in this regard—sentimentality will be the death of you as a writer, I've told them. But now I want to be sentimental—I want to write all the terrible prose I've been telling my students not to write—in a journal, on the back of an envelope, somewhere—I want to be able to gush now that gushing is called for.

By the time we came back from Prague, we had decided to get married. She was between teaching jobs and free to go wherever she wished, so she moved from New York to Philadelphia. But we were playing a game, I guess you'd call it, wherein we wanted to see how long we could keep our happiness to ourselves. Neither of us told anyone about the other, other than that we were dating someone, and we found this liberating—for once in our lives we felt no need to include anyone else in our happiness. Our plan was to elope later that summer and then show up at the homes of our family and friends and say, "I'd like you to meet my husband" or "I'd like you to meet my wife." This was not a selfish or impish decision, but a peaceful one, and the result was that the world, which every day had been finding new ways to fall apart, became very small, and the universe—all those forces that conspire for or against us, or both, depending on how one sees things—was, without question, on our side. We felt blessed and made fun of ourselves for using such a word—but we really didn't care. I would go so far as to say that we feared nothing except the loss of the other, which is the same as saying we feared everything.

There was hope, if you are looking for hope, in that I kept looking, even after the wounding range did not work. I was never suicidal but was convinced that the rest of my life would not be much of a life at all, a thought that gave me my only consolation, for the opposite—a life filled with happiness and love and a renewed interest in the world—seemed much worse. I was looking for a pain worse than the pain I was feeling. One problem with getting shot, as I saw it, was that the pain did not last long enough; the other problem was that it was, for the most part, localized—the pain in my shoulder did not move to most other parts of my body. I decided that maybe I needed something on a much larger scale, so I went to the new interactive Holocaust camp, where, as the brochure states, one can "experience what it was really like for those who suffered in the camps."

There were a few hundred people there the day I went. After we paid our fee for the weekend, our heads were shaven and our clothes and belongings taken from us; we were given instructions not to speak. Men dressed as Nazi soldiers crowded us into a train; there was barbed wire over the windows. The soldiers spoke what sounded to me like fluent German; they yelled at people as they pushed them onto the train. I heard one say in English, but with a German accent, "Do you think this is a joke? This is no joke—this is real!" A few people started crying, an older man fainted; when some of us moved to help him, we were told to stay where we were or we would be shot. Not long after the train pulled out of the station, everything went dark; we were made to stand huddled together for over an hour, and when the lights came on we could see that the scenery outside had changed—we had arrived at the camps. A woman standing near me had gotten sick; someone had defecated on the floor. The soldiers ordered us out of the train then made us march into the camp, where we were lined up against a barbed wire fence. We were broken up into work groups of ten; my group's job was to transport heavy machinery from one end of the camp to the other, about three hundred yards, using only a rickety wooden cart we had to take turns pulling. After five hours of work, we had not yet moved half the machinery; one of the soldiers dropped a moldy piece of bread in the dirt at our feet and told us we had to share it, but the bread was too hard to break, so we passed the piece around so that each of us could take a bite, if he or she wanted, which I did not. We worked for another four or five hours, into early evening, and then we were given a small bowl of soup, which was just warm water and grass; I was thirsty, so I drank the water. When we finished moving all the machinery, the soldiers told us we had to move it back. We kept working until two or three in the morning, at which point we were led into barracks, where we slept two to a bed. My body was exhausted and sore—at least they had done that for me—but I could not sleep; it had something to do with having a body pressed against me, an older man who told me twenty times if he told me once that he had lost his mother in the camps and that was why he was doing this—he wanted her to look down and see that he was suffering the way she did. First, I wanted to ask him where exactly his mother was looking down from; then, I wanted to tell him that he would never suffer the way his mother had, nor had his mother ever suffered the way he had upon losing her. The only difference was that his mother's suffering had ended, but his went on. I told him none of this, of course—who was I to question why anyone else did what he did? "Did you lose someone in the camps?" the man asked me before he fell asleep. "No," I said. "Are you Jewish?" he said. "No," I said. "What made you do this?" he said. "I don't know," I said.

In the early morning, before light, we were roused from our beds and sent out to move the same machinery we had moved the day before—back and forth. My hands were bleeding, my feet sore, and there was a dull but constant pain in my shoulder, where I had been shot a few months earlier. The soldiers shouted at us and pushed us around, but a few of us they beat severely; some people fell and were kicked until they stood; others were taken behind one of the barracks, after which we would hear one or two shots ring out; then the person, limp and apparently lifeless, was dragged or carried past us and tossed into a hole one of the work groups had dug. By this time I was well aware which workers were employed by the camp—most of them, no doubt, actors desperate for work. I was surprised, however, when one of the soldiers came and dragged away the man I had shared a bed with—I had believed his story about his mother. He was made to stand over the hole, whereupon he was shot twice, a scene realistic enough to shake up those who were able to forget this was not real. Late afternoon we were told we would be given showers, which I knew, from having read books on the subject, meant we were going to the gas chambers. They ordered us to take off our clothes and leave them in a pile. We were given bars of soap and led to a room that looked like what gas chambers look like in movies about the Holocaust. The room barely held all of us, but somehow we managed to crowd near the center. One woman was frantic—she began screaming that this wasn't really a shower, that we were all going to be killed. But she was a terrible actress. By this time I just wanted to go home—the physical labor did its trick, for a time, but the suffering one might have hoped to re-create here could never be re-created anywhere, for the suffering in the real camps, I imagine, had been less about physical pain and starvation and more about seeing one's loved ones suffer and die, and about not knowing when, if ever, the suffering would end. When we heard gas coming through the pipes near the ceiling, some people started to cry—not from any real fear of dying, I assume, but from what the sound of the gas made them think about. The actors employed by the camp—there were perhaps a dozen or more with us in the chamber—screamed and tried to claw their way up the walls to the small window near the ceiling, where light came through. Gas kept filling the room; the actors coughed and made choking sounds, and eventually they fell to the floor and played dead—their eyes and mouths open. We were left this way for quite some time; some people were hugging each other, but no one spoke. I made sure I made eye contact with no one. After the soldiers opened the door, they dropped their weapons, removed their helmets, and told us we had all perished. They ordered us to file out of the chamber, one person at a time. On our way out, we were each handed a piece of paper, upon which had been written the name of someone who had died in a *real* concentration camp.

Every night for weeks I woke from a dream she was alive and sleeping next to me. The first few times, I got up and looked in the bathroom. Her toothbrush was still there, her contact lens case, her face soap. I sat on the fire escape, even when it was raining, and looked down for her car on the street. There I would smoke and remember the dream she had that I died. She was crying out in her sleep, so I woke her and told her it was okay, it was just a dream, but I could see that she was terribly afraid, so I rubbed her head where she told me her head hurt—she had been getting terrible headaches.

"You were gone," she said.

"Where did I go?"

"Nowhere," she said. "You were just gone—you weren't anywhere."

"You *do* know that someday I'm going to die, don't you?"

"Yes."

"Are you ever afraid that *you're* going to die?"

"No," she said. "I have a strong feeling I'll live a very long life."

"Well, lucky you," I said.

"But I don't want to be old without you," she said.

"You'll be sorry when you have to change my diapers."

"Can't we hire someone to do that?"

"Sure," I said. "We'll go into a rest home together."

"That sounds lovely," she said.

"Listen," I said, "I promise not to get struck by lightning, okay?"

"I'm sorry," she said. "I get this way sometimes when I'm happy."

She cried for a little while, in her quiet way of crying, and then I rubbed her head until she fell asleep.

Years ago, when people felt the way I did, they jumped out of airplanes or swam with sharks—anything to feel close to death but alive. Today there are many more options available—options that don't involve death but, rather, pain. Death seems easy when one loses everything, including the ability to feel one's grief. But one needs the right *kind* of pain—the kind that gets you from the inside out.

There are places you can go to feel virtually anything, and so I went to one of these places—there is one in New York, one in Tokyo, one in Amsterdam—where a single injection can give you almost any experience you want. It's a form of hypnosis, or so I've been told. There is a menu of sorts—one injection allows you to feel what it feels like to be in love, even if you are not in love; another injection can make you feel the guilt of having just killed someone; another makes you feel what a junkie feels when going through withdrawal; there is an injection to make you believe you are gay, another to make you believe you are straight; there are injections to make you feel what having late-stage brain or stomach or breast cancer feels like, or what having Parkinson's or Alzheimer's or Lou Gehrig's disease feels like, or what it's like to be a paraplegic or quadriplegic, or what it feels like to have a heart attack or a diabetic stroke, or to drown or burn or starve to death, or to fall to one's death from a roof, or to be eaten alive by a bear or stung to death by killer bees, or to die in a plane crash or be run over by a truck, or to feel what it's like to be a dog or a rat or a chimpanzee, or a one-month-old baby or a hundred-year-old man. This is all legal now—it's considered by most to be a medical extension of virtual reality. Everything is supervised by physicians, and one cannot have more than one "experience," as they're called, in any six-month period. I don't know the science of it, but, then again, I don't really care to know.

I chose to feel what it feels like to lose a child, which I've heard is one of the worst things, if not *the* worst thing, a human being can experience.

The New York facility looks like it may have once been a factory. There are seven floors, each devoted to its own type of experience—first floor, Birth/Childhood; second floor, Adult Pleasures; third floor, Physical Pain; fourth floor, Emotional Pain; fifth floor, Animal Experiences; sixth floor, Death/Grief; seventh floor, Monthly Specials. Each floor is divided into subcategories—on one, for example, Labor Pains, an experience many mothers-to-be like to purchase for their husbands; on three, Nailed to Cross, popular with religious devotees and Goth teens; on five, Shark-Feeding, or Fly-Mating; one of the special experiences the month I went was called Artist—after being injected, one was able to paint, or rather to *believe* one was painting, a work worthy of a place in the Guggenheim's permanent collection.

But I was concerned only with the sixth floor—specifically, its subcategory Death of Child. They asked me to fill out the requisite forms asking why I was seeking out this particular experience, were there any experiences the facility did not offer that I might be interested in in the future, did I want to receive promotional materials for upcoming specials and events, et cetera. Not only did I have to sign legal papers, but actual lawyers sat down to go over the fine print with me. I pretended to listen then signed where they told me to sign. A pale, balding man with a clipboard came into the room and went over the details.

"Do you want the child to be a son or a daughter?"

"Either is fine," I said. "No, wait—a son."

"Do you want the child's mother to be present?"

"Yes."

"Would you prefer the experience to include the actual death, or would you rather the experience begin after the child is already dead—say, at a wake or funeral?"

"I'd like to experience the death."

"Would you like the death to be something violent and surprising like a car accident, or would you rather your son die from, say, a prolonged illness?"

"I want the death to be quiet and painless."

"Do you have any preferences as to what the child looks like?"

"I suppose he should look something like me—dark hair, brown eyes."

"How old—"

"Wait," I said. "Give him light brown hair, very curly, and green eyes."

"That's fine," he said. "And how old would you like your son to be?"

"I'm not sure—I guess three sounds about right."

"And finally, what would you like your wife to look like?"

"A little shorter than me, thin but not too thin, green eyes, light brown hair—curly and long but not too long."

"We should be ready for you in about an hour, Mr. Holden."

They put me in an isolation waiting room—no magazines, no music playing, no windows, just a folding chair to sit on. The purpose, I was told, was to give me time to think about what I was about to experience—to get my mind prepared for the drug they would inject into my body. There had been a few incidents—*very* few, the lawyers told me—in which clients weren't mentally prepared for the experience, and so the results were, to use their word, unexpected. "The human brain is very powerful," they told me. "Far more powerful than the drugs we use. As with any form of hypnosis, if the brain is unwilling, there is very little we can do."

About twenty minutes later, a nurse came in and gave me a pill. "What's this?" I asked.

"It's just something to relax you."

"I'm relaxed," I said.

"I'm sorry," she said, "but it's part of your agreement that you follow our procedures to the letter."

I put the pill in my mouth, and she gave me a cup of water, which I drank quickly. I then opened my mouth and moved around my tongue to show her I had actually swallowed the pill.

"Very good," she said. "Just a short while longer and they should be ready for you."

By the time the doctors arrived—there were two of them—the pill had made me tired enough that I was lying on the floor. "Hello, Mr. Holden," the older doctor said. "I'm Dr. Steinberg, this is Dr. Aziz, and we'll be administering and monitoring your experience today. In a few moments, I'm going to give you an injection in your arm—it may sting just a little—and then we'll lead you to the experience room. We won't be in the room with you—we want the experience to be as pure as possible—but there will be cameras in the room, and we'll be close by should you need our assistance in any way."

Dr. Aziz was silently readying my arm for the injection—extending it, tapping for a vein. He had a way of breathing slowly in and out through his nose that relaxed me.

Dr. Steinberg continued, "As I'm sure you've read in the contract, there is no way of knowing what the specifics of your experience will be. What happens is largely a matter of what you bring to the experience. Certainly, we can create the situation and make it as real as anything else you've ever experienced in your life, but what you feel during and as a result of the experience is mostly up to you. In other words, if I were to light a match and hold the flame to your skin, your skin would burn—there is no question of that—but whether or not you feel pain is another question entirely."

"Mr. Holden is ready," Aziz said.

"Do you have any questions or concerns?" Steinberg said.

"No, I don't think so," I said.

As Steinberg was bringing the needle to my arm, I said, "I'm just curious, how long will this experience last?"

"That depends," he said, "on how you react to the set of circumstances you've requested. What one does and feels during any given experience will vary from person to person. To do and feel whatever you're going to do and feel might take only five virtual minutes, but then again, it could take five hours. In ten seconds real time you will be able to experience sixty seconds virtual time. We do not allow the experience to exceed one hour real time. Does that sufficiently answer your question?"

"Yes," I said, and I held out my arm.

I remember the prick of the needle, and then both men led me out of the room and through a maze of white hallways. Something in the walls seemed to be moving; it was almost as if a movie were being projected onto the walls, but I couldn't quite see what it was. But I felt that I could see through things. Through my shoes and socks and the skin and flesh of my feet, I could see bone. I could see inside Aziz's throat and past Steinberg's shirt to his sagging chest. Then, when I looked away from Steinberg, Aziz was gone. When I looked back to where Steinberg had been, he was gone too, and I was in my son's bedroom. My wife was lying in bed with our son. He had been sick for over a year, and now we were just waiting. He was in and out of consciousness; every time he opened his eyes I wanted more than anything else that he would see me and know I was with him. I sat on the edge of the bed and rubbed his head, which was warm; I pulled down the covers because I wanted to see his chest moving. My wife was whispering something into his ear. But you must understand that this wasn't just a scene I had been made to be a part of—some boy dying, some woman who was supposed to be my wife lying with him. This was *my* wife and *my* son, and this moment—his death—was not limited to this moment: As I sat on the bed, I had within me years of memories of having lived with them—of having watched her give birth to this boy, of having fed him and taught him and watched him smile and crawl and walk and run and do all the things children do—and so this moment was not sad so much as it was happy.

After a while, my wife got out of bed and asked if I wanted to spend some time with our son. I lay next to him and put my hand on his stomach. His breathing was the breathing of someone in restless sleep trying to break free from a dream or from fever—quick, shallow breaths—so I put my mouth against his ear and breathed slowly and evenly with the hope that his body would follow my lead, similar to the way a husband might coach his wife to breathe when in labor. "He's actively dying," my wife said, and I knew she was right—there was no panic, no mad rush to save him—we were there merely to witness his dying and to help him through it, if we could. I couldn't help looking at his face—his nose and the shape of his mouth were mine. His hair and eyes were my wife's—his fingers too. His breathing became slower. My wife lay in bed on the other side of him; we closed our eyes and waited until we no longer saw his chest rise or heard breath come from his mouth. It was very peaceful, and even after he passed we stayed where we were; there was no one to call to tell, no reason at all to move, and soon I fell asleep.

I woke what seemed like hours later to Dr. Steinberg standing next to the bed and Dr. Aziz listening to my heart.

"My son died," I said.

"Yes," Steinberg said. "He was supposed to die—that's what you wanted."

"But it was happy," I said.

"Is that what you wanted?"

"No," I said. "I mean, I don't know."

"Sometimes," Steinberg said, "we don't realize the full effect of an experience until weeks or months, perhaps even years, later."

"Are you real?"

"Yes," Steinberg said.

"They were real too," I said.

Steinberg looked away from me; he wrote something on the chart in his hand. "We'll need to keep you under observation," he said.

"They were real," I said.

"Dr. Aziz will periodically check your vitals, and we'll have to run a few tests, but if everything looks fine, we'll be able to release you."

"I didn't think I would feel happy," I said.

"Before you leave," Steinberg said, "you'll have an opportunity to fill out an evaluation form—there you can provide us with a full account of your experience."

"I have a question," I said. "A few questions, actually. Is there any chance I'll have flashbacks? I mean, will I be walking down the street next week and see—or think I'm seeing—my son or my wife? Will I be able to tell what's real and what's not real? And what about withdrawal—will I crash in a few hours?"

"I'm afraid I'm already late for another client," Steinberg said, "but the answers to your questions should be in the literature we'll provide you upon your release."

After Steinberg left, I looked at Aziz. "Everybody reacts differently," he said. "Some people have side effects, some don't. There might be fatigue, maybe a loss of appetite. A small percentage of people temporarily reenter the hypnotic state. But really, there's nothing you need to worry about."

On the train from New York to Philadelphia, I wasn't sure if anything I was seeing was real. Everything seemed lighter, thinner, almost transparent, and people talking sounded like people talking underwater. I closed my eyes and put my hands over my ears, and I didn't care if people were staring at me. At one point I began to panic, so I went into the bathroom and sat on the floor and tried to breathe. Eventually, someone knocked on the door, and I went back to my seat and closed my eyes.

During my walk home from the station, the first stage of my breakdown—the period during which my only consolation was that I would never again experience joy, or anything close to joy—ended with laughter, and the second stage—the real beginning of my grief—began. I knew precisely when it happened—it was a seemingly small moment that would have meant very little otherwise. I was walking through the park when I saw a little girl, perhaps three or four years old, long curly blond hair, sticking her finger into a dog's ass. With every poke of her finger the girl made a sound like, "Wheeee! Wheeee!" The dog, a black Lab going gray in its face, looked back at the girl but did nothing to get away—perhaps it was too old to care, or, who knows, maybe it felt good. What made me laugh, really, was the girl's father's reaction when he saw what she was doing. "Christie!" he said. "My God, Christie! What are you doing? Don't do that!" He looked around nervously to see if anyone was watching. Then he turned to his wife and said, "Did you see what she was doing?" "No," the wife said, "what did she do?" "She was putting her—" the man began. "She was sticking her finger—" he said, but he couldn't seem to finish. Instead, he crouched to pet the dog. "Poor Georgia," he said. "What happened to Georgia?" the man's wife said. "I'll tell you later," he said. He turned to his daughter. "Christie!" he said. "Don't put your finger in your mouth—that's filthy!" "What happened?" his wife said. "Just take her somewhere and wash her hands," he said.

I went over to pet the dog—I wanted to make sure she was real. Her hair felt like dog's hair, and she panted like a dog. I wasn't sure if everything around me was real—the people, the trees, the ground beneath me—but I knew my hand and what my hand was touching were real, so I kept petting the dog, I would not stop petting her, not even when the man touched my shoulder and said, "Hey, it's okay, really, everything is okay—she's fine, she's all right now."

man throws dog out window

Before we looked up to see the dog falling splay-legged toward us, we heard a woman scream. We are ashamed now to say that not one of us walking to lunch, nor any of us standing smoking, thought the scream an indication of something truly grave happening. Those walking did not break stride; those smoking, with a flick of a finger, tapped off ash, then breathed in more smoke. We thought: a mouse out from under a fridge. Or: a woman tickled. Or: shower water turned cold. It was not until the scream did not stop that we—all of us at once, it seems to me now—looked up and saw the dog. We were concerned first, though briefly, with taking in what was happening, with getting the story right; we imagined the pleasure of being able to tell our husbands and wives and children at day's end. Then, because to each of us the dog seemed to be falling directly overhead, we ran for cover: Some crouched under awnings; some simply put their hands up, as if this could protect them; some of us ran into each other, knocked each other over. We had been sent so quickly into a panic that only a few of us noticed the two gunshots and that the woman's screaming had stopped after the first.

The dog's descent took no more than a slow count to five, or so we told our families and neighbors that evening. There was no panic on the dog's face that we could see; she pedaled her legs as if swimming. No one looked long enough to see the dog bounce up from the cement, though we told our families and friends that the dog bounced once before coming to rest. Its legs, we saw later, before one of us covered the body with his jacket, were bent in the way the limbs of dead broken things are bent—snapped back, snapped apart. If it were not for the blood around the dog's mouth and one eye being more open than the other, it could have been a stuffed dog, its fall the result of a child's tantrum, the scream the scream of a frustrated mother, nothing more.

Beginning later that evening, and continuing for weeks, we heard the rest of the story of the dog's death, which is a story we continue to tell and get pleasure from telling. It is a story we tell to friends at dinner parties and to strangers in doctors' and dentists' waiting rooms. "Have I ever told you about the dog that almost fell on my head?" Or: "Were you living in this neighborhood when the incident with the dog happened?" Or: "What do you think it would take for a man to throw a dog out a window?" We like to begin with these types of teasers, questions to make listeners lean in close. Only after people are sufficiently intrigued, perhaps to the point at which our walking away and refusing to tell the story would be painful to them—only then do we begin, "Before we looked up to see the dog falling splay-legged toward us, we heard a woman scream." Except in rare cases—people afraid to speak with strangers, or people in a hurry, or people who suspect from the first sentence that our story will be too violent—except in these cases, people usually lean in closer, cover their mouths with their hands. They want to know why the dog was thrown out a window, and once they know why—I'm talking about the facts, this happened, then this, then this—they again ask why, and for this question we have no answer. Eventually, the listener becomes the teller, passes the story along to a cousin at the funeral of a great-aunt or to a woman pushing a stroller in line at the bank, and in this way the story, or rather our hope that we will find the answers we seek, never dies.

The story we tell—and we all tell a somewhat similar version, with only slight variations—always focuses on the dog. I do not mean to say that we do not cover the story in its entirety—the woman who owned the dog, the man who threw the dog to its death—but, rather, that the dog always seems the story's center of gravity—no pun intended, we assure you. At first we told the story in a circular manner, which was the only way we could, given that new facts were revealed daily. Once we had all the facts, or *most* of them, since there is no way of knowing what is true and what is hearsay, and since we know that even in stories that seem to have clear beginnings and endings, there is always the possibility of new information or a new way of looking at or telling the story—once we had *most* of the facts, we began to piece them together chronologically and told the story from what we knew as A to what we knew as Z. But lately we have chosen, more often than not, to tell the story from what we know as Z to what we know as A, or some variation thereof that moves, in general, backwards. Much better, we've been thinking, to allow what happened last to illuminate, to help us redefine, what happened first.

So we continue now with blood around the dog's mouth, one eye more open than the other. Before the police arrived, a man removed his jacket and covered the dog's body. Some people walked past without turning to look, some stopped long enough to see that under the jacket was a dog, not a person, but most stayed, asked questions, looked up to see, or try to see, where the dog had come from, which window, what happened, did someone leave the dog home with a window open, did the dog jump, was she chasing a bird on the windowsill? No, there was a scream—maybe the woman who owned the dog saw that the dog was about to fall. Then why isn't she down here now? Maybe she's calling the police, maybe she fainted. But what about the gunshots? What gunshots? There were two, didn't you hear them? No, I was too busy running for cover. Do you think someone was trying to shoot the dog and the dog jumped to save herself? Why would someone want to shoot a dog? I don't know, why would something like this happen period? And so on. The voices of all the people who formed a circle around the dog blended into one voice trying to answer its own questions. Most of us did not return to work, or if we did it was only to begin telling what we knew, what we didn't know. Those who left eventually returned to the street, where the dog lay stiff. Our coworkers, and in some cases our employers, came with us: They did not want to have to be told what was happening; they did not want to have to tell their families and neighbors, "Listen to what I *heard* happened near where I work," but, rather, wanted to say, "Listen to what I *saw*."

The police were there asking questions: What did you see, what did you hear, are you sure, here's my card, call me if you remember anything else that might help, et cetera, and we in turn asked the police what *they* knew, but they told us they were sorry, they didn't know much more than we did. But at least some of them—those who had gone into the building and into the apartment the dog had fallen from—had to have known more. What they knew, what they were beginning to piece together, we learned later that afternoon, on TVs in our offices, or from people on the street with cell phones, and hours later, on the evening news, and on the car radio during the next morning's commute, and from all these sources, and from hearsay, during the days and weeks to follow.

Sleep that first night was restless, filled with dreams not about dogs falling, or even about dogs in general, but about the usual strange things and places dreams are about—a phone ringing somewhere, it's important that we get to the phone, where is the phone, it's a matter of life and death to find the phone; eyes peering out at us from hedges bordering a garden filled with mice; in a library the size of an entire city, every page in every book empty; our dream selves waking in bedrooms with neither ceilings nor walls nor floors, the bed and bureau floating in a night that was not night but a sunless day; a phone ringing, hurry, we must get to the phone. Our children came to us in the night and asked if they could sleep with us. We asked if they were having bad dreams; they said yes. We asked had they been dreaming about the dog; they said no. But we understood that their dreams, regardless of what they seemed to have been about, *had* been about the dog, and so together we slept restlessly and woke tired, and it was a relief to go to work in the light of day; it was even a relief, we'd all agree, to see the bloodstain on the street where the dog had fallen and to know that the terrible dreams we had had, and what we were feeling in general, were about the dog—something tangible, something we felt we could point to, think about, deal with, and that would eventually pass through us, a slight bump in our lives—and were not about something more frightening we could not name.

By the afternoon someone had created a memorial for the dog, whose name, we discovered, was Cookie. Near the bloodstain people left posters that read: WE'LL MISS YOU, COOKIE and PUPPIES GO TO HEAVEN TOO and JUSTICE FOR COOKIE! Someone, perhaps a friend or relative of Cookie's owner, left dozens of photos, beginning when the dog was eight weeks old, small enough to sit in her owner's hands, and ending "two days before the tragedy" (as the note attached to the photo told us), when Cookie was three years old. By the end of the week the memorial had grown; not only were pedestrians stopping to read the posters and look at the photographs and ask questions, but bicycle messengers and motorists were finding it difficult not to stop to see what the circle of people—there was almost always a circle of people—had gathered to see. People who owned German shepherds or Labs or shepherd/Lab mutts, which is what Cookie had been, left photos of their dogs; some left chew toys and collars and slobber balls. Those who had been particularly disturbed by the incident brought their dogs to the memorial. While the dogs sniffed the bloodstain, wagged their tails, and let people pet them, their owners said to each other or to the reporters covering the tragedy, "Dogs feel grief too, you know," or "That was my Ridley's pal from the dog park," or "I would kill anyone who ever tried to harm my Samson," or some such statement expressing sadness or anger or outrage or any combination thereof.

Doctors performed an autopsy and concluded that Cookie had not ingested any poisons, nor had she been beaten or burned or harmed in any way prior to her fall, and that the cause of death, as most suspected, was "bodily trauma due to an impact while traveling at a fatal velocity." Those who visited the memorial took up a collection to help pay for the cremation; half the ashes were scattered in the dog park, half were kept in an urn, which the collection also helped pay for and which became the centerpiece of the memorial.

Every day new information came out about the events leading to

Cookie's death, and every day, at work or at the memorial, or at night, at the dinner table, we told each other what we knew, asked what we didn't know. We continued to wake from dreams thinking about the dog. We thought of our days in terms of the dog's death—one week after, three weeks after, a month.

We learned what happened last first, what happened first last. When we told what we knew, we did not merely restate facts, for we understood that to capture our listeners' attention and, more important, evoke their emotions, we had to dramatize—to speculate, if you will—to fill in those details that, though they could not be confirmed, were, in a sense, or could have been, true. For example, the first facts, or I should say the *last* facts, were that a white male, S., thirty years old, of below average height though strong for his size, a security guard by profession, during an argument with his girlfriend, V., that had been escalating for close to an hour, in a moment authorities have described as temporary insanity, picked up her shepherd/Lab mutt, Cookie, who had been the subject of the argument, or if not *the* subject then certainly a contributing factor, and threw the dog, which weighed sixty-five pounds, out the open living room window. Not long after the dog had fallen, S., no longer temporarily insane, for he was now fully aware of what he was doing, especially given V.'s scream and the commotion below, took a gun from between his back and the back of his belt and, without hesitation, shot V. in the center of her chest then shot himself in the face. These facts are grisly enough: We feel no need to exaggerate, nor do we feel the need to go into too many details about what position V. fell dead in (you can imagine for yourself that perhaps her eyes were open, one arm extended above her head in the gesture one might associate with a ballerina doing a pirouette, one hand holding her shirt near where the bullet went through), or what S.'s face looked like (there was no nose, no lips, no upper teeth), or where his blood splattered (it formed a Pollock-like pattern on the wall behind him, on the TV screen, on the glass fronts of the picture frames atop the desk V. sat at to write letters and pay bills). There is no need, really, for this kind of storytelling. We are more concerned with—and have been since our first telling—the whys, if there *are* whys, and less concerned with who, when, where, and how. Who, when, where, and how can be summed up briefly and neatly, as above, whereas why is a more complicated and therefore more interesting and important question—the kind of question that wakes us in the night to rooms that do not seem to be rooms we know, to people sleeping next to us who seem not quite real—things we need to touch to see that they have substance.

The argument, or rather this last phase of the argument, since it had been going on, off and on, for more than six months, began the night before Cookie died, when S., putting aside his pride, called V. one more time to ask why she had "chosen" the dog over him. Had V. answered the phone, she might have told S., as she had many times, that she had not "chosen" the dog, it was more the case that—silly as she knew it sounded—she loved the dog as a mother loves her child; she had taught the dog everything it knew and had watched its personality develop and knew truly that her dog was in many ways a reflection of her Self, and even the thought of giving Cookie away to someone who could never love her as V. did made her depressed, and her decision to keep Cookie, and to put off moving in with and eventually marrying S., had less to do with "choosing" the dog over S. than with trying to find a way to have both in her life—she could keep Cookie, and S. could remain her boyfriend, and they, V. and S., could maintain the relationship they had had for the past two years, and maybe someday they could find a way for all of them to live together—maybe someone would come up with new allergy and asthma medications S. could take, or maybe he could try (she had asked him several times to try, but he had not) some natural or herbal remedies or acupuncture. Or maybe someday, who knows, they would make enough money to buy a house large enough so that Cookie could have her own space, an addition to the house, something like a kennel, but for just one dog, and V. could go into this space anytime she wanted to play and snuggle with Cookie, and before she came back into the main section of the house she would change her clothes and wash her hands, which she knew was something she hadn't been exactly careful with lately, and she was sorry for that, but her relationship with the dog, as she'd told S. before, was different when he was around—she wasn't as affectionate, she was anxious about getting every last dog hair off her clothes and hands, not to mention having to change her socks three or four times a day, there was *always* dog hair on the bottoms of her socks, and every time she got into bed with S. he would ask if she was "contaminated," which used to be a word that made V. laugh—it made light of what otherwise could have been a sensitive issue—but was now more a word S. hesitated before using, for he feared his use of it (his checking up on her) had become annoying, though V. would reassure him that *he* was not annoying, it was more the *situation* that had become annoying, at which point S. would become hurt, he saw no difference between him and the situation, so V. would take back the word *annoying* and say that the situation was *frustrating*—she had meant frustrating. But, as we said, V. did not answer the phone—she and S. had gone back and forth about this subject too many times for her to bear going back and forth about it again. The more they argued about it—and this is what she told him when he showed up at her apartment the day she died, and which was part of what sent him into a rage he could not come back from—the more they argued, the more secure she felt in her decision not to give away the dog. (Several times S. had used the phrase "get rid of," so V. would make sure to say "give away" or "give up" or "find a new home for," and would also make sure, especially in the middle of an argument, to emphasize these words.) Why, she asked him, should she *give away* a dog she loved as a mother loves her child, when the man she would be giving up the dog for was too self-centered to understand what the love of an animal meant and was, she reminded him, too lazy to look into alternative medical options, such as herbs or acupuncture or even hypnosis, all of which she had reminded him about many times, but never in a nagging way, more in a genuinely-concerned-for-the-future-of-our-relationship way? This last question was what sent S. further into the rage he was already in, which in turn led V. to say, "Do you expect me to give up my dog for a man who becomes so violent?" "I've never been violent in my life," S. said, or could have, and so said in the story we told. "Do you want to see me violent? I'll give you me violent right now, if you want." At this point, we believe S. was only thinking about throwing his car keys across the room or breaking the glass of a picture frame against the floor. It was only when V. said, "Look at yourself, I rest my case," that S. snapped. We don't know the textbook psychological dynamics of temporary insanity, though we like to describe what happened as follows: The rational part of S. left his body, and the animalistic raging part of him, which had been buried way back in the most inaccessible part of his brain, or soul, if you want to look at it that way, took over. He was, in a sense, blind and deaf and, had he lived, would not have remembered (unless maybe under intense hypnosis) the moment he grabbed the dog, ran to the window, and threw her out. Only when S. heard V. screaming did he begin to understand not only that something terrible was happening but that *he* had something to do with the terrible thing that was happening; only then did his psyche begin to shift from "temporarily insane" to "sane but enraged and murderous," which some might say, *we* might, is more easily understood yet less easily forgivable. He must have shown up, we believe, with some murderous, or at least violent, intent, for between his back and the back of his belt was a gun he'd owned since having been robbed in his home three years earlier: Yes, he could have brought the gun with the intention of shooting holes in V.'s wall or desk or coffee table, or maybe with the intention of just waving it around and threatening to harm V. or more likely himself, a cry for sympathy or love, but we must assume that a man who owns a gun is prepared to use it for more than just evoking sympathy or creating drama, especially a man enraged about his girlfriend's not having answered or returned his calls, and even more so, if we can get back to the genesis of this story, about his girlfriend's having "chosen" her dog over cohabitation and possible matrimony with him, a human being, as he often reminded her he was (and resented having to remind her), with feelings that went *way* beyond (he never failed to place emphasis on the word *way,* at which point V. would ask if he knew that for a fact, had he ever read a single book on the psychology of dogs?)—his feelings, he claimed, went *way* beyond the feelings of a dog. A dog, S. told V., is loyal to the human that gives it food and rubs its belly—that's it, there was no such thing as dog love, how dare she compare her love for a dog with the love a mother has for her child? If that was the kind of mother she was going to be—a mother who treats her child like just one more thing to feed and snuggle with and teach tricks—then good riddance, he had no intention of spending his life with a woman who didn't know the difference between human babies and puppies that peed on the rug and pooped on the floor and even ate their own poop and expected you to clean up their mess and two minutes later wanted to jump in bed with you no matter if you wanted them to or not and didn't seem to give a rat's ass if you were lying there with your nose dripping and air barely getting into your lungs or if you, a human being, had to go out in subfreezing weather and walk home to your own bed without dog hair and then spend the next week bending over backwards to make things right with your human girlfriend, who for some reason was hurt that you "chose" to leave when you "knew damn well" that leaving would make her feel guilty. No, he told her, he wasn't so sure he wanted to spend his life with a woman who couldn't tell the difference between four- and two-legged creatures. S. had a habit, though, of backing away from these pronouncements when he saw that they were not going to change the way V. felt but were pushing her closer to her dog and farther from the thought of a life with him.

As you can see, we were as thorough as possible in telling the story; we left no detail we knew, or felt we knew, out. We kept working backward. Next we told of the period during which it had been decided by V., through S.'s urging, that V. would indeed give away the dog. What prompted S.'s urging V. was the fact that S. and V. were in love, and loved each other deeply beyond their being in love, and had what they called a "great working relationship" as a couple, by which they meant that even when they had "bumps" (they did not like to call them fights), they did not raise their voices (V. had been the one to remind S., when he started to lose his temper, that that wasn't the way *they* worked as a couple), nor did they rest until the "bump" had sufficiently been smoothed out, sufficiently meaning neither S.

nor V. walked away from their "discussions" carrying any residual hurt or anger that might "bubble up" maybe weeks or months later through no or very little provocation. V. was in therapy—she had been for years and saw her therapy not as a "taking care of problems" but more as "maintenance" or a "preventative measure"—and so she was the one who often took the lead in their working through things: If the subject of V.'s most recent ex-boyfriend came up—let's say V. saw him in the park and he told V. how great she looked and asked if they could get together for coffee sometime and pretended not to remember S.'s name—V. would hold S.'s hand and ask him how he felt, and he would feel comfortable and relaxed telling her his Truth, which was always something V. wanted to hear and which S. came to look forward to sharing with V., and she was very good about not judging him and would tell him that what he was feeling—even if it was a sign of jealousy or pettiness—was perfectly human, and she "understood" and thought no less of him, and in this way S. was able to at least begin to work through some of his core issues. (Because V. was so physically attractive and S. was what most woman might describe as "cute" in that way women describe men not very physically attractive but with "great personalities" as cute and because he was a security guard in a museum and V. worked in an art gallery and was herself a sculptor whose abstract sculptures S. did not understand—because of all this, plus, of course, V.'s very obvious love for her dog, S. was afraid he was somehow not worthy of V.'s love, even though she had given him every indication, especially the way she held his hand when they worked through his feelings, that he was *more* than worthy of her love.) There were even times when V. had been the one who was jealous or petty or the one starting to raise her voice, and S., through what he had learned from watching V., was the one to remind V. that there was no need to raise their voices, they were a much better couple than that, or that V. would feel better if she just told him the Truth about what she was feeling, and he, S., would never judge her, nor would he love her any less, and in this way, they would have said, and anyone who knew them could see it when they were together, they had become a "working couple" in a relationship that not only gave them room to grow but made that growth possible, and they would fall asleep most nights making sure at least one part of their bodies touched, and if they woke in the night and one had unknowingly shifted to his or her side of the bed, the other would shift too and make sure they were touching, and they would wake feeling almost embarrassingly happy to be part of something so meaningful, and they would do all the "sappy" things couples do when they're in love, such as kissing and saying "I love you" and "I'm so happy" and "I never want to be without you," and so on, and their worry, when they had worry, was not "Will he cheat on me?" or "Will she leave me?" but, rather, "Will something terrible happen to one of us?" by which they meant a terminal illness or fatal car accident, which were the only things they could think of that could possibly come between them and which they had to reassure each other about. All this is to say that when S. raised the subject of the dog—more specifically, how would S. and V. ever live together and/or get married when there was no way S. could live with the dog, even with a large space and V.'s constantly cleaning and changing her clothes and washing her hands—V. reacted by getting sad, but only briefly, before reassuring S. that as important as Cookie was to her, S. was more important, and together they would find a solution to their problem.

For several months after it had been decided, S. was the one who spent his energy looking for a new home for the dog—not because he didn't like the dog but because he had come, as he told V., to actually love the dog. He did not use the word *love* in relation to the dog in the same way V. used it; he did not mean he loved the dog as a parent loves a child, or as an uncle loves his niece, or as a friend loves his friend, or as any human loves any other human; he meant, simply, that he had come to love having the dog around: Yes, despite not being able to sit on the couch because that was where the dog liked to sit; despite the fact that S. spent some nights with a runny nose and unable to take a deep breath even though V. had done her best, usually, to dust and clean; despite the dog's habit of following S. around and wagging her tail at him so that hair from her tail got on his jeans and got in his eyes when he touched his jeans then rubbed his eyes; despite the dog's fear of rain such that on rainy days she would not go outside and so pooped on the rug and S. had to look at the poop, if it was his day off, until V. came home to clean it up; despite the dog's crying when she was bored or hungry or her barking when S. or V. turned on the vacuum cleaner or when she, the dog, heard another dog barking outside or in a nearby apartment; despite all these things, maybe *because* of all these things, S. had come to love the dog—keeping in mind, of course, *his* definition of love in relation to a dog, not V.'s. What we are saying here—and we mean this not as a defense of S.'s actions—is that S.'s search for a home for the dog was not, as we see it, a selfish act but was motivated by a genuine concern that the dog be happy, by which he meant—and V. would have agreed with this—that the dog had someone to give it, rather *her,* food and water, and bring her to the vet when she was sick or needed shots, and take her for walks and to her favorite dog park, where she could see her dog friends, and every once in a while buy her a chew toy or slobber ball, and give her a bath when she needed a bath, and never hit her, and buy her favorite peanut-buttery treats, someone who maybe had a yard the dog could run around and dig holes in, and, even better, someone with children and/or another dog. At some point during S.'s search, he became convinced—he could never tell V. this—that the dog might even be happier in a backyard-type suburban home rather than a one-bedroom city apartment in which the dog had to lean her paws on the windowsill and stretch up as much as she could just to get a glimpse of what was going on down on the ground. S. found himself asking strangers at the museum if they were interested in owning a dog, and when children came in packs from nearby schools, S. would sometimes ask them and their teachers, and if anyone expressed interest he would ask where they lived, had they ever owned a dog, did they feel they could take on the responsibility, et cetera, and he found himself telling them all about the dog, even using her name (usually, when referring to Cookie, he simply said "the dog"), and described her, Cookie, in the most flattering ways, and meant what he said—that she was, it could not be denied, a very lovable dog, and that to see her running around a dog park chasing other dogs, or rolling in mud, or play-wrestling with and gently nibbling other dogs' necks, was something even *he* felt could add years to a person's life. But whenever he came home from work and called V., or went over to see her, and would tell her he had found the perfect home for the dog, V. would quickly find something wrong with the proposed home or owner: "If she's a surgeon, she needs to be on call, who knows what hours she works, she can't give Cookie what she needs." "I don't want Cookie living with cats—you know she's afraid of cats." "I don't want her living in Ohio—that's too far, I want to be able to visit her." "The man was wearing a cowboy hat? What kind of a person wears a cowboy hat in summer in a museum in New York City? I don't want Cookie living with a person like that."

So at a certain point, S. told V. that finding a new home for the dog was *her* project now—he was tired of having his ideas shot down. V. was hurt that S. felt he needed to put it that way—after all, she was only looking out for Cookie's best interests—but she agreed to be more proactive in finding the dog (sometimes she used the phrase "my girl") a new home. Still, S. had to keep reminding V. that in a few months his apartment lease was up, and he had already given notice, and she needed to find a home for the dog sooner rather than later, and V. would say, "I know, I haven't forgotten, I've spoken to a few people," and S. wanted to ask V. who specifically she'd spoken to because he suspected V. was stalling, which made S. even more bitter and insecure, and it was at this point, we believe, that, rather than expressing his anger and insecurity, S. began storing up these feelings: He would lie in bed, especially those nights he slept alone in his own apartment (V. said she didn't have too much time left with Cookie and wanted, if S. didn't mind, to give Cookie as much of her love and attention as possible during these final few months), and imagine showing up at V.'s apartment with a truck filled with everything he owned and V. standing curbside with Cookie, and S. saying, "Why are you crying?" and V. saying nothing, and S. saying, "You didn't find her a home, did you?" and V. saying, "Can't we just try it out for a few months, please? I'll clean twice a day, I'll give her a bath every night, I'll keep her off the couch, I promise, I'll have someone take her on weekends, but I just can't give her away, I'm sorry, I tried." Before he fell asleep, alone, S. would imagine the tirade he would unleash: He would make V. feel as terrible as possible; he would remind her that he'd sold his bed and bedding and cookware and TV and two of his favorite lamps V. said didn't go with her lamps and some of his artwork they agreed they didn't have room for; he would remind her that he didn't have a place to live now, that his apartment was no longer his, someone at that very moment was moving in, and now he had no choice but to put what was left of his things in storage and stay with a friend, or else get a room in a hotel, or else leave everything in the truck and pay for however many extra days he'd have to rent the truck before finding a new place to live, which would be impossible now that it was the first of the month, because there was no way (he'd tell V.) he was moving a single piece of furniture or one of his rugs or his clothes or shoes (the dog liked to chew shoes) into that apartment as long as that dog was still living there, and V. (in S.'s fantasy, that is) would cry and say she was sorry and admit that she was the cause of S.'s current situation. But as soon as V. began crying and showing genuine remorse, S.'s anger (lying in his bed) began to subside. No, he wasn't finished feeling angry; he had only just begun to feel angry. So in the revision of S.'s fantasy, V. did not cry but, rather, became angry with S., called him a selfish bastard, something like that, which allowed S. to scream at V. more, which was what he really, deep down, wanted to do. And so S. would fall asleep these nights, and wake the next morning, feeling angry with V. but happy to know that at some point, if V. didn't do what she had promised, S. would have an opportunity to make her feel pain in return, which was small compensation, S. knew, considering he loved V. and wanted to spend his life with her.

But S. didn't even get the satisfaction he imagined he'd get. There was no curbside drama; he had not yet sold his bed, nor had they discussed which lamps and what artwork he would keep. V.'s realization that she could not give away Cookie was not last-minute enough to warrant the kind of tirade S. had hoped he'd be able to unleash on

V. One month before S. was to move in, V. sent an e-mail to everyone she knew, including S., explaining that "due to allergies" she was looking for a new home for Cookie. (She did not say "due to S.'s allergies" or "due to the fact that she loved S. and they were going to live together" or anything to make S. feel that V.'s decision to live with S. was anything other than tragic). V. used phrases like "this is a painful decision" and "sometimes in life we need to make choices even if we might not feel entirely ready to make them" and "this will be one of the saddest things I'll ever go through," all of which S. knew was meant for him and which likely made everyone else who received the e-mail (S. felt) hate him. When he called V. that evening, she was crying. She explained, as he knew she would, that she simply couldn't do it. Sending the e-mail made it more "real" for her, and only then did she begin to imagine someone coming to pick up Cookie and how she, V., would feel watching the elevator doors close in front of Cookie and her new owner, or how she would feel dropping off Cookie at her new owner's house and having to drive away knowing that from that moment on Cookie would no longer be her dog, Cookie would be "just some dog someone else owned who someone else would get to love and feed and snuggle and watch grow old and be with when she died." V. was in such a state over not being able to hold Cookie when she died maybe ten or twelve years in the future that S. didn't feel he could get even the least bit angry; losing his temper would make his already remote chance of moving in with and having a life with V. even more remote. He told her he was hurt, but he understood it was her decision and she should call him when she felt she was ready to talk about the future of their relationship, which he admitted to her *he* wasn't so sure about, and told her he didn't know how much longer he could go on this way, which he said more to try to make her worry than to express something he was genuinely feeling. As soon as he hung up the phone, he knew he had missed his chance to fully express his hurt and anger. Now he would have to wait for another appropriate moment when he could make the case (in the moment, that is) that he was hurt and angry. He wasn't the type of person to call V. out of the blue and start screaming at her;

he needed immediate provocation in order to feel justified in his emotions.

But when V. did not fall for S.'s "I'm not sure about our future" and "You know, after a while, my feelings are just going to shut off and it will be too late," when she returned his calls with less frequency and cried less and less about the situation (the "situation" now being the possible loss of S. rather than the possible loss of Cookie), when she didn't get emotional when S. claimed he was "on the verge of making a final decision" about their future, S. had no choice but to resort to getting angry without immediate justification. He began calling V. during the night, or early morning, when he couldn't sleep, and yelling at her for making it such that he couldn't sleep. Any problems he was having—he hated his job, he was depressed, he'd lost weight, he'd gotten a terrible haircut—he fairly convincingly (in his mind) explained to V. how they were *her* fault. But by this time—by the time S. was finally able to express his hurt and anger—V. had successfully turned off her emotions in relation to S. Her tone of voice was clinical; she would say things like "I'm very sorry you feel the way you do" and "I hope you understand that it was not my intention that you feel hurt" and "I really hope you're able to work through the feelings you're having" and would often begin her sentences with "What I hear you saying is" and would proceed to summarize what S. had just said though in such a robotic, sterile way it made what S. had just said sound more like the foolish whining of a too-sensitive baby than the justifiably angry emotions of a man who had been (as S. felt he'd been) mistreated. In short, it was much too late—they had already begun a fatal trajectory leading to the events of this story.

We like to begin our story, as you can see, with the events closest to where we are now—with, as some might call them, the darkest, most sordid details of the incident. Only then do we continue our story with the years leading up to the dog's death—the quiet nights S. and V. were happy merely lying in bed together, the dog content on the floor outside V.'s closed bedroom door. Or the first time V. went away for a weekend and asked S. if he could take care of Cookie, and S. slept in V.'s bed without her and even let the dog sleep on the floor beside the bed, and didn't mind when he woke to the dog licking his hand to be let out to pee, and didn't mind the next morning when he woke to the dog in bed with him, and was perfectly happy to wash V.'s sheets and pillowcases, and for the first time the tightness in his lungs felt something other than restricting—pain suffered gladly, a sort of play version of what dying for someone might feel like. Or we tell about the time S. surprised V. by petting the dog and letting the dog lick his hand just before he got into the shower, if only to show V. that if it were not for his allergies and asthma, he would love the dog as she did. Or the times S. and V. brought the dog to the dog park and S., even wearing new shoes, went into the muddy part of the park and didn't get upset when Cookie jumped up and left paw prints on his pants. We like to tell of the nights S. woke to tell V. he dreamed she'd hurt him—he walked past her, she did not know him, or pretended not to know him—or the nights V. woke to tell S. she dreamed he hated her—there was a knock on her bedroom door, she was afraid to answer, she knew it was S., she was terrified, and when she opened the door he was standing there with a knife. These nights, V. would tell S., or S. would tell V., that the other was loved and would be loved forever and no one would be hurt—what they had was untouchable, unbreakable. These smaller, perhaps less dramatic but no less important, parts of the story, we like to tell last. Some people prefer we begin in the beginning; they like us to end with the memorial for Cookie, which they say makes them feel sad, yes, but also something else, a feeling they struggle to name but eventually describe as the feeling of not being alone in their grief, if we may call what these listeners feel "grief." Others prefer the way we have chosen here to tell the story—what happened last first, what happened first last. We may choose to include even those moments that seem far removed from the last day of Cookie's, S.'s, and V.'s lives—Cookie's birth among a litter of pups that looked just like Cookie, or the day V. went to the pet store and brought Cookie home, or even the day almost thirty years earlier when S. saw a dog for the first time but did not know the word for dog and so pointed and opened his mouth. Yes, we prefer to end with a period of time during which none of what happened seemed even remotely possible, not even in S.'s and V.'s most irrational nightmares or darkest what-if daydreams, which at some point or other we all find ourselves having, if only to test how or if we'd survive the worst things that can happen, or perhaps to feel relieved upon "waking" to the realization that, though these terrible things can happen—yes, theoretically, they *can*—they will, we know, happen to someone else: The world is a safe place; we are loved; we close our eyes at night knowing come morning we will open them and the skin of our dearest, touching us, will be warm.

story

I am writing about what happened this afternoon in the park because I want my son, just three years old, to remember what he saw and maybe a few things he did not see.

Years from now, he might say to me: "You know, I have this memory of something happening in the park when you brought me there when I was a boy. Something about another boy a few years older than I was. I remember the police, and people watching, and I think you were involved. I think I remember you were very upset about what was happening."

Or, more likely, he will forget what happened this afternoon entirely. More likely, his brain will file what happened in, as I call it, his "lost memories" file.

And that is why, when my son is a young man, I will ask him: "Do you remember that time in the park when you were three years old?"

"What time?"

"The time with the other boy."

"I don't think I remember."

"Would you like to remember?"

If my son becomes the type of young man—and I hope he does—to say yes, he would like to remember, I might say:

"I brought you to a park in Queens—the park closest to our apartment. This was when your mother was working and I was not. One of our favorite things to do—me because during the day I was lonely, you because you liked birds—was go to this park. It had rained that morning. I remember having to remove wet leaves from the steps of the sliding pond, and having to stand behind you, braced, as you climbed the steps and as you stood at the top of the slide, and having to make a great effort to shake the thought that it was possible, perhaps likely, that you might fall—which was a thought, from the moment you were born, I could not help having.

"The one thing you did not like about going to the park was the people. If a person, adult or child, walked too close to where you were playing, you would scurry back to me. I liked to sit on a bench and smoke, and watch what you were doing and what the other people in the park were doing. I liked going to the park because there were people there, and if I did not go to the park I might see no human beings—other than you, of course, and your mother when she came home—the entire day, and when this happened—and too often it happened—I would become very much aware of the passing of time, and the sun setting would become—and I feel silly saying this—would become, I guess, a very dramatic, a very difficult, moment for me, and during the night, when I could not sleep, when I felt I could do nothing but press my face against the window screen and watch for people walking on the street below, and when I did not see any people, or when I saw people who for some reason or other triggered in me even more loneliness, even more of this sense of time passing, I might smoke more than a few cigarettes and press my lips against the screen and breathe through the screen and see how long I could follow the smoke before the last traces of it would disappear, and I remember thinking that I would always, until the day I die, remember these silly moments I spent breathing smoke through the window screen, and I used to promise myself that the next day, no matter what, I would take you to the park, or somewhere outside, where we could be around other people.

"I'm sorry for being so roundabout about this. All this is to say that my reason for wanting to go to the park was very different from yours. I liked to watch people, or at least to know they were out there

—living and breathing, as I was, maybe a bit lonely, as I was. You liked, mostly, to watch birds. In fact, on the day I'm talking about, you were trying to talk with the pigeons walking around the fountain people threw pennies in for good luck. You reached your hands out to the pigeons and tried to make the sound they were making, and you would get very close to them before they flew away.

"There were children swinging on swings: One girl, older than you, stood on the seat of a swing and would not listen when the woman I assume was her mother asked her to please get down before she fell and broke her neck, and I remember watching this girl for some time, and the way my stomach would turn when her body was horizontal and it looked as if her sneakers might very easily slide off the wet seat or she might swing all the way over. There was a boy beating a tree with a plastic bat; there were children hanging from their knees from the monkey bars; there was a man playing handball; there was a young woman who had spread a blanket and laid out sandwiches and fruit and bags of chips, and then she took a thermos out of her bag and removed the lid and I saw steam rise from the opening of the thermos and that was how I remembered it was fall and soon it would be cold.

"It was easy to get distracted watching what everyone else was doing, and it felt right to be there, out in the world, with all these humans who were going about their lives, and I remember being able to take a clean deep breath, which was something I was not always able to do.

"But then—and this is what I want to get to—a boy walked into the park. I was watching everyone watch this boy. It was as if I could see—though I know I could not really have seen this—every adult in the park move the slightest bit closer to every child. This was a young black boy—no more than six or seven years old—and these people, I would guess, were shocked to see him, since there had never been—or at least I had never seen—a black person in this park, or even on any of the streets in the surrounding neighborhood. There was quiet. Maybe not quiet, but rather the sense of quiet. The boy was not wearing a shirt. He was wearing white jeans rolled up at the bottom. There were no laces in his sneakers. He walked through the park and did not look at anyone, nor did he look away from anyone. He leaned against the small building that used to be the park's rest room. The doors and windows had been boarded up. He stood there with his face pressed against the brick of the building. He was doing something with his hands, I could not see what. And then I saw a puddle forming on the ground near his sneakers and knew that he was urinating, and I saw that you had stopped chasing the pigeons and were watching this boy, and I remember wondering what you were thinking.

"The woman who had laid out sandwiches and fruit and chips moved away from her blanket to retrieve her two children from where they were digging in the dirt, and I saw the boy walk past this woman's blanket, and I saw him reach into the bag she had left on the blanket and take out what looked like a wallet and continue walking through the park.

"I could no longer take a deep breath. I didn't know if I was supposed to stop the boy, or say something to the woman, or if I was to do nothing, say nothing—if I was just to watch you chasing pigeons and be happy that I was out there in the world with people, regardless of what they were doing.

"The boy did not leave the park, as I imagined he might. He stood in the playground area, where I could see him clearly, and then he opened the wallet and began looking through it. I did not see him take out any money. Everything he took out—cards, photographs, tiny pieces of paper—he put back in. He sat on the ground near the monkey bars with the wallet on his lap.

"I decided I should say something to the woman who owned the wallet, but I did not want the boy to get in any trouble. At some point I had decided that what the boy had done was harmless and that it was likely that he wasn't even aware of what he was doing—that he had had no intention of stealing someone's money or valuables, but rather that he was simply looking for someone to notice that he was there in the park that day and that, in general, he was alive and capable of acting on the world in a way that might make the world react, and I wanted the woman whose wallet the boy had taken to understand what I had decided about the boy, and to agree with me, and to come with me to ask the boy kindly to give the wallet back, and to ask his name and where he lived, and if he had any family, and how he had ended up in this neighborhood, and if there was anyone we could call to pick him up, and I stood from where I had been sitting and began walking to where the woman, unaware that her wallet had been taken, was unwrapping sandwiches for her children, and in my mind I was practicing what I wanted to say and how I wanted to say it so that this woman would not panic and would understand what I thought—just from observing the boy for no more than five minutes—I had come to understand.

"But before I reached this woman I saw a police officer, led by several people, approach the boy and say something to him, and then the boy tried to run away, and the officer grabbed his arm and held him, and the boy started yelling that the officer should leave him alone, he didn't do anything wrong, he had found the wallet on the ground, he didn't steal anything, and the boy was struggling so much that the officer had to put handcuffs around the boy's wrists, and by this time everyone in the park was watching, including you, and I wondered what you were thinking and what the effect of your watching all this might be.

"When I saw that the boy was crying, I walked over to where he was and asked what had happened. One of the men standing there said he had seen the boy take the wallet from someone's bag and had found the police officer and that now the boy was saying he had found the wallet on the ground and had been looking through it to see if he could find the name of the person who owned it. I told this man and the officer that what the boy was saying was true, that I had watched him pick up the wallet from the ground and sit near the monkey bars and look through the wallet and not touch any of the money inside and never make a move to leave the park, but the man said that he was certain, there was no doubt in his mind, he had witnessed the boy reach into the bag and take out the wallet and walk away, and another man standing there said yes, he had witnessed the same, and then two other people said they had witnessed the same, and I asked, then, if there was any way we could just return the wallet to its owner and find out where the boy lived and bring him home and give him a warning, and someone said no, that would send the wrong message, the boy should not have been in this park in the first place, what was he doing there, and if we let him go then the next time he'll tell his friends and next week there might be five or ten of them running around the park stealing wallets and doing who knows what else, and I said—"

I said nothing.

It was morning, not afternoon, and it was winter, not fall, and it was six months ago, not today, and I was the one, not my son, trying to talk with the pigeons.

I do not have a son. I was alone in the park. There was no police officer, were no people standing around.

I can go no further with this story. I do not know what happens next. I wrote the beginning six months ago, and I have been waiting to find out what happens next, and I have discovered that nothing happens next—or rather nothing will happen that involves my fictional son in the park on some fictional fall afternoon with some fictional people eating fictional sandwiches and a fictional police officer putting fictional handcuffs around a boy's wrists.

This is only a means of getting to something underneath—to that which, sadly, I might not want to write, and you might not want to read, without the use of characters, an implied narrator, an A-leads-to-B-leads-to-C setup.

Sometimes this is what happens: A writer reaches the end of the story, and what he has set down is simply not enough. The story has failed. The writer gives up.

The characters must be killed off; the implied narrator must be killed off.

The story becomes an essay.

The writer blurts out what he has always been afraid to blurt out:

1977. I was playing the piano in the house I grew up in in Queens when I heard a noise that sounded like someone scratching at the front door. I looked up and saw through the stained glass what I thought was the shadow of a man. I called my father, who came from wherever he was and looked through the window. He told me to stand away from the door. With his fist he banged the door—in an attempt to frighten away the man, I assume. When he saw that the man was not frightened, my father kicked the door, then yelled something like, "Hey you, get out of here before I call the police." Still the man did not leave. My father opened the door and discovered that the man was trying to eat the plastic corn my mother had hung in celebration of Thanksgiving, which was only a few days away. My father said, "Get the fuck out of our neighborhood. Go back where you came from, back where your own kind live." When the man did not leave or say anything in response, my father closed the door and called the police. I heard him say the phrase "some black man" into the phone. The police came. The neighbors gathered to watch. The police told the man he had to go with them, but he did not want to leave our stoop. He did not want to let go of the plastic corn. The police spoke to the man some more; they tried to reason with him; they told him everything would be all right and no one would get hurt if he would just put down the plastic corn and leave with them. The man did not seem to hear what they were saying. My sister and I stood inside the house, where we felt we would be safe, but from where we could see what was happening, and laughed. Finally the police officers wrestled the plastic corn from the man's hands, put handcuffs around his wrists, and led him away. The neighbors watched, some smiling, some with their hands on their hips. The next day in school, my sister and I told our friends—as many as would listen—and together we all laughed.

1992. To help pay for college tuition, I worked summers as a security guard at a retail store on Fifth Avenue. One day the security manager asked why, after working at this store for three summers, I had not caught a single person stealing. He told me that, since this would likely be my last summer working there, he wanted me to walk away from the job able to say I had made at least one collar (his word). Several days later I heard the manager's voice in the plug in my ear.

He had spotted a 90 (the code number we used for a black man) who was a possible 39 (the code number we used for a shoplifter). He was watching from the floor above. He told me that this man was trying on lizard belts and that he had seen this scam a million times—he was certain this man was going to take two belts from the rack, put them both around his waist, and return only one belt to the rack. The manager told me this was my chance to get my first collar. He said, "If you see him put back two belts, leave him alone, but if you see him put back only one belt, wait until he puts his hand on the revolving door and then grab him." He said, "I'll be right here. As soon as you grab him, I'll come down and give you backup." He said, "Don't let him scare you. If he screams and yells and tells you he didn't do anything, don't let him go. And watch that he doesn't try to kick you in the balls. I've seen this guy's type. These 90s—they like to make a lot of noise, and then they try to kick you in the balls." The man was standing very close to the belt rack. He looked behind him and then to either side and then he moved even closer to the rack. I could not see exactly what he was doing with his hands. One of the sales associates asked the man—in the way she asked people she knew would never buy anything—if he needed any help, and the man said no thank you but seemed nervous, and I saw him return one belt to the rack, and then in my earplug I heard the security manager say, "Did you see that? He only put back one belt. He probably has it around his waist. Now wait to see if he puts his hand on the door." When the man put his hand on the revolving doors, I grabbed his arm and told him he had to come with me. The man said he was not going to come with me, that he had done nothing wrong, that I was—that every person who worked at this store was—a racist, and that if I did not remove my hand from his arm he was going to sue me and everyone associated with the store. The man pulled open his jacket. "I don't have anything," he said. The employees and customers close enough to hear or see what was going on stopped what they were doing. "You'll have to come with me," I said, and the man said, "No—that's just it. I don't have to go anywhere with anybody." He pulled his arm away and tried to leave, and I stood between him and the door, and he shook his head and said I was making the biggest mistake I would ever make, and then the security manager was there, and he grabbed the man's arm, and within a matter of seconds three other security officers were there, and soon we were all leading the man off the sales floor and into the lobby of the building and onto the elevator and up eight floors to the loss prevention office, where I was told to handcuff the man to the security manager's desk. I was then told to find the belt the man had been trying to steal. I looked under the man's jacket, then under his shirt, and then I pulled down his pants and looked there. When I could not find the belt, each of the other security guards looked, and when no one could find the belt this man had been trying to steal, the security manager looked—under the man's jacket, under his shirt, inside the legs of his pants. There was no belt. "I told you," the man said. "I didn't try to steal anything." "I know you," the security manager said. "I've seen you in here before." Then the security manager took me aside, where the man could not hear us. "Listen to me," he said. "I want you to go down and look on the floor near the belt rack. I'm sure that's where he ditched the belt." "What if I can't find a belt on the floor?" I said. "You'll find one on the floor," he said. "Okay," I said, "but what if I don't happen to find it on the floor?" "Listen to me," he said. "You're going to go back to the store and you're going to find a lizard belt on the floor near the belt rack—the exact one you and I saw this 90 try to steal—and you're going to bring it up here. Do you understand what I'm saying?" "I think so." "Good," he said. "Hurry up," he said when I had not moved. "You have to get here before the police." I went down and saw nothing on the floor near the belt rack. I stood where the man had been and faced the belts. When no one was looking, I took a black lizard belt from the rack and walked out of the store and into the lobby and took the elevator to the loss prevention office. "I knew you would find it," the security manager said to me. "Where did you find it?" he said so that everyone in the room could hear him. "Did you find it near the door? Is that where he ditched it?" "Yes," I said. "I found it near the door." "I'm going to sue all of you," the man said, and then I was told to take his picture and a picture of the belt, and when they had developed I was told to put them into the box that contained pictures of all the people the security officers who had ever worked at this store had caught stealing. The security manager showed the man the box and said, "Every one of these people left here screaming that they didn't do it, that they were going to call their lawyer, and every one of them was successfully prosecuted." The man turned to one of the other security officers, who was black, and said, "I can't believe *you* can stand there and watch this." A few minutes later the police came. I was told to remove the handcuffs from the man's wrists. The man stood up. The police put their handcuffs around his wrists. Before the man left, he looked at me and would not turn away, and then he laughed, and as the police were leading him out, and even after they were gone and the other officers were congratulating me on my first collar, I could still hear him laughing.

2000. I was sitting in the park. It was morning, not afternoon, and it was winter, not fall. I was trying to talk with the pigeons, who were pecking the ice inside a fountain, and I remember looking into the fountain and ashing my cigarette onto the ice and thinking, for some reason, that I would always remember ashing my cigarette onto this ice on this day in this park, and I saw all the pennies people had thrown into the ice, when it had been water, for good luck. I could have been the only person in the world, for all I knew, until a black boy no more than six or seven years old walked into the park. He was wearing something torn on his back—something I would not call a shirt. He did not seem to notice me. He walked into the playground area, stood near the seesaw, pulled down his pants, and urinated onto the ground. I watched him pull up his pants and walk around the park. He played with something on the ground, picked it up, smelled it, dropped it. He sat against the fence; he rubbed his hands together. Seeing the boy rub his hands together and then blow on his hands helped me remember that my fingers were cold and some of my toes were numb. My nose was running, and I did not have a tissue. I remember, in my head, cursing the fact that I did not have a tissue. I stood up so that the boy might see me. I cleared my throat so that the boy might hear me. He did not look up. I did not ask him his name, or if he lived somewhere, or if he was alone in the world, or how he found himself in this park on this day at this time.

I walked home.

It felt good to be inside and to take my boots off and to rub the feeling back into my toes. I turned up the heat, and then I drank a cup of hot tea.

But then I remembered the man who tried to eat the plastic corn my mother had hung from our front door, and how when the police tried to lead him away he sat on the stoop and spoke to the plastic corn, and how my sister and I laughed at him, and how the next day at school we told the story in such a way that our friends laughed at him, and in the warmth of my home, more than twenty years later, I could not shake this man's face from my mind.

And a little while later I remembered how the man who had not tried to steal a belt laughed at me, and how when I got home from work and my father asked how my day was, if anything interesting happened at work, I did not answer, and how I went to my room and smoked cigarettes and pressed my lips against the screen and breathed smoke through it and followed the smoke until the last traces had disappeared, and told myself that the next day at work I would say something to someone about what had happened, I even went so far as to write down what I intended to say and practiced how I was going to say it and decided at what time of the next day I would seek out the person I wanted to speak to, but the next day everyone was talking about my first collar and how it was about time and how, since I was going to be a writer someday, my first collar might make for a good story, especially with the way the man had laughed at me, which might make for a funny part of the story, and the time I had set aside to speak to the person I had decided to speak to passed, and the rest of the day passed, and the rest of the week, and the rest of the summer, and the people I worked with threw a party for me and wished me luck in graduate school and reminded me to write a story one day about my first collar, and to never forget them, and to never forget the promise I had made to include them in one of my stories.

Eight years later, in the warmth of my home, with a cup of hot tea in front of me, I could not shake this man's laughter from my mind.

And then I thought of the boy I had seen just a few hours earlier in the park, and I knew I did not want to forget him—suddenly it became very important, maybe the most important thing, to find a way to never forget him—and so I sat down to write this story.

if the sky falls, hold up your hands

If you've never witnessed a human life expire, perhaps you won't believe me when I tell you that the experience, at least in my daughter's case, seems to be quite peaceful. Dramatic, yes, but quietly so. Breathing not like the breathing the living know. Fingers clinging to the top of a bedsheet pulled up high as if to cover what the body's negotiating beneath. The sensation that with every breath the room is expanding and with the final breath expanding more. To the dying, if you are the only person with them, you are everything—the entire world. You are the last thing they let go before letting go. You hear their last words, the final sounds their bodies make. You are the only witness to something that can't be explained, yet you must try to explain it.

Lois died two weeks ago, in her own bed, in the carriage house she rented on a horse farm in Chestnut Hill, a section of Philadelphia most people don't think of when they think of Philadelphia. Bakeries, used-book stores, flower and cheese shops. She worked at home, where she carved wood and stone into miniature animals and flowers, painted them, and sold them to a store in town. She didn't consider this work, and I would have to agree with her. She made enough money to pay her rent and live the simple life she'd decided to live after her divorce five years ago. All this and more she had to explain to me because we hadn't spoken in fifteen years.

I don't blame you for wondering how a man doesn't speak with his daughter in fifteen years. I'd like to enter into this record the following story from my childhood, not as an excuse but, rather, as one more part of my attempt to understand. My mother's mother, a kind but feisty Irishwoman, didn't speak to her brother for the last fifty years of her life, yet they lived only two blocks from each other in South Philadelphia. When I was a boy, I used to deliver his paper. I came home one day and told my mother that a man on my route looked just like my grandmother, and my mother said, "That's because he's your grandmother's brother." My mother told me not to mention this to my grandmother because she and her brother hadn't spoken for many years. When I asked my mother why, she said, "It's difficult to explain. Sometimes these things happen. People just stop speaking to each other."

When I delivered my grandmother's brother's paper, I would stare at him as if his face would reveal some long-kept adult secret my mother was afraid to let me in on. But he was just an old man who looked like my grandmother. A bit grumpy, a lousy tipper. One day, after I'd been delivering his paper for more than a year, I asked him. I hadn't planned to say anything; it just came out of my mouth, as if someone else were speaking. "Why don't you talk to your sister?" He looked at me for a while, moving his hands around in his pockets, then said, "Who are you?" "I'm your sister's grandson." "Which sister? I have three." "Mary," I said. He counted out my money in nickels, plus three pennies for a tip, always three pennies, then said, "Say hello to Mary."

I ran through the rest of my route that day, tossing papers onto people's lawns, against their doors—it didn't matter, I had to get home. No, not home—I went straight to my grandmother's house and, out of breath, said to her, "Your brother you don't talk to says hello." She brushed imaginary crumbs off her housedress then went into the kitchen to stir stew. I followed her. "Did you hear what I said? Your brother says hello. I deliver the paper to him—that's how I know." Without turning from the stove she said, "That's nice, thank you."

That night, when I told my mother what I'd done, I expected her to bring me door to door telling the neighbors what a great son I was, reuniting brother and sister after so many years, salvaging a relationship that didn't seem salvageable, all because I was brave enough to ask a question I probably wasn't supposed to ask. But my mother told me it wasn't a good idea to "drag all that up" and that I should have minded my own business. Neither my grandmother nor her brother ever mentioned it again—there was no tearful reunion, no making up for lost time. My mother explained to me a few days later, when I wanted to try again, that my grandmother and her brother were never going to speak, that's just the way it was, and that sometimes people who have no intention to speak will say things like "Say hello." The last thing my mother said about the subject was, "It doesn't mean they're bad people. Some people are better off not speaking. You're just a boy—you can't understand that yet."

One thing I do understand, better late than never, is that you can't really know anything before it happens. Doesn't matter what it is. Years ago, had someone asked if I'd ever get divorced, I would have said never. Had someone asked if I'd ever get fat. Never. Would I ever lose my hair? Never. Would I ever drink so much I'd have to quit drinking? Never. Would I ever smoke so much I'd have to quit smoking? Never. Would I ever become a man who doesn't speak to his daughter, his only child, for fifteen years? No way. Never. Yet I've become a man who's done these and many other things I was sure I'd never do. Now I won't make any more promises without the understanding that my promises are subject to change. Even if I make them in good faith.

I will get to my daughter's death—what we said to each other after fifteen years of saying nothing, what it was like to watch her body expire—but right now I'd like to tell you about why we stopped speaking. It's what's on my mind, it's the part of this that's weighing on me at the moment, so I'll tell that part now, without further delay, as objectively as my memory and conscience will allow. The last day we spoke there was a lot of screaming. In fact, during the years leading up to the last day we spoke, there was a lot of screaming. Will you ever become a man who screams all the time—at his wife, at his kid, at other drivers, at people in the bank? Never, never, never. Yet I did. At first it was just me screaming, but then I dragged my wife into it. When she refused to fight back, I got my daughter to fight. It got worse as Lois got older. Fifteen, sixteen, seventeen—those were difficult years. I can admit now that I screamed to feel better, and therefore it was selfish. Screaming released the pressure inside my head, but this release was incomplete until someone screamed back. Only then would I stop. My wife was a fair screamer, but my daughter was better, in volume and duration. I would get my daughter so worked up that she would cry and shake and call me monster, pig, asshole—to hear her swear at me was also a kind of release—and here I would become so calm and collected that it was hard to believe I'd just been screaming. I would say to her, "What's wrong with you? Look at yourself—you're crazy. You need help." And at these moments—my daughter coming at me half-blind with tears and anger, waving or having already thrown a shoe or glass—at these moments, even she could not deny that what I was saying was true—she *was* crazy, she *did* need help. My sudden calm was the gasoline for the fire she'd become.

It's difficult to remember the specifics of what we fought about—even the last day we fought—but I know that my anger, whatever the specifics, was about the two jobs I had to work to pay for the house and the vacations and the private school Lois went to, all of which my wife did not agree were beyond our means. This was my true anger no matter if I was screaming about a pile of unwashed dishes or a bra slung over the shower door or Lois feeding cookies and ice cream to the dog she begged me to get her even though I thought a dog was a terrible idea and knew I would end up taking the dog out and giving her a bath and taking her to the vet and working overtime to pay for the cast on her broken leg and even holding her when we had to put her down, for which neither my wife nor my daughter ever thanked me.

As you can see, I still have a lot of anger. Probably always will. One promise I made to my daughter when she died—not to her, but inside my head—was to work on my anger. But what do you do with anger once it's inside you—I mean, once it's inside your cells? You have to release it somehow. For me it used to be smoking and drinking and screaming. Since Lois died, I've been trying a batting cage every other day. Sixty years old, and I'm wearing one of those double-earflapped Little League helmets. I swing and swing until I hit one hundred solid—foul tips and weak ground balls don't count. Kills my arms and my back, tears up my hands, but it helps—I haven't screamed in two weeks, though I've wanted to.

The point is: I don't remember what we were fighting about the last day we fought. I remember that whatever I said to Lois triggered what I would call a brief nervous breakdown. It wasn't a true breakdown, when you're out of sorts for months or years; hers lasted only a few days. But it had all the signs of a true breakdown—her eye started twitching, she was pulling out her hair in clumps, kicking the wall, yelling nonsense, half-sentences she'd lose her breath before finishing. It was frightening, yet I did nothing to stop it. In fact, I made it worse when I said to my wife, "Look at your daughter. Take a good look at her. I've worked my ass into the ground all these years, and this is what we have to show for it." Then I said to Lois, "I feel sorry for you. You're a sick young woman. You really need help." That was when she fell to the floor, curled into a fetal position, and hyperventilated. She said she couldn't breathe and her arms were tingling and she had a pain in her chest and was sure she was dying. I told her she was being a drama queen—that got her every time—and she told me I was killing her. My wife held a paper bag over Lois's face, but that didn't help. "Stop being such a baby," I said to Lois. "You're not dying." My wife took the car keys and helped Lois outside. I kicked a hole in my closet door, then kicked the door off its hinges. I ran outside and tried to get into the car, but the doors were locked. My wife started to pull away. I banged on the hood and yelled at the car. A few of the neighbors parted their drapes to look. I stood in front of the car and told my wife that she was going to have to run me over if she wanted to take Lois to the hospital. She unlocked the door, but I said, "I'm driving. Get in the back." During the ride my wife kept telling Lois, "You're going to be okay," Lois kept saying, " He's killing me. I can't do this anymore." All I could say was, "This is it—this is the last fucking straw."

In the emergency room they attached wires to Lois's chest. They gave her a paper bag to breathe into, but she threw it on the floor. Her heart was beating wildly—almost two hundred beats per minute. They pulled down her pants and gave her a shot in her hip. Seeing her struggle to keep her eyes open, but then give up, reminded me of watching the dog be put to sleep, and I found myself watching Lois's chest to make sure she was still breathing. A psychiatrist came to speak with us. My wife said, "Our daughter's been under a lot of stress lately. She's applying to colleges this year." He asked if Lois had been using any drugs like cocaine or speed or LSD, and we said no, not that we knew of. We took Lois home and laid her on the couch, where we could watch her, and for the next day she kept going in and out of sleep.

Two days later my wife asked for a divorce. I did what I did best—I acted angry and hurt, and was. I went around the house slamming doors. I broke a picture frame, two lamps, the toilet seat. With a bottle of my wife's perfume I cracked the bathroom mirror. I picked up the living room rug and turned it upside down. I packed my clothes and left. (That was the last time I saw my wife without a lawyer present—except at Lois's funeral, where we were properly cordial and compassionate with each other.) After I was gone, I expected my wife to call and say she'd changed her mind; I expected Lois to show up at my hotel to say she was sorry, that she was the reason her mother had asked me for a divorce, and that she would do whatever she could to patch things up. But no one called; no one showed up at my door. After the divorce was final I gave up on my wife, but I always expected Lois to show up.

The next time I saw her was about a year after the divorce, during her first year at Penn State. It was early evening, and I was standing by the window having a drink, staring out at nothing in particular, when I noticed a car stop in front of my building. The driver, a young woman who looked vaguely familiar, was staring at me. The car's windows were down, and I could hear music. There was another young woman in the front passenger seat and someone in the back. Then I heard a voice that sounded like Lois's saying, "Turn down the music." She looked up at me from the backseat—she was thinner, her hair longer and streaked blond—but I quickly looked away, checked my watch, sipped my drink. My heart wasn't beating faster than normal, but I could feel every beat—everything was that still and quiet. Then I heard Lois saying to her friend, "Go! Just go! Forget it!"

You would think a father would be sad after such an incident, but I was elated—borderline triumphant. There was no doubt in my mind that Lois had found out where I lived and come looking for me—not to knock on my door, not to speak with me, but just to see me, to see that I was alive. Over the next few years I caught her driving by three more times—twice alone, once with a boy who threw a beer can out the car window and said, "We should do it right here." But even that wouldn't have gotten me to go out there; there was simply no way I was going to be the one to break the silence. I would have called the police, yes, but I would not have gone out. That she cared enough to drive by made me confident that she would make the first gesture—a phone call, a letter, a birthday card—and therefore I would always have the upper hand. But after she finished college—I was sure she would call me before her graduation to ask me to attend, but she didn't—I never saw her drive by again. After the last time, with the boy, I watched from my window every night for a month. I can admit now—I should have told her this before she died—that I actually considered installing a surveillance camera in case she drove past when I was at work. I wanted to know that she was okay—that was part of it—but I wasn't in touch with anyone in her life. Even if I had been, I'm not sure I would have allowed myself to ask about her. This was ten years ago, before I even knew or cared about the Internet. Once I bought a computer and had access to the Web, I was able to find information about her—her address in Philadelphia, her phone number, the names of her roommates, where she worked, where and when she had art shows, et cetera. A few times I considered showing up at one of her shows, but that would have meant losing the game I wanted so desperately to win.

One night from these years stands out. I kept waking from but eventually falling back into a dream in which a group of fanged children were chasing me with small pitchforks. The last time I woke from this dream I felt a sharp pain in the center of my chest. I've never feared death—not consciously—but upon feeling this pain I ran to the door, opened it, and leaned against the frame, trying to breathe. I opened the door because if I dropped dead someone would see my body in a few hours when they were heading to work. If I died inside my apartment, alone, my boss wouldn't have known whom to call—I always leave the "Notify in Case of Emergency" line blank on any forms—and by the time I missed however many days of work you need to miss before your employer calls the police, my body would smell, and I didn't want that—there was something terribly and finally sad about not just dying alone but about my body decomposing on the floor while the world outside went about its business. I left the door open—the pain hadn't gotten worse, but it hadn't gotten better either—and came inside. I dialed my daughter's number—at least I hoped it was still her number—but quickly hung up. I told myself that if the pain in my chest became even the slightest bit worse, or if it spread to my arm or back or neck, I would press redial. I stood there holding the phone for close to an hour, then I sat with the phone, then I lay down with it and closed my eyes. When I woke, the sun up, the phone still in my hand, I felt—after I felt lucky—embarrassed. Not so much of my panic as of having almost called Lois. I had trouble sleeping the next few nights—I was afraid to close my eyes—and to solve this problem I went out and found a girlfriend—my first since the divorce. I'm not talking about a woman to have a drink with or have sex with—I'd had a few of those since my marriage ended. I'm talking about a steady girlfriend—someone who sleeps over most nights and can call an ambulance if you need one.

Over the years I received three phone calls from or concerning my daughter. The first was ten years after we'd last spoken, when Lois was twenty-seven. Her mother called me—the first time I'd heard her voice since the divorce. My first thought was that someone had died. I barely had time to consider who when my ex said, "I'm calling about Lois." "What's wrong?" I said, trying not to sound too anxious. She explained that she wouldn't be calling if it weren't important. Lois was getting married in a few weeks, she told me. I was certain she was going to ask me to walk Lois down the aisle or at least to show up at the ceremony, but instead she said, "I don't know if she's doing the right thing. There's something about this man—he has a terrible temper and he doesn't have a job and he doesn't let her go out with her friends and he's making her move to Florida. I can't get through to her—no one can—and I just thought that, since you're her father, you might give her a call and speak with her."

I asked her if "my daughter's stepfather" hadn't been able to get through to her.

"If you're going to drag that into this," she said.

"I'm not dragging anything into anything," I said. "If she wants my advice about who she should or shouldn't marry, she's more than capable of finding my number in the phone book or getting it from you."

"But she won't call. You know she won't."

"That's not *my* problem," I said. "She can call if she chooses—no one's stopping her."

"That's just it," she said. "This guy is the type to stop her. We're all worried about her."

"It's her choice whether or not she calls."

"This is your daughter," she said. "This is one time you have to stop playing this game. It's been ten years. You don't know who she is. She has problems you have no idea about."

"And whose fault is that?" I said.

"Not yours," she said. "Nothing is ever your fault."

"None of this would be happening if you hadn't chosen to end—"

"Oh God—forget it!"

"If you hadn't chosen to—"

"Forget I called. Forget you have a daughter."

"Don't hang up! Let me finish what I want to say!"
"Good-bye."
"I swear to God, if you hang up!"
"Good-bye."

The second call was from my daughter. We spoke, literally, but we didn't really speak. About a year after she got married and moved to Florida, she called pretending to be a telemarketer. I knew who it was right away, even though her voice shook. At the time I told myself her voice was shaking because she was nervous about calling me. When I spoke with her a few weeks ago, before she died, I found out that I wasn't the one making her nervous; it was her husband. My ex-wife had been right about him—he didn't work, he maxed out Lois's credit cards, he didn't allow her to leave the house without him, unless she was going to work, and he was arrested once, just before she left him, for trying to strangle her.

"Hello, may I speak with Mr. Paul Gruber?"

"Speaking."

"Good evening, Mr. Gruber. I'm sorry to bother you."

"Then why are you bothering me?"

"Well, I hope I'm not bothering you, but this is a very important election tomorrow."

"Who are you calling for?"

"Mr. Paul Gruber."

"No—who are you working for? Who are you trying to get me to vote for?"

"I'm not calling to get you to vote for either candidate, just to vote."

"But who do you work for—the Democrats or the Republicans?"

"It's my job to call registered Democrats to encourage them to vote, but I'm not asking you to vote for either—"

"What's your name?"

"I'm not supposed to give out my name."

"I'd like to speak to your supervisor."

"My supervisor isn't here."

"I'd like to know your supervisor's name."

"This is just a friendly call encouraging you to vote tomorrow."

"I don't vote anymore."

"Is there anyone else in your household who's eligible to vote?"

"I'm the whole household."

"Do you have any children over the age of eighteen no longer living at home who you might encourage to vote?"

"No children."

"Thank you, sir. I'm sorry to have disturbed you."

The third call came from Lois on my sixtieth birthday. This was the call I had been waiting for—she was going to tell me she was sorry, enough was enough, this had gone on too long, life was short, it was now or never, time to bite the bullet, bury the hatchet, all those clichés, I was ready to hear all of them—I was her father, for God's sake, and I was sixty years old, and it wasn't right for a daughter not to speak with her father—she was going to invite me out to lunch, for a drink, for coffee, to her house for dinner, whatever I wanted.

Instead, she said, "Father, I'm dying."

I thought she meant "dying" figuratively, as in: I'm not feeling well, I'm going through a very difficult time, I feel *like* I'm dying.

When I asked her what was wrong she said, "Nothing's wrong. I'm dying."

"Is this supposed to be funny?"

She said, "I'm very sick. I won't be able to call you after this. I have people taking care of me, but I want it to be you."

I always thought it would have been me calling her from my deathbed. Or, knowing me, I would have had someone else call. I would have hinted around enough—at least I hope I would have—and a neighbor or my doctor or my girlfriend would have called my daughter and said, "Your father doesn't know I'm calling you—he'd be angry if he knew—but he doesn't have long, and I think it would be nice if you came to see him one last time." That way I would have been able to save face up to the very end. The one who gets the call has to suck it up and comfort the dying. Has to weep, has to say, "I'm sorry" or "I'll miss you" or, even worse, "I've missed you. It shouldn't have taken this." I was sure it would have been her, not me, saying those things. Not that I ever said them. Though I think she knew. She had to have known—I showed up, I took care of her as best I could, I was with her when she passed.

One small thing I regret, in addition to all the larger things, is that I asked for her address. I actually said to her, "I have no idea where you live," though I knew exactly where she lived and how to get there. I went right away—as soon as I hung up the phone. I knew she wasn't lying—I could hear the truth in her voice—yet on the drive to Chestnut Hill I prayed this was a joke she was playing on me. I would show up and she would have a nice laugh at my expense. She would say, "Is this what it takes for you to give a damn about your daughter? You *knew* that was me who called four years ago! I just wanted you to ask how I was doing. I wanted to tell you what a mess I was in in Florida. And that was *before* he tried to hurt me—you could have helped me!" When I imagined this possibility—that the joke would be on me—I figured out ways I could turn it on her. "What kind of a cruel person are you that you would tell your father you're dying? I told you this the last time I spoke with you, but let me say it again—you're sick!" Even as I was driving to see her, I was still trying to win, trying to maintain the upper hand.

But when I got there I saw that this was not a joke. She was bald, and her face was swollen; she was so thin she had no breasts. She was using a cane. The only thing I could say was, "My God, what happened to you? Your face isn't your face."

"It's not the face you know," she said. "Every atom in my body is different from the last time you saw me."

"You're not dying," I said. "We'll get you the best doctors."

"I've had enough opinions," she said. "I'm dying. I've already accepted it."

"We can do something."

"There's nothing to do," she said.

"I'm taking you to a hospital. Why aren't you in a hospital?"

"I don't want to be in a hospital," she said. "I want to be here."

"You're not thinking straight. You don't know what's best for you."

"The only thing I'm asking you to do is stay with me. There are a few things I need to teach you."

I drove home to get some clothes and my razor. I considered calling my ex but couldn't bring myself to do it. I stood near the phone, wondering whom I might call, but there was no one. Even my girlfriend, who's good company at night, isn't the kind of person I could call about this. We know each other, but don't. I actually thought of calling the police, but I had no idea what I might say to them. I'm calling because my daughter is very ill and refuses to go to the hospital? Yes, maybe I could spin her refusal to seek medical attention as a kind of slow suicide. But no, that would be ridiculous—you can't force someone to see a doctor. There was nothing for me to do but go back to her and do whatever she asked.

Lois said a lot of things over the last two weeks of her life that I'm not sure what to make of. There were piles of books on her desk with titles like *Be Here Now* and *Breathe the Universe, Be the Universe* and *Wherever You Go, There You Are.* One thing I'm proud of is that I did my best to listen and not judge. Whatever she said, I tried to understand. Whatever she asked me to do, I did. She told me there was no difference between us, that the energy inside me was the same energy that was inside her. She told me that after her body was gone I shouldn't be afraid to talk to her, that the words I speak, even these, contain living energy, and that this energy will reach her because it *is* her.

She told me, "The atoms that make up our bodies will create new suns, which will heat new planets and give life to new life-forms."

I asked what she needed me to do for her.

She said, "There's nothing we're supposed to do. Everything flows back to where it came from. We were all there from the very first explosion."

"I don't understand."

"You are the sun, the stars, and the ocean," she said. "Close your eyes and listen."

"I don't hear anything."

"Listen," she said. "That's you and me and everything that ever was."

"What do you want me to do for you?"

"There is no future," she said. "Every moment grows out of the void. Every moment is the great surprise."

"But what should I *do* for you?"

"My death is a gift," she told me. "I'm sharing it with you right now, if you can bring yourself to take it."

"Please let me do something for you," I said.

"If we could speed up time," she said, "we would see that everyone is the same—fetus to baby to child to adult to old person to bones to dust."

"For Christ's sake," I said, "will you allow me to do something for you? Look at you—you need help. Please, let me *do* something!"

"Breathing happens," she said. "Then one day breathing stops. We don't ever have to make an effort."

She told me she believed in the "reincarnation of energy." She believed that when you die your "life force" goes somewhere else and hangs around with other life forces and together they decide what they want to be in the next life—something they haven't been before, some new and beautiful experience they will carry with them, not fully known, wherever they go, whatever form they take, throughout each subsequent life—an emperor, a sculptor, a mother of twelve, a boy born in an alley, a chimpanzee, a gazelle, a sea urchin, a cicada, a marigold, a single cell in a sandbur. She explained that our life forces, before they took human form, had chosen together to be father and daughter, that this was the human relationship they needed at this exact moment in time in order to grow, and that in some other life her life force might need to be the mother or uncle or best friend of my life force, and that we're all the same life force anyway, just broken into pieces when we need to be.

"We were supposed to have the exact lives we've had," she said. "Every moment, every detail, has been part of a plan. We were supposed to have every difficulty we've had. We were supposed to become strangers. I was supposed to call you exactly when I did, not a moment before. You're supposed to be here."

"I'm here," I said. "Just tell me what I can *do* for you."

* * *

She wanted me to walk with her. When I asked where, she said, "Nowhere." I lifted her out of bed, washed her face, helped her dress, then followed her outside. We were in the city of Philadelphia, but everywhere there was grass and flowers and dirt roads. "Where are we going?" I asked, and she said, "Here," and we would walk a little more—past the stables, alongside a cornfield—and I said, "Lois, please tell me where we're going," and she said, "Here," and we continued walking.

After an hour we stopped where rainwater had formed a puddle at the side of the road. Lois asked me to take some water in my cupped hands, and I did, and then she asked what I had in my hands, and I said, "Water," and she said, "No, that's *you* in your hands. You're a drop of water." I threw the water at her—not really at her but near her, maybe some of it splashed on her shoes, I don't remember—and said, "I am not a drop of water! Do you hear me? I don't know what's gotten into you or who's been filling your head with all these ideas, but I am *not* a drop of water! Now will you please let me bring you to a doctor?"

She asked me, then, to do as she was about to do, and she began walking in slow motion—so slowly that at times I wondered if she was moving at all. I asked why she was doing this, but she didn't answer. I felt bad about just having yelled at her, so I tried to do what she was doing, to lift my leg so that I could not tell I was really lifting it. It must have taken me a full ten minutes to lift my leg and another ten to bring it back down, and then the other leg, and she told me to notice how my arms were also moving, and how many different muscles I was using, and to imagine living my life, for the rest of my life, this way.

We walked like this for an hour, but we had moved only a few yards. Then, just as slowly, she led me back to the rainwater puddle. She sat next to it, and I did the same, and this took almost an hour, and she put her face close to the puddle and began reaching out her hands to cup the water, and I did the same, and this took maybe a half-hour, and when my hands were almost touching the water it was very difficult to resist plunging them in—I was suddenly very thirsty—and from the moment my hands made contact with the water to the moment I brought the water to my mouth was another half-hour, and the act of sticking out my tongue was another half-hour, and we said nothing while we were doing this, and I saw that Lois would not allow her tongue to touch the water, would not allow herself the satisfaction of quenching her thirst. She took twenty minutes parting her hands so that the water would fall back into the puddle, and when I did this, when I saw the water fall from my hands, I began to cry, if you can believe it, because I had forgotten that I had the capability of moving faster than the speed at which I was moving, I had tricked myself into believing that this was the speed at which life moved, and that it would be another several hours before I would be able to reach my hands into the water and bring the water to my mouth and stick out my tongue and quench my thirst. I sat there unsure of everything—where I was, who I was, what would happen next—but then I felt something cold and wet on the back of my neck and turned to see that it was my daughter, no longer in slow motion, pouring water on me, and I said, "Can we please go back now?" and she said, "We can never go back," and then she began walking in the direction from which we had come, and I followed, and after what seemed a long time we arrived back at her house, where I helped her change, and then helped her into bed, and then I sat on a chair and watched her sleep.

She liked to smell things—flowers, my clothes, my hands before and after I washed them. She liked to touch dirt, my hair, my face. She could stare at her own fingernail for an hour. She believed only in the present and wanted me to believe in the same. "When you are filling a glass with water," she told me, "you are only filling a glass with water, nothing more, nor have you ever done anything else, nor will you ever. In fact," she told me, "you are not even filling a glass with water, you are only holding the glass so that it can be filled—that is your only purpose in this world, now or ever—to hold that glass. No," she said, "you're not even holding the glass, you're doing nothing, your hand is simply where it is, the glass is simply where it is, the water is flowing where it is flowing, and everything has been, and always will be, this way." For a moment I looked at my hand, and saw that it was part of the glass, and the glass part of the water, and the water part of the faucet, and the faucet part of the rest of the sink, and the sink part of the house, and the house part of the earth, and the earth part of the air, and the air went up and away into space, where everything else was. My hand went numb, and I dropped the glass.

The morning she died, she told me she was ready. She said she knew death was close because there was an angel in the room—an Indian boy standing by the window. She said the boy was playing—he was jumping up and down and waving to her.

She kept going in and out, in and out.

She woke and sat up in bed, though she hadn't sat up all morning. She asked if I remembered Chicken Little. When she was a girl she had read Chicken Little and was scared. "I used to ask you what to do if the sky falls," she said. "I was so scared, I don't know how many times I asked you. You always told me not to worry, the sky would never fall. But the little Indian boy just told me that the sky is always falling, and there is no reason to be afraid, and here is what you must do."

For a long time she went in and out, her breathing labored, sometimes ten or more seconds between breaths.

She woke—I didn't think she'd wake again—and told me she'd been in the corner of the room watching us and that during the time between breaths she became larger and larger—she had no form, yet she was expanding out from the corner of the room in all directions. Eventually, she became the entire room. Then she expanded out the window and up into the air. But with every breath she became smaller until she was only the corner of the room again, and now she had breathed herself back inside her body on the bed. "Death," she told me, "is when you stop breathing and don't come back. Death is when you're in the air flying above everything, and then you become the air, and then you become everything."

She woke three more times.

The first time she looked at me and said, "Don't worry about the past. The past doesn't matter—it's all a fiction. Our entire lives we've been in first grade. We're just here to learn the basics."

The second time she looked at me and said, "Now I'm *your* father."

The last time she didn't open her eyes, but said, "Beautiful little humans."

The week before she died, she told me there was a place you could go to be born again and asked if I would take her there. I didn't ask what she was talking about or if she had been seeing things or hearing voices—didn't ask her where we were going or why or for how long or, once there, what I was expected to do. I helped her into the car and began to drive: I turned when she told me to turn; when she told me to stop, I stopped. Even as I'm writing this, I don't know if what I saw was real. I don't know if places like this really exist. Yet I saw it. I was there. I *was.* And what I saw was—there is no other way to say it—my daughter being born. They knew her there; maybe they were her friends; maybe she had done this before. They took us to a back room, and inside was a large version of a womb. I did not see inside the womb; I did not want to see. From the outside it was shaped like an egg. My daughter took off her clothes, then I helped her into the womb through an opening that closed behind her. My daughter was immersed to her neck in water and what looked like mucus and blood; I could hear the recorded beating of a human heart. I was told I could press my hand against this womb, which I did, and I felt my daughter kicking. I kept my hand on the womb, and whenever my daughter moved, I moved with her. After a long time had passed, maybe two hours, I noticed water and blood leaking from the womb, and the people who ran this place—a man and a woman—put on gloves and stood at the opening and said I could stand with them, and within a few minutes we were able to see her head, and they braced themselves and said, "Push, we're right here, we're waiting," and then I could see my daughter's face, which was covered with mucus, and they held her head and said, "Push, we're here, we love you," and then slowly my daughter, the rest of her, came out—I'm not sure where she found the strength—and the man and woman caught her and carried her to a table, where they rubbed her chest until she breathed, for she had not been breathing, and wrapped her in a blanket, and asked me if I wanted to come and look at her, and I did, and when I saw her I wasn't sure what I was supposed to say, so I said, "I don't know what's happening. I don't know what's real anymore. I'm scared," and they, the man and the woman, told me it was going to be okay, everything had turned out all right, everything would always turn out all right, and then my daughter looked at me and spoke her first words—

"Father," she said. "Don't be afraid."

ABOUT THE AUTHOR

Nicholas Montemarano was born in Brooklyn in 1970 and grew up in Queens. He is the author of a novel, *A Fine Place.* His short fiction has been published in *Esquire, Zoetrope, DoubleTake, Agni, The Antioch Review,* and elsewhere. His stories have been reprinted in *The Pushcart Prize XXVII: Best of the Small Presses* and *Scribner's Best of the Fiction Workshops 1999* and have been cited as Distinguished Stories in *The Best American Short Stories* for 2001 and 2002. He has received fellowships from the National Endowment for the Arts, The MacDowell Colony, Yaddo, and the Edward F. Albee Foundation. He teaches at Franklin & Marshall College in Lancaster, Pennsylvania.